SINFUL SACRAMENT

RETRIBUTION SERIES
BOOK 7

MORGAN JAMES

ABOUT THE BOOK

EVA

I knew Fox would find me; it was only a matter of time. But I won't give in without a fight. He owes me the truth, and I'm determined to get answers no matter what it takes. I'm not at all prepared for what I discover, and I'm forced to acknowledge that no one is as innocent as they appear.

Each day brings us closer to finding Araña, the man Fox has been hunting for decades—until the unthinkable happens, and a shocking betrayal shatters our hopes for the future.

FOX

One minute everything was perfect. The next, Eva is ripped from my life, kidnapped in broad daylight, gone without a trace. But they don't know me. I'll dismantle Araña's empire piece by piece, kill a thousand men to bring her back to me.

The closer I get to revealing the truth, the more tangled the web of deceit becomes. They say the devil comes in many forms—but this was one we never expected…

Villainy wears many masks;
none so dangerous as the mask of virtue.

~Washington Irving

PROLOGUE

FOX

Anger. Relief. Desire. They all mingled in my chest, the emotions fluctuating so rapidly I could hardly keep up.

Forty-seven days had passed since I'd last seen her. It felt as though everything had changed yet stayed exactly the same. From my concealed spot where I'd been watching her for the past four days, I studied Eva as she moved behind the bar.

I clamped down on the urge to stalk inside and force her to come with me. I wanted nothing more than to drag her back home, back to my side where she belonged. Instead, I closed my eyes briefly and drew in a deep breath, then focused once more on her beautiful features. Even though she was too far away to see clearly, I vividly remembered the slope of her jaw, the satiny softness of her skin beneath my fingertips. The slight dusting of freckles across her nose and cheeks, and that stubborn little chin.

Those pretty green eyes that flashed with fire when she defied me.

Most of all, I remembered the way she made me feel. Whole. Content. Like my entire existence revolved around her. Just seeing her again, knowing that she was safe and hale, eased the pressure on my chest. Immediately on the heels of the intense relief came the anger. She'd run from me without a single word. I wanted to know why—and very soon, I was going to find out.

I turned the black king over in my hands, the carved ridges of the crown familiar beneath my fingertips. My queen had fled, putting miles between us like the spaces on a board. She'd made her move—but now it was my turn.

A slow smile curved my mouth. "Checkmate, angel."

ONE

"Last call."

I held back a yawn as I cleared the sticky, empty glasses from the table, then wiped it down before heading back to the bar. I dunked the glassware into the tub of sudsy water and threw a look down the bar to the handful of men still seated on the stools as I scrubbed the glasses and set them aside to drain.

From his spot in front of the tap, Bryce glanced over his shoulder at me. "Can you get the trash together?"

"Sure. If you want, you can finish up and I'll take it out."

One honey-colored brow lifted. "You sure?"

I nodded, deeply appreciative of his concern for me. He knew how much I hated being alone outside in the dark. But I was a thousand miles from home—and *him*. It was time to move on. I forced a smile. "I'll be fine."

"All right."

After the whole ordeal with Fox a month and a half ago I had disappeared from Chicago with literally only the clothes on my back, hopped into the cab of the semi, and hitchhiked to Omaha. Bryce had welcomed me in with open arms and given me solace working in the bar and staying in his friend's duplex. He watched over me like a big brother and had never made a single untoward comment. There would never be anything romantic between us, and if it bothered him at all, he never said a word.

My heart still felt bruised, and my mind was even worse. I stayed mostly behind the bar, away from the patrons, where I could avoid the flirtatious remarks occasionally flung my direction. If anyone ever came on too strong, Bryce stepped in, always my savior. He had deemed himself my protector, and I appreciated it immensely. I owed him so much for helping me to get back on my feet.

For the first several weeks after I'd first arrived, alone in my small, dark duplex where no one could see, I cried myself to sleep each night. Even though Fox had betrayed me, even after everything, I still missed him. What we'd shared had felt real.

Despite the fact that he had initially taken me captive, in the end it had seemed like a real relationship, a connection born of mutual attraction and desire. There'd been plenty of those—but no trust to speak of. Against all odds I'd gambled and put my faith in him—and lost. I still felt the sting of hurt down into the marrow of my bones.

I wasn't sure I could ever get over the fact that he lied to me. He had every opportunity to tell me he knew who my parents were, but he'd chosen to keep that from me. I wasn't sure whose betrayal hurt worse—Fox's or my father's.

My father, who I assumed would have been beside himself with grief and worry, had apparently known where I was all along. He'd willingly handed me over to Fox and cut all ties with his only remaining daughter. Part of me wanted to ask him why he'd done it; the other part of me wanted to cut him as ruthlessly from my life as he'd done to me.

I felt alone and adrift in the world with no one to turn to. Outwardly, I was moving on. Inside, I still felt stuck in the past. I missed Fox, missed the way he made me feel. I had even debated several times reaching out to him or going back, but I could never quite bring myself to do it. Fox had attempted no communication, and I wasn't sure if that dismayed me or not.

He had connections all over the US; I was fairly certain that he would have found me and dragged me back to Chicago if he'd wanted to. I could only surmise that he'd decided he had better things to do than track down the errant woman who'd run from him. I'd escaped my captor; it was exactly what I'd wanted. But then why did I feel so empty?

I finished drying the glasses, then wiped my hands on my apron before untying it and setting it aside to toss in the laundry later. Making my way through the bar and kitchen areas, I collected the bags of trash, then glanced at the clock. Bryce had yelled last call fifteen minutes ago, and now only two men lingered at the bar. As I twisted up the bags, they downed their drinks then pushed the empty glasses toward Bryce, who collected them and dumped them into the soapy water.

An older man who went by the name Tyrone lifted a hand my way. "Have yourself a good night."

My mouth automatically formed a smile, though I didn't feel a flicker of happiness. "See you tomorrow."

With a nod, he turned and loped out the door. He was a perpetual fixture in Bryce's bar, and he sat in the same seat every day from seven o'clock in the evening until we closed at two in the morning. I felt bad for him, having learned a few weeks ago that, after forty-two years of marriage, he'd lost his wife to pneumonia two winters ago. He had no one to go home to, no one to take care of him.

I often slid him extra food, and I comped it by covering the cost of the meal with my own tips. I had a feeling Bryce knew, because occasionally my pay would be a little higher to compensate for the difference.

Once I had gathered all the trash bags together, I pushed out the back door into the alley. A security light to my left illuminated the dumpster, and I used a brick to prop the door open before carrying the bags over and tossing them in, one by one. The lid shut with a bang, and I dusted my hands on my jeans before drawing in a deep breath of the muggy early summer air.

A soft scuffle behind me had the hairs on the back of my neck lifting, and I whirled around, immediately on edge. My eyes scanned the dark alley but found nothing. I replayed the sound in my mind over and over, trying to place exactly what it was, where it'd come from. It had sounded almost like… a footstep. I slowly began to edge my way toward the door, scanning in all directions.

Suddenly, a clatter rose from a steel trashcan of the travel agency next door, and a scream caught in my throat. I slapped one hand over my heart as a mangy black cat hopped down and strode forward, a scrap of food clenched between its teeth.

Breathing heavily, I collapsed against the jagged brick wall and blinked back the tears that had sprung to my eyes. God, I needed to get a grip. Because on the heels of the initial fear I'd felt, hope had welled up. Hope that he'd found me. Hope that he'd cared enough to come for me. But he didn't. Forty-seven days had passed since I'd walked away from him. Forty-seven days without a single word, without any indication that he wanted me back. He wasn't coming.

Shaking off my wayward thoughts, I strode back into the bar then closed up behind me, making sure that the door was securely locked. By the time I made it back to the bar, Bryce had already washed the remaining dishes and set them aside to dry. He threw a look my way. "Ready to head out?"

"Yep." I grabbed my purse from under the bar. "Trash is taken care of."

"Awesome, thanks." Bryce reached over and flipped a switch that turned off the neon lights in the windows displaying the names of various brands of beer, then grabbed up the deposit envelope to drop off at the bank on his way in tomorrow.

"Come on." He dug his keys from his pocket as he rounded the bar. "I'll drive you home."

It was a nightly routine for us, and though I'd told him a hundred times he didn't have to do it, Bryce insisted on making sure I got home safely every night. I didn't bother to argue with him, just fell into step as we locked up and headed to his car. The duplex I currently rented was only a couple of blocks away, and five minutes later, I climbed out of Bryce's car, gave him a little wave, then headed into the house.

Once I was inside, I watched through the window as he pulled away from the curb and headed home to get some sleep before he had to be back at the bar by noon tomorrow. As soon as his taillights disappeared down the street, I prepared for the night ahead. A small table stood against the wall just inside the entryway, and I pulled it in front of the door, effectively blocking the entrance.

A vase took up residence in the middle of the table, and I slid it forward, balancing it precariously close to the edge. The table itself wouldn't stop someone from getting in, but if the door was opened, it would hit the table and send the vase crashing to the floor. Since there was no security system, the noise would at least give me some warning if someone decided to break in.

As soon as everything was in place, I made my way to the bedroom and kicked off my shoes. My hand automatically went to the pocket of my jeans, where I fingered the small silver cufflink within. I'd carried it with me every single day, like a talisman of sorts. My heart ached as I set it on the nightstand next to the bed. Even if Fox wasn't physically here with me, I still had a piece of him.

I shook off my melancholy and strode to the bathroom, stripping my clothes off as I went. My shirt reeked of beer, and the perpetual scent of greasy fried food clung to my hair. I flicked the handle of the shower faucet over to its hottest setting and waited for a moment as the old pipes warmed up. Soon, steam rose into the air and I gratefully climbed beneath the spray.

Tipping my head back, I allowed the hot water to wash

over me, and I reveled in the feeling. I scrubbed at my skin, washing away the grime of the day and leaving the fresh scent of eucalyptus in its place. I poured shampoo into my palm, then lathered and rinsed my hair. A subtle shift in the air had goosebumps sprouting along the backs of my arms, and I froze. The apprehension I'd felt in the alley came back full force, sweeping over me like a tidal wave and rooting my feet to the floor of the tub.

Slowly turning my head, I glanced through the translucent curtain. The room beyond was hazy, but I saw nothing out of the ordinary. I leaned forward slightly and peered around the edge of the shower curtain, my eyes scanning every inch of the tiny room. The door stood open exactly as I'd left it, but I heard no movement from the hallway.

I let out the breath I'd been holding and tried to steady my nerves. What was wrong with me? Tonight especially I'd felt particularly on edge, but I couldn't pinpoint the reason why. Nothing out of the ordinary had happened. No one had come on to me, no one had even looked at me sideways. So I couldn't quite tell why I felt like there were eyes on me at all times. Maybe it was a manifestation of my own feelings presenting themselves.

Part of me was still conflicted about the situation with Fox, but I knew I'd done the right thing. Had I never spoken with Daddy, Fox probably would never have told me the whole story. I'd still be there, playing house with a man who'd withheld the truth—that he'd practically stolen me from my father.

That knowledge had plagued me every day for nearly the past seven weeks. Part of me wanted to demand every detail. But the other, far more rational part of me told me it was better this way. My father and Fox were men cut from the same cloth. They were both manipulators who did what was best for them; to hell with whoever or whatever got in their way.

The two men I'd cared for most had both betrayed me in some fashion—and I would never let it happen again.

TWO

FOX

The night was silent and still, not a stirring of life present at this predawn hour. I slid up the window sash, dropped my bag inside, then pulled myself over the sill and into the room before closing it up again. A smile curved my mouth at the sight of the booby trap she'd placed by the front door. Good thing I'd left the window unlocked when I came into her place earlier.

I paused, ears cocked as I listened intently. The sound of water running in the bathroom met my ears, and I smiled. Right on time. I'd studied every single move she made for the past four days. Each morning she rose at 10:30 on the dot. At noon, I followed far behind as she made her way to the bar on foot.

She returned around half past two in the morning, always dropped off by the man who owned the bar. Jealousy curdled my stomach at the thought of him and the fact that he'd been here with her for the past seven weeks. I couldn't help but wonder if he meant anything to her.

Pushing thoughts of him away, I glanced at the front door and shook my head. Each time she was in for the night, she would pull the small table in front of the door, a vase balanced on the edge. Once she was satisfied it was in place to alert her of any intruders, she showered, checked her windows and doors, then went to bed so she could wake up and do it all over again. She would be pissed when she found out I'd been here all along, watching her, waiting. It filled me with a twisted sense of satisfaction.

On silent feet, I made my way through the living room and down the short hallway to the bathroom. Just being this close to her was exhilarating, and I lightly rubbed a hand over my chest to soothe the tightness that had taken up residence at the sight of her.

She stood under the spray of the water, head tipped back as she rinsed the soap from the long blonde strands. The outline of her body through the clear shower curtain was blurry, but I recalled every tantalizing inch of flesh. Steam wrapped around her body then curled toward the ceiling, practically inviting me to step into the tub with her.

Part of me wanted to throw back the curtain and sweep her into my arms before she had the chance to evade me again. I could only imagine how that would play out; my little hellcat would probably drown us both in her attempt to fight back. A smile curved my mouth. It was tempting, but I needed to be on her good side. Or, at least, not completely on her bad side.

I drew in a deep breath and pushed from the doorjamb, forcing myself to bide my time as I meandered into her bedroom. I'd been inside earlier, but I hadn't paid much attention to the room itself; now I took in every detail—or lack thereof. There were no pictures, no personal effects, hardly any clothes to fill the closet or drawers of the tall dresser in the corner. Pulling the king from the inner pocket of my jacket, I set it on the top of the dresser where she'd be sure to see it.

I turned in place, my gaze sweeping the room once more. For a woman who'd come from wealth, it was almost staggering how little she now owned. I wanted to give her the world if only she would give me the opportunity. She'd never asked for a single thing—except the truth. I owed her that and more, and I would do everything in my power to make it up to her. But first, I had to find a way to get her to listen to me.

Taking a seat on the edge of the mattress, I tried to steady my nerves. My gaze drifted to the nightstand, and my heart slammed against my ribcage when a silvery reflection on the wooden surface caught my eye. I reached out and picked up the cufflink I'd lost the night of the engagement party. It glinted in the faint glow of light spilling in from the hallway as I turned it over in my hands, remembering the last night she and I had spent together. I couldn't begin to imagine why she kept it, but I chose to see it as a good sign.

The water in the bathroom shut off, and I quietly crossed the room to conceal myself behind the open door. I'd be damned if I would give her the chance to run. Eva entered the bedroom less than a minute later, and I heard the flick of the switch a split second before the bright glow of the overhead light illuminated the room. She moved forward, her back to me, her gorgeous curves now covered by the threadbare white towel wrapped around her.

I knew the exact moment she saw it. Eyes glued to the chess piece, her steps faltered then jerked to a stop in the middle of the room. Her arm twitched by her side, almost as if she wanted to reach for it but forced herself to stop. I could practically hear the wheels turning in her head, and anticipation swelled in my chest as I shut the door, closing her in with me.

At the sound of the latch hitting the striker plate, Eva whirled around. She reared back and a gasp left her mouth as one hand went to her heart, the other to the bed behind her for support. With my gaze locked on her face, I watched her eyes widen, the gamut of emotion flickering in those green irises mimicking those roiling in my stomach.

It was like she couldn't believe I was really here. Hell, I could barely believe it myself. Day after day, I'd dealt with crushing disappointment, no information and no leads as to where she'd gone. It felt like I'd waited forever for this moment.

"Hello, Eva."

She blinked rapidly, like she was trying to wrap her mind around the fact that the words coming from my mouth were real, and I wasn't some apparition conjured up in her mind. "Fox?" she finally managed to croak out.

A grim smile curved my mouth as I pushed off the wall and strode toward her. "Yes, Eva, it's me."

She took a step away, her hand tightening on the towel knotted around her chest. "Get the hell out of my house."

Such a fighter. I bit back the smile that sprang to my lips as I watched her, muscles tight with tension, eyes full of wariness and... hope? It had always been this way between us; her going on the offensive, putting on a show of defiance even when she didn't mean it. I slowly shook my head. "You don't really want me to leave."

Her eyes narrowed. "Why are you here? Why are you doing this?"

I wanted so badly to reach for her, pull her into my arms. But I was still too keyed up. Part of me wanted to punish her for leaving the way she had. Ignoring her question, I opened my hand, palm up, holding the cufflink up for her inspection. "You kept it."

Her eyes dropped to my hand, then blinked before she met my gaze again. For a long moment, we stared at each other. Now that I was here, the anguish of the past seven weeks slipped away. It felt like just yesterday that I'd held her in my arms, kissed her sweet lips. I could still see her in my mind's eye, clad in the green cocktail dress, her arms wrapped around me when I bared my soul to her. Of course, she didn't know that. She hadn't given me the chance.

Her body trembled like she was ready to flee at any second. Her gaze darted toward the dresser on the opposite side of the room, but she couldn't get dressed without me seeing her, and I sensed she wasn't quite ready to risk that just yet. Besides, I liked her like this—bare, vulnerable. She had so many walls up to guard herself, and clothing would be another added layer of protection.

"Why did you run?" I tried to control my voice, but I knew I failed when Eva's eyes narrowed.

"Why the hell would you care?"

Irritation flashed inside me, but I shoved it down. "Do you know how worried I was?"

"Right," she scoffed. "Worried that you wouldn't have me at your beck and call anymore."

"Goddamn it, Eva." I swore one of these days she was going to push me over the edge. "Tell me why the hell you ran."

"You lied to me."

"I—" I started, but she cut me off, eyes sparkling with anger.

"You betrayed me in a way no one else has."

"You're right," I ground out. "I omitted the truth. But you should have come to me. You could have asked me, but instead you assumed the worst. You always do."

She cocked a brow, a challenging glint in her eyes. "Well, it was the truth, wasn't it?"

"No," I snapped. "It wasn't. You heard something you didn't understand and chose to react based on one side of a story. But you're missing half the information—my information."

"What else do I need to know? You knew about my father the entire time." She threw an angry look my way. "Doesn't sound like I'm missing anything except why the hell you felt the need to lie to me about it."

I stared at her. "It's not that simple."

Her mouth took on a bitter curve. "I was nothing more than a pawn to you—to both of you. You never cared about me."

I lunged forward, grabbing her wrists. "That's not true, and you know it. If I didn't care for you, I wouldn't be here right now. I would have let you go, content with the fact that you were away from that asshole of a father of yours."

"Why did you do it?" She yanked against me, but I

refused to let her go. "He knew I was with you. And you took your anger for my father out on me."

She was right. "Eva, I—" Damn it. I knew I needed to tell her the truth, but I wasn't ready. I eased my hold on her wrists. "I never wanted to hurt you, angel."

Her eyes flamed with anger as she wrenched free. "That doesn't change the fact that you lied to me!"

"You're right," I bit out. "I did lie to you. And I swear to God, Eva, I would do it all over again if it would keep you from being hurt."

She threw her hands in the air. "That doesn't even make sense."

"I wanted to tell you. I just…" I raked one hand through my hair. "I just needed a little more time."

"So tell me now."

Her defiant little chin tilted upward, and a spark of something ran through me. "Damn it, Eva. Your father left you with me, and I took advantage of the situation. Can't we just leave it at that?"

"You came all this way to track me down and you expect me to just fall in line without any explanation at all —only because you tell me I need to? I don't think so."

She spun away from me, and I grabbed one wrist to stop her. "Don't."

She threw a mutinous look my way, and I sighed. Goddamn it. "Please. Just… sit. I'll tell you what I can."

It took every ounce of willpower to release her. I slowly retreated, eyes on her the entire time as I settled on the mattress. Looking torn, she pulled the towel more tightly around her, then sat primly on the edge of the bed, keeping a good foot of space between us. She didn't say a word, only fixed that intense green gaze on me, and I took a moment to order my thoughts before speaking. "I did what I thought was right at the time. I wanted to shield you from the truth."

She snorted a mirthless little laugh. "Whatever the truth is, I don't think I could trust you even if you told me."

I glared at her. "That's exactly the problem. I lied to you because I couldn't bear for you to know the truth—that your father had practically fucking handed you to me on a silver platter to save his own ass."

Her brow drew together, and she shook her head. "But… he told me you'd kill him if he tried to intervene."

The hurt in her voice cut through me like a knife. "That's true—but not for the reason you think. He traded you in exchange for me relieving his debts."

Surprise and disappointment flickered in her eyes. "That doesn't make sense. Debts for what? Why would daddy need money?"

How the hell could William have fucked this up so badly? Fixing my gaze on the wall over her shoulder, I blew out a breath. "Your father's business has been hemorrhaging money for the past couple of years, so much so that he's ready to lose it."

I watched in my peripheral vision as my words sank in. Her mouth opened then closed again before she finally spoke. "And these debts… Did you loan him money?"

Christ. I rubbed my temples with one hand and finally turned my gaze to her. "Yes, but it's more complicated than that." Her brow furrowed in confusion, and I continued. "Do you know what I do?"

"You've never deigned to tell me, but I have my suspicions."

The challenging look she tossed my way made me want to pull her across my lap and spank the sass right out of her. I clenched my hand where it rested on my thigh, biting back the urge to paddle her ass red as I took a calming breath. "It took me a couple days to figure out who you were. Miranda—the woman who runs Noir—ran a background check on you."

"What's Noir?" she interjected.

"A club," I said curtly, not wanting to explain.

"What kind of club?"

Goddamn it. This was not at all how I'd planned for this to go. I should have known it wouldn't be that easy. With Eva, it never was. When an idea popped into that pretty little head of hers, she latched onto it like a dog with a bone. Curious, bright green eyes cut into mine, and I exhaled deeply. "It caters to the BDSM community."

She jerked at the implication, and I spoke quickly before her mind could run away with her. "I own it—that's the extent of it. I do not play or interact with any members beyond the necessary."

I could practically hear the wheels turning in her head as she processed that. "Is that... Do you... like that sort of thing?"

"Not really, no." Though I readily admitted the fact that I loved to dominate and control Eva, I wasn't a true Dom. "I opened the club back before the scene really blew up because I was curious. I wanted to experiment. I'd never..."

How the hell could I even begin to tell her everything that had molded me into the person I was? It took me years to deal with the shit I'd endured, and I had no intention of divulging that kind of horror to Eva just yet.

I tried a different tack. "Remember how I told you I don't like to touch or be touched?" She nodded, and I continued. "I was young and curious, but women in the real world weren't exactly receptive when I approached them."

Her brows drew together. "Why?"

This was a whole other issue I wasn't quite ready to get into just yet. "I couldn't touch them, so… I wore gloves." There was no mistaking the mixture of surprise and confusion in her gaze, so I spoke quickly to head off any other questions. "At the club, no one judged. It was just another quirk, a strange idiosyncrasy."

She nodded a little at my explanation, but I knew it would come up again later. Her face twisted a little in something like revulsion. "And my father…?"

"Does not belong to Noir." I bit back a chuckle at the relief that flashed in her eyes. "That's where my other dealings come into play. Beneath Noir is a room where I hold card games on weekends. It's extremely lucrative and exclusive. Wealthy men and women come from all over to attend."

"Like an underground casino." One dark brow rose toward her hairline. "Is that legal?"

Not in the least. "The city council and I have an… understanding."

She closed her eyes briefly before meeting my gaze again. "So, what does my father have to do with all this? You mentioned something about Spencer before…" She trailed off, no doubt remembering one of the last times we'd spoken. "Were they trying to get you shut down?"

"No." I shook my head, not entirely sure how to tell her without hurting her further. "Your father first attended one of my games a couple of years ago. Unfortunately, his pride and arrogance outweighed his skill, and he ended up deeply in debt."

She turned a confused look on me. "I can't… He…" I knew she wanted to deny it, but she couldn't quite find the words, and I shook my head gently.

"He was in far over his head and came to me for a loan. I obliged."

Her eyes narrowed on me. "You gave my father money when you knew he wouldn't be able to pay it back?"

I understood her anger, but I couldn't take it back even if I wanted to. "It's business, and it happened long before I even knew of you."

"Still," she insisted. "What about the people who can't pay you back? What do you do then?"

"I don't kill them, if that's what you're asking," I said tartly. "Believe it or not, killing someone doesn't exactly help me get my money back."

Her lips pressed into a firm line but she didn't say anything, so I continued. "There are multiple forms of payment besides money. Information. Connections. Everyone eventually finds a way to settle their debt. Your father, though… He refused to tell his wife about his losses, and he was not in possession of any information I needed. When you showed up, I reached out to him." I rubbed the bridge of my nose with my thumb and middle finger. "I threatened to keep you, and he… consented."

Her gaze darted away, but not before I saw the shimmer of moisture there. I still wasn't sure precisely what William had told her that night. Obviously, she'd discovered that her father had known all along where she was but had chosen not to help her. It killed me to tell her the truth, but I owed her that much.

"So," she said, her voice breaking, "he traded me to you."

"In so many words," I acknowledged. "Yes."

She gave her head a little shake and stared at her hands clasped in her lap. "I never thought…" She trailed off, then started again. "When we lost Elle, things changed so much. It was like this huge shadow fell over our house. But instead of bringing us together, it drove us all further apart. Daddy pulled away—probably gambling," she said bitterly.

"My mother turned her focus to her constituents, putting all of her effort into her campaigning. And I…" She bit her lower lip. "I felt… hollow. I was in school, but I lost my drive, my focus. I spent days in this fog of grief, just trying to survive. The weight of her loss settled over me until I couldn't take it anymore."

She shifted slightly but stared off into space like she was lost in the past. "Then one day I overheard Spencer talking to Daddy."

I wasn't a fan of Eva's father, William, but Spencer Masterson was a prick of the highest order. Had he not been a public figure I would have put him in the ground the day I discovered he'd lifted a hand to his wife. I wasn't ready to say anything to Eva, though, so I swallowed down my reaction.

"When he said your name, it was like something clicked." She finally lifted her gaze to mine. "I knew exactly what I had to do."

"Revenge," I said softly, and she nodded.

"I… I had to do something. I couldn't sit there and just

watch her memory fade away a day at a time. I wanted to punish someone."

I breathed deeply through my nose, recalling in perfect detail the moment I'd first seen her skulking through the trees behind my home. She'd come for revenge, needing to lash out at someone. "Me."

She nodded a little, looking lost and forlorn.

"I would take the hurt away if I could." For the first time in almost two months she was mere inches from me, and I wanted so badly to pull her against me. Through sheer force of will, I managed to clamp down on my control. She would come to me in her own time, on her own terms. And when she did, I would be right here waiting.

THREE

EVA

The events of the past few months lined up in startling clarity, sending a dagger of hurt spearing through my heart. I recalled those first couple of weeks in Fox's home, cut off from the world, from my friends and family. Except, if what he said was true, he wasn't the cause of it.

I turned to him. "So, what about my apartment, my school work? Did you have anything to do with that?"

He shook his head. "I assume your father arranged for your things to be packed up and taken home."

Even though he'd confirmed my suspicions, the knowledge still hurt. I could almost forgive him for trying to protect me as he'd said. But I wasn't ready to let go of my anger just yet. I'd been in danger—we both had. And I wasn't sure I could live like that. I needed something else to focus on besides my father's betrayal.

"So…" His brows lifted a millimeter, and I continued. "Tell me about this club you own."

The knowledge that he was involved in something like that had blindsided me. In retrospect, it probably shouldn't have. Considering the way he craved control, it seemed like it would be a good venue for him. But the thought of him even being around other like-minded men and women made me uncomfortable. He swore he'd never slept with anyone else during the time we were together, but would the temptation eventually overcome whatever tenuous bond we'd constructed?

He seemed to read the thousand questions in my mind, because he gently rubbed his temples. "As I said earlier, I haven't slept with anyone but you since you showed up at my house. In fact, until recently, my only interactions were with a friend I've known for years."

A friend? "What's her name?"

"Eva..."

My name was a warning, but I couldn't help it. "I need to know."

He sighed. "Her name is Marcella Levieva."

The name sounded familiar. "Isn't she engaged to Sebastian Moreau?"

A dark look crossed his face. "They're not engaged."

"So you were fucking a woman under her boyfriend's nose?" My voice rose several octaves, and Fox sent me a sharp look.

"It's not always black and white. They've been on-again, off-again for years."

"Because that makes it better," I said sarcastically. I was seriously beginning to regret this conversation.

"I can't take back what I've done in the past," Fox said, his tone low and deep. "But I promised you the truth."

He was right, but I continued to curse my own

stupidity. I dropped my gaze to my hands and clenched them tightly in the fabric of the towel. "All right. And what does this have to do with the club?"

"There's something you don't know about me."

Oh, God. I braced myself for whatever he was about to impart.

"I have visions."

"Visions?" I snapped my head up to look at him, my gaze sweeping over his face. There wasn't a hint of mirth in sight. "Like... premonitions?"

"Sort of. You see the lines that cross my palm?" He held it up for my inspection, and I nodded. "We all have them, but I'm one of the unfortunate few who derives anything from touch. If I place my bare hands on someone's skin, I can read what's in their heart—the things they've done or plan to do."

"Oh." A myriad of thoughts flitted through my mind. How many times had he read my thoughts—my plans? The memory of my escape came back to me, along with a hundred other moments in time, and I felt my cheeks heat.

His lips quirked. "There's only ever been one person I'm not able to read." He paused, his dark gaze boring into mine. "You."

"Me?" But... "Why?"

"I don't know. But you can't imagine how... freeing it feels to be able to touch someone without being bombarded with flashes of images. Some call it a gift, but it's more like a curse."

"I can't even imagine," I said slowly.

He closed his eyes briefly, and a pained expression moved across his face. "Until I was in my mid-twenties,

I'd never had a relationship with a woman. I didn't know how to deal with my sexuality."

I stiffened, completely unable to think, to move, to breathe. He hadn't…? I opened my mouth to speak the dozens of questions forming on my tongue, but he shook his head.

"Not now. Please."

Though I wanted so badly to press for answers, the quiet plea in his voice stopped me cold. I reluctantly backed down with a nod, and Fox steered the conversation back to the club. "I wasn't able to touch anyone, but I needed to explore my needs. I wore gloves so I wouldn't have to. And, in the club, it wasn't out of place."

I nodded a little at his explanation, and he elaborated. "I was trying to learn about myself, trying to just be… normal. But I figured out I didn't exactly fit in there, either. I don't really know how to explain it, but…"

He trailed off, and I was silent for a long moment as I absorbed everything he'd told me. "You don't have to justify it. I don't know what you went through, and I can't begin to imagine how it affected your life."

I was left with more questions than answers. I was more than a little irked that he'd kept such a huge part of himself hidden away from me, especially since I seemed to have no effect on him at all. Why hadn't he opened up to me? His enemies would no doubt see it as a weakness, but did his men know of his affliction? Almost surely, since they worked with him every day. The knowledge that he felt he couldn't trust me with that information stung.

I crossed my arms over my chest. "So you own a sex club. But that doesn't explain why someone shot up your house."

Fox's lips pressed into a thin line as he regarded me. "The men and women I've been looking for are incredibly evil. Human trafficking is a very lucrative venture, and the people involved don't take kindly to having their business disrupted."

I flinched at the cold, lifeless tone of his voice but was unable to tear my gaze away as his hands moved to the buttons of his shirt. While he spoke, he began to free them from their holes, one by one. "I was adopted when I was six. The man who took me in lived on a secluded estate with no neighbors, no one to run to for help."

Oh, God. The way he said that sent my heart beating furiously, and my lungs felt tight as I tried to draw in a breath. I watched, rooted to my spot, as he shrugged the shirt off his shoulders and allowed it to slip down his arms. "What—What did...?"

I couldn't form the words, but I didn't need to. Fox already knew exactly what I was asking. He turned, and the sight of the scars stole my breath and stopped my heart. Silvery-pink lines crisscrossed his dark skin from beneath the waistband of his pants all the way up to his shoulders. He'd told me that his childhood hadn't been good, but I'd never expected this. Why hadn't I seen them before? How—?

A barrage of memories slammed into me, and I saw every prior interaction in perfect hindsight. I'd touched his hands, his face... but never his back. He'd never let me close enough. The knowledge that he'd kept this from me, coupled with the revelation of his visions, was like a stake had been driven through my chest. There was so much about this man that I didn't know—that he wouldn't let me see.

I forced my heart to harden even as I wanted to break down and cry. "Is that supposed to make me pity you?"

He slowly rotated, meeting my gaze and reading straight into the depths of my soul. "I would never ask for your pity—only your understanding. The man who raised me was only one of the men involved. Once he was gone, I vowed that I would bring down the entire operation."

It made so much sense—the secrecy, the danger. But that only made me vacillate more. This would be a never-ending quest for justice. These men were wealthy and incredibly well-connected, and Fox was the only thing standing between them and their prey. They wouldn't hesitate to take him down. They'd already tried—how much longer could he evade them? We'd been lucky to survive the first time. I couldn't bear to see him hurt, let alone die before my very eyes.

I cleared my throat, swallowing down my conflicting emotions. "I admire what you're trying to do. I think it's very noble, but I can't…" My words trailed off as he took a step toward me. "What are you doing?"

"I've waited almost two months for this moment. You have no idea how relieved I felt when I finally found you. I've come all this way, Eva—for you."

He stopped right in front of me, so close that I could feel the tips of his shoes touching my toes. Everything inside me tightened at his nearness, and I curled my toes into the carpet as his mesmerizing dark eyes bored into mine. "Tell me you don't want me."

I tightened my arms around my waist. I couldn't very well lie to him. Deciding that silence was the best course of action, I lifted my chin and stared at him.

A tiny smile quirked his mouth. "You belong with me."

Anger flared, hot and fierce. "I don't belong to anyone."

"I said you belong with me, not to me," he corrected as he lifted one hand and stroked my cheek. "I want you, Eva, and I know you want me."

"No." I jumped up from the bed and stomped away, crossing my arms over my middle as if it would help to contain the swirling mass of confusing emotions within.

"Come here."

There really wasn't anywhere I could go. I turned and glared at him, notching my chin up.

"Come. Here." Each word was slow and deliberate, and my body ached to heed his command. My heart throbbed in my chest as I fought the magnetic pull between us. His eyes fixed on mine, he stared deep into my soul, reading my every thought.

No longer able to deny him, I threw my arms up. "Why?"

"Because I told you to."

"Go fuck yourself."

"Watch your mouth," he snapped, but I saw the glint in his eyes—he knew my heart wasn't in it.

My need for him trumped my anger, and it'd been so long since I'd felt his hands on me. "You won't touch me," I taunted.

"Careful, Eva," he warned. "I am about two seconds from pulling you over my lap and spanking that pretty ass red."

"I'm not yours to punish," I shot back.

"You will *always* be mine." Faster than I could react, he grabbed the corner of the towel where it was knotted against my chest and ripped it from my body, then flung it to the ground. Wrapping one hand around my wrist, he tugged me over his lap and into position. His erection was a thick, hard ridge pressing up through the material of his slacks, and a little thrill ran through me. Right here—this was where I belonged.

His hand coasted over my bottom, the firm pressure unlocking something inside me. A shiver of need worked its way down my spine. It'd been too long.

"You ran away from me, Eva." Fox's voice floated over my shoulder. "You left me without a single word. You need to be punished."

One hand squeezed my ass roughly, and I drew in a sharp breath at the spike of need it sent through me. I'd been in the wrong for running away; I would gladly accept responsibility for that. "I was counting on it."

Even though I was prepared for it, the hard blow still caught me off guard, and I flinched. The sting of pain radiated outward, turning to a simmering pleasure. I shifted on his lap, pushing my hips upward, welcoming the next stinging slap. He alternated between cheeks until it felt as if I were on fire, both inside and out.

His touch brought tears to my eyes and they slipped free, running down my temples and into my damp hair. I cried as he spanked me, allowing the pent-up emotion of the last seven long weeks to leave my body in a cathartic cleansing. With Fox here, I felt whole again. I'd missed him so much it hurt.

With each swat, the negative emotions left my body, and my world began to right itself. When it was over, he levered me to my feet, then turned me to face him. Standing between his knees, tears cutting tracks down my cheeks, I stared at him. He seemed to know exactly what I was feeling, because his huge hands lifted to cup my face, and those dark eyes stared at me for what felt like an eternity as his thumbs swept gently along my cheeks, wiping away the last of my tears.

"Don't ever run from me again, Eva. I couldn't stand it."

At his words, it felt as if a dam inside me had broken. I threw my arms around his shoulders, burying my face in the crook of his neck. He wrapped his arms around my waist and lifted me so I straddled his lap. I was still angry, but right now, I was just so damn relieved to see him. "I missed you. Every single day. I..." I cut off with a small sob, and his arms tightened around me, holding me close.

"I know, angel. I know."

The connection between us was palpable, and I could no longer deny the desire I'd felt the second I saw him standing by the door waiting for me. I turned my head and spoke against the base of his throat, my lips brushing his pulse point. "I need you."

We struggled out of our clothes, and a moment later fell to the bed together in a tangled heap. There was no need for foreplay, only the burning desire to have each other right that second. He kissed me hard, a brutal claiming of my body and soul. One hand moved between us, testing my entrance to see if I was ready for him. He let out a little growl as his fingers slid through my slick folds. A moment later, the broad, hard head of him was there, pushing inside and filling me up, stealing my breath and my heart in one swift motion.

FOUR

FOX

Coming home.

That was the only way I could explain the way it felt to be back with Eva. The sharp claws of anxiety that had clutched relentlessly at my throat for the past seven weeks loosened their hold, and I could finally breathe again. I reveled in the rightness of the feeling, all of me inside all of her. She was back in my arms, and the gaping chasm in my chest began to fuse together once more.

For the first time since we'd met, Eva and I were both completely bared—stripped of clothing and insecurities and any lies that had once lain between us. Eyes locked on hers, I pulled out and rolled my hips, plunging back inside her hot channel. I never wanted this feeling to end. I wanted to draw it out for hours, days, never let her go again.

I dipped my head and kissed her, my tongue sweeping over hers as I thrust in and out. Her legs curled around mine, and her heels dug into the back of my thighs, urging me closer, deeper. Her hands slid from my biceps down to my ribs, and my breath stilted as she trailed them over my back, her fingers skimming over the gnarled flesh of my scars.

I froze momentarily, and a shudder rolled down my spine. I felt incredibly vulnerable and exposed… Yet with Eva's hands on me, the pain of the past finally began to recede, leaving only her and me in this moment.

I kissed her hard, hoping she could feel the depth of the emotion neither of us were ready to admit just yet. Coasting one hand down her body, I slipped my arm beneath her left leg and lifted it over my shoulder, opening her to me. Her back arched as I thrust inside, sinking deeper than before, and her fingers curled into my flesh as she held on for dear life.

"Oh, God…"

"Christ, Eva…"

Our words mingled together as we panted hard, our skin slick with sweat, need and desire driving us higher and higher until her inner muscles began to contract. I picked up the pace, pushing her over the edge, and she let out a stifled cry as she buried her head in the crook of my neck. Sheer bliss took over and I let go, pulsing two months' worth of emotions deep inside her.

My body shook, and I fought to hold myself upright. But Eva was having none of it. Arms and legs still wrapped around me she tightened her grasp, and I gladly gave in to the need to hold her and be held. Rolling to my back, I kept her wound around me, our bodies pressed so close I could feel the rapid rise and fall of her chest with each breath she took.

For what seemed like forever we lay there quietly, the only sound our combined breaths leaving in shallow pants. It had always been this way between us. Carnal need, unquenchable desire. But there was still so much broken between us, and I didn't know if we could ever fix it.

"How's your side?" Her hand tentatively coasted along the ribs on the right side of my body, checking the old injury.

I caught her hand and lifted it to my mouth, then kissed her fingers. "Like it never happened."

She nodded and was silent for several seconds, seemingly lost in thought. "How did you find me, anyway?"

A bittersweet smile curved my mouth. "Did you really think I was just going to let you go?"

She lifted one shoulder where she still lay draped over my chest. "I actually was kind of surprised you didn't get to me faster. I waited for several days when I got here, watching over my shoulder, but you never showed up."

I couldn't see her face from where we were positioned, but I thought I heard a trace of sadness in her voice. "Were you disappointed?"

She was silent for nearly a minute. "I don't know. Maybe. I… After Rodrigo told me to go, I began to think that maybe you really believed it was for the best."

The reminder sent another surge of anger through me. "He's lucky to be alive."

She propped her chin on her hand and turned her head so she could look at me. "He was just trying to protect you. He thought I was distracting you from everything you've been working so hard for."

"Those assholes have been around since long before I was born, and more will take their place after I die. But there's only one of you. I swear, I was ready to tear the whole city apart before we finally caught wind of where you might have gone."

Her brows drew together. "Did someone see me?"

"An informant of Johnson's happened to be at the gas station the night you left. He saw a woman in a dress getting into a truck, and once he heard who I was looking for, he came forward. Told us the truck had a faded four-leaf clover on the side, so we tracked it down."

Her eyes widened and she lifted her head to better see me. "You didn't...?"

I was already shaking my head. "I ran his name, but I never spoke with him. We discovered from dispatch records that his next stop was in Omaha, so we checked it out. There weren't too many places in between where he could stop without throwing off his schedule, so I guessed you would take the most direct route to a place as far away as possible."

She gave a little nod and settled back onto my chest. "I just... It was so much to process. It's still a lot to process."

"I know." I sifted my fingers through her long pale hair. "I should have told you. I just couldn't bear to see you hurt, especially after everything you'd already been through."

She peered at me. "I would have stayed with you. All you had to do was ask."

"Each minute with you was a gift. I didn't deserve you then, and I don't deserve you now, but I can't let you go."

A myriad of emotions flickered in her eyes. "I just... I don't know how we can move on from this."

"You were scared, and I understand that. Araña was lashing out after I'd intercepted a shipment intended for some of his buyers. I put you in danger, and that was unforgivable. But I promise, Eva, I won't let that happen again."

I needed to convince her to give me another chance. I'd told her once that I wasn't responsible for Elle's death, and I hadn't been lying. But I think she seriously had her doubts. "The night we went shopping for your gown... I told you I wanted to take you away. Do you remember that?"

She tipped her head slightly, a turbulent expression in her eyes. Of course she remembered; it was one of the last times I'd seen her, right before she'd run away. She nodded slightly.

There was so much about my life that she didn't know, and she would never just take my word for it. She needed to see things for herself to truly understand and believe. "I have a home on a small island in the Caribbean. I wanted to take you there months ago—come with me now."

"What?"

"We'll leave tonight." She blinked owlishly, and I grabbed one hand. "Trust me, Eva. I want to show you something."

FIVE

EVA

I was caught between wanting to laugh and cry. It was everything I'd dreamed of hearing two months ago. But now? I had no idea. So much had happened since then. I sat up a little and stared down at him, conflicted. "What is it?"

He dragged his fingers lightly up and down my arm. "I can't tell you. Some things you just need to see for yourself."

What the hell did that mean? My irritation bubbled to the surface again. "That's cryptic as hell. I don't understand why you refuse to tell me."

He smiled a little. "That would ruin my plans for you."

Doubt began to creep in, overshadowing the relief and happiness from only moments ago. Regret for falling right back into my old habits rose up like a tidal wave. I refused to go back and be some trophy for him to bring out and parade around on his arm whenever the hell he felt like it.

Sex had always clouded the issue with us, and I was no longer certain that this was the right thing to do. "I can't just leave. I have a job here."

"You work in a bar." He rolled his eyes, and my temper flared.

"It's still a responsibility. Have you ever done anything for yourself, or do you just throw orders around and expect people to follow them?"

He scowled at me, his hand pausing its path along my arm. "I've worked damn hard to get where I am today. You have no idea the things I've done."

The way he said it sent a little chill down my spine, and I fought the urge to shudder. Pushing down my apprehension, I fell back on the anger swelling and growing inside me. "Then you know I can't just walk away yet, regardless of what you command. I need to give Bryce my notice."

His eyes narrowed at the other man's name. "Is this Bryce more than just your boss?"

I turned toward Fox, ready to smack him. "How dare you ask me that? I literally just"—I made an agitated gesture with one hand—"fell into bed with you—a mistake I'm really starting to regret right now, let me tell you—and you have the gall to ask if I've been seeing someone else? Fuck you, Fox."

I clambered from the bed and yanked the sheet around me, but Fox stopped my progress, his fingers curling around my wrist. "That's not what I meant."

"It's exactly what you meant!" I exclaimed. "Here's a newsflash, asshole: I'm not yours."

He let out a little growl as he bounded toward me and grabbed me around the waist. "You will always be mine."

"The hell I will!" I struggled to get my free hand wedged between us as I fought to hold the sheet up with the other. I shoved at him, but he didn't move an inch. "Let me go!"

"Not a chance." I let out a little shriek as he scooped me up, sheet and all, then sat down on the bed and settled me in his lap, arms wrapped firmly around me. "Not until you listen to me."

"There's nothing you can say right now to—"

He slapped one hand over my mouth, and I sucked in an outraged breath before snapping at his palm. Fox was too quick, though, anticipating my move and snatching his hand away before I could sink my teeth into his flesh.

"You ran out on me without giving me a chance to explain everything."

His voice was low and husky, full of some unnamed emotion, and it irked me that I even cared how he should feel right now. I steeled my heart against him. "What else is there to explain?"

He stared at me for several seconds. "A lot."

I glared at him, my face only inches from his. "You always do this," I snapped. "You think you can just wrestle me into submission, talk me down and reel me back in. Well, it won't work this time. I won't let you just drag me back."

"If that's all I wanted, I would have done it four days ago."

I stared at him, completely taken aback. "You've been here for four days?"

How had I not known—how could I not have felt his eyes on me? The scene in the alley earlier came back to me, stirring my ire. "That's exactly what I'm talking about. You sit and wait and plan as if what you want is the only thing that matters. To hell with everyone else, you just manipulate everything to your advantage."

His nostrils flared and his jaw clenched but to his credit, Fox remained silent, absorbing my words.

God, this was so like him to just show up and start making demands again. He'd been here for little more than an hour, and already he was acting like he ran my life. He thought I would just gratefully take his word for it and trust that everything would be okay? No way. I'd come too far to regress the very second he walked back into my life. "Why?"

"Why what?"

I threw him a dark look. "Why do you want to drag me out of the country to some island?"

"Because I think it will be good for us."

I shook my head. "That's not good enough."

His eyes darkened. "Goddamn it, Eva, I swear I'll—"

"What?" I snapped. "You'll throw me over your shoulder and cart me off?"

Fox glared at me. "Probably not the worst idea considering your attitude."

"My attitude?" I parroted, incredulous. "Oh, right, forgive me for being a little upset when you suddenly show up after all this time and demand I go with you."

I didn't give him a chance to speak up as I continued. "And you didn't just come to my door like a normal person—you broke into my home so I had no choice but to acknowledge you."

His chest rose on a deep inhale, and I could tell he was trying desperately to clamp down on his anger. I wasn't sure if that was a good thing or not. I wanted him just as angry as I was; I wanted him to feel what it was like to not get his way for once.

"Why should I go?" I repeated.

"I've already explained—"

"You haven't explained shit," I exploded. "You won't tell me a damn thing other than I 'need to go.' Well, I'm not going!"

I slid from his lap with the intent to put distance between us, but Fox jumped to his feet and yanked me back to him. "Stop being so damn petulant for a second, and—"

I shoved against his chest, but he only fell back half a step. "This is not being petulant. This is being smart and making sure I don't rush back into something I shouldn't. You want me to go with you?" He stared at me for several seconds, not bothering to answer my rhetorical question. "Then prove it. You show me how much you care about me like you say and I'll consider going with you."

He let out a little laugh that held no mirth. "You've been here for almost two damn months. You really think a couple days will change your mind?"

"I don't know," I snapped. "But you can either take it or leave it."

His dark eyes flashed to mine and held for a second before he spoke. "I'm staying."

"Fine." I fought the urge to squirm. It would be so easy to just give in to him, do what he wanted—and what a huge part of me wanted as well. But I couldn't allow my feelings for Fox to cloud my judgement. Whatever decision I made, I was going to make sure it was the right one. "But no sex until we figure out whatever the hell this is."

His face darkened. "After everything we've been through, now you're kicking me out of your bed?"

Despite the slight twinge of guilt I felt at his statement, I stiffened my spine and stared him down. This would be a huge concession for me. If I decided to go back with him, I would be walking away from my job, my new home. If we had any chance of moving on at all, then he needed to show me he was willing to do whatever it took. "I told you I would think about going away with you. I could have turned you down flat, but I didn't. I'm trying to be open-minded here, and I need you to do the same for me."

He waited for nearly a minute, and his words were quiet when he finally spoke. "If that's what you need, angel. I would do anything for you."

I wasn't sure what else to say in that moment, so I glanced at the clock. A soft groan filtered from my mouth when I saw how late—or, rather, early—it was. "I need to get to bed."

Fox released me, and I moved around the bed and climbed under the covers. Fox stood and hovered next to the mattress for a moment, staring down at me. "I want to sleep next to you."

It was already close to dawn, and I felt bad sending him back to a hotel or wherever he was staying. At least, that's what I told myself as I flipped back the covers. "Fine. Just remember to keep your hands to yourself."

I rolled away from him, my heart racing as I stared at the wall. A minute later, the bed dipped under his weight, and a draft of cool air hit me as he pulled the blanket up.

I slept fitfully, waiting to feel him creep closer. But he was true to his word. He never reached for me, just as I'd requested. I wasn't quite sure why, but it pissed me off even more. By the time I woke up the next morning just after ten o'clock., I was cranky and exhausted.

Fox watched me intently as I began to dress. "Want a ride?"

The word 'ride' brought dirty images to the forefront of my mind. No, damn it. I would *not* cave. My weakness for him pissed me off even more. "I don't need a ride."

"Okay." I could hear the trace of mirth in his tone, as if he knew I was declining his offer on principle.

"I won't be back until late," I snapped as I grabbed up my purse. "You'll have to find something to entertain yourself while I'm gone."

"I'm sure I can find something."

He sounded so nonchalant that my fingers twitched with the urge to slap him. How could he be so unflappable while I felt like a mess inside? What the hell was wrong with me? "Lock up when you leave."

With that I stormed out, slamming the front door harder than necessary, then set off at a brisk walk down the sidewalk. The day was cool, but it didn't diminish the heat of my anger. Admittedly, it made no sense. My emotions were all over the place: I loved him, but I despised what he'd done. He'd promised to give me what I wanted, yet it wasn't enough.

What bothered me most was that I couldn't quite figure out why he'd given in to my demands. Was it because he truly cared about me, or was he just doing it to appease me? Was this a temporary change to get me to come back, after which he would revert to his old ways? The more I agonized over the answers, the angrier I got.

God, I was so screwed up. I stopped and leaned against a building, tipping my head back to stare up at the sky. A smart woman wouldn't even consider going back to a situation like that. So why did it excite me so much? I'd fucking missed him. And that, right there, was the worst part of it all. Despite everything he'd said and done, I still felt so much for him that it was overwhelming.

I couldn't have sex with him again. We'd always been compatible in bed, but it was outside the bedroom that our communication was lacking. I would have to keep him at a distance until I was sure I wanted to be with him.

SIX

FOX

She wasn't going to get rid of me that easily. I felt her eyes on me the second I stepped into the bar. Some animals gave off pheromones to warn predators away. Now that same instinctual chemical wafted off Eva in rippling waves.

Avoiding the bar, I took a seat at a small table in the corner with my back to the wall so I could keep an eye on everything around me. In my peripheral vision, I watched Eva gesture animatedly for a second with Bryce before finally dragging herself out from behind the bar and over to my table.

Not meeting her gaze, I glanced at the handwritten sign behind the bar listing the night's drink specials. "What do you recommend?"

"Another bar," she said without inflection.

I bit back a smile at her obvious reluctance to serve me. No way in hell was I going to give her the satisfaction. If she wanted me to somehow prove to her that I was in this for the long haul, she was about to see more of me than she ever dreamed possible.

"Tempting, considering the service." I lifted a brow at her, and her eyes narrowed further.

She didn't move a muscle, didn't even blink as she stared at me. "What are you doing here?"

"Having a drink."

Her eyes flashed. "The hell you are."

"Why not?" I gestured with my chin around the mostly empty bar. "Looks like you could use the business."

Her cheeks flushed red with anger. "You here to spy on me some more?"

"Just doing what you asked, angel."

"I asked for space," she responded tightly, "not for you to come loiter where I work."

"You asked for time, not space," I corrected. Not that I would have given it to her anyway. I'd waited almost two goddamn months to see her again. If she thought I was just going to throw in the towel at the first sign of trouble, she was out of her mind. If that were the case, I'd have gotten rid of her the moment she stepped foot in my house. Lucky for her, I loved a good fight.

I moved back to the topic at hand. "What's your best whiskey?"

"Maker's Mark," she stated flatly.

I held back a grimace and nodded. "Make it a double."

I spent the next several hours watching Eva move around behind the bar, cleaning and taking care of patrons. I felt her eyes on me from time to time, and she eventually came back over to my table.

She swiped my empty glass from the table. "I'll take this for you and get your bill."

"Actually, could I have some water, please?"

The look in her green eyes told me she'd rather skewer me than bring me water, but she stalked off to retrieve it and returned less than a minute later. She plunked the glass down so hard the liquid sloshed over the rim.

I lifted a brow her way. "Napkin?"

Without a word she pulled the bar towel from her shoulder and flung it my way before spinning on a heel and striding away.

As I cleaned up the mess, I bit the inside of my cheek—to keep from laughing or lashing out at her, I wasn't completely certain. God, I wanted to paddle her ass until she was so red and tender she couldn't sit for days. Maybe while I was back there, I'd find the stick she had shoved up her butt.

Though she continued to flit around the bar, she didn't stop by my table again. The owner, Bryce, made a cursory stop once when he noticed my water was empty.

"Can I get you another?"

"No, thank you." I tipped my head toward the woman currently avoiding me like the plague. "I'm just waiting for Eva to finish up so I can take her home."

His eyes were full of questions, but he only nodded in response. "Let me know if you need anything else."

At the end of the night, I crossed to the bar and slid a hundred across the polished oak surface.

Eva's eyes widened at the sight, and red flared over her cheeks. "I don't want your damn money," she hissed.

"You apparently don't want anything from me, angel."

Spinning away and ignoring the money on the bartop,

Eva flounced into the kitchen, leaving the doors swinging wildly in her wake.

The man seated on the stool to my right slid a look my way. "Trouble in paradise?"

I snorted and shook my head. "You have no idea."

SEVEN

EVA

I swore I was going to kill him. I didn't even have to look up to know that the man who'd just stepped into the bar was none other than Fox—also currently known as the bane of my existence.

For the past three days, he'd shown up about halfway through my shift, then stayed until close and walked me home. Most of our time together had been spent in tense silence as I refuted every attempt at small talk.

I was more on edge than when I found out he'd broken into my house, and I was loath to admit that sleeping next to him every night but not allowing any intimacies between us had pushed my control to the limits. My temper was rapidly fraying, and I was ready to scream. The knowledge that it was my own doing offered no consolation.

At the end of the night, we silently trudged back to my

place. Fox locked the door behind us, and I spun toward him. "What the hell are you doing?"

He lifted one brow as he started to move past me toward the bedroom. "Getting ready for bed."

"You know what the hell I'm talking about." I planted my hands on my hips. "You drove halfway across the country and broke into my house instead of approaching me like any ordinary, sane person would. You spend every night sitting at the bar because you don't trust me, and—"

He whirled toward me. "That's bullshit and you know it."

I continued as if he hadn't even spoken. "This—this shit right here—is exactly why I left. I won't be treated like a prisoner, like I'm nothing more than a piece of property to you, you controlling bastard!"

"What the hell do you want from me, Eva?" Fox stormed forward, closing the distance between us, eyes dark with some unnamed emotion. "One minute I'm too unfeeling, the next I'm too controlling. This is exactly what you asked of me. You wanted me to prove I was serious— whatever the hell that means. You've never had a fucking problem telling me exactly what the hell you wanted before, just make up your goddamn mind!"

"Stop pressuring me! You've been breathing down my neck every single night." Fury simmered to the surface at being put on the spot. "I told you I need time to think about it."

"Do you prefer this over the life I can give you?" He swept his arms wide. "Is this what you want?"

"It's better than where I was." As soon as the words left my mouth, I wanted to call them back. Had I not been looking directly at Fox I would have missed the stricken expression that moved over his face. It was gone a split second later, replaced by a cold, hard mask. Shit. "I didn't mean that."

A muscle ticked in his jaw. "You must have, otherwise you wouldn't have said it."

Deep down I recognized the truth of it. I'd spewed the words out of anger, saying the most hurtful thing I could think of to make him feel the way I felt. Confused. Hurt. Frustrated. "I'm sorry."

Silence fell heavily between us and I held my breath, waiting for him to walk away from me. Neither of us spoke, yet Fox made no move to leave, either.

His gaze dropped to the floor. "Is there any chance of you coming with me, or have you already made up your mind?"

There was a vulnerability to his tone I'd never heard before. No, that wasn't true—I'd heard it once before, right after the invasion at his house. I drew back on that moment, and my heart constricted as I shook my head. "I haven't made up my mind. I just… I don't know what to do," I finally admitted.

We stared at each other for nearly a minute before he spoke. "I'm asking you, Eva—please give me this chance."

I lifted a brow. "You don't want to drag me back to Chicago with you?"

"Of course I do." He took a tiny step forward and settled his hands on my hips. "I would keep you with me forever if I could."

My heart gave a hard thump, and I swallowed hard. It was so reminiscent of our last few weeks together that it was becoming harder and harder to keep my emotions in check. "What about me? What if I decide I'm not happy there?"

I felt his hands tighten infinitesimally where they rested on my waist, almost as if his body had reacted automatically at the idea of letting me go. Silence stretched between us, and I could practically hear the thoughts rolling around his head as he fought to come to some sort of conclusion.

"Come to the island with me first. If you're still not happy, then… I'll let you go."

Something twisted inside me. It was exactly what I'd asked for—so why did hearing it hurt so much? It didn't make sense even as I thought it, but I didn't want him to just let me go. I wanted him to fight for me. After everything we'd been through, I wanted him to prove that he would give me the freedom I wanted and needed.

I tried to dissect my feelings as I stared at him, his gaze focused on the floor like he couldn't even look at me. He was normally so strong, so self-assured. I'd never seen him like this, almost as if he were afflicted by some kind of misgiving. Doubt, maybe? Was he truly worried that I would walk away forever? I didn't want to, but we had to find a way to meet in the middle. I refused to be a captive any more—but I did want to be with Fox.

"I meant what I said," I said softly. "I'm not yours to command. I won't be merely your possession."

Dark brown eyes finally lifted and searched mine. "I don't want to clip your wings, angel. I want you to come fly with me."

His words sent a little shiver of pleasure down my spine. I hoped what he said was true; I didn't want to give up everything I'd worked for over the past couple of months only to fall into the same destructive pattern with Fox. I wanted him to love me the way I loved him.

Over the past several weeks I'd begun to question whether I truly loved him or if I was just a casualty of Stockholm Syndrome, developing feelings for my captor. Deep down, I knew that wasn't the case. The moment I'd seen him lurking in my bedroom, relief like I'd never known had spread through me. But my love alone wouldn't be enough to save us.

"I'll go with you," I said slowly, "but only on a probationary period."

It sounded like a business transaction even to my ears, and a faint smile curved his mouth. "Is that right?"

"Yes," I said primly, determined to stick to my guns. I would *not* throw myself at him. No matter how much I wanted to.

His thumb swept along my side, teasingly soft and sensual. "It's a deal."

After another long sleepless—and sexless—night, I went into the bar and began to open the register while I waited for Bryce to show up. He slowed when he saw me and his astute gaze swept over my face, as if searching for answers. "You good?"

"Yeah." I sighed. "Can we talk?"

He nodded and led the way to his office. I sat in the chair and began to speak. "I really appreciate what you've done for me, going out on a limb and helping me when you didn't have to. But…"

"You're leaving."

I bit down on my lower lip. "I think so, yes."

One brow lifted. "You want to talk about it?"

I shook my head. "No. I just... I'll pay you back for everything. Things have... changed."

"In the past twelve hours?" My cheeks burned at the memory of seeing Fox again for the first time in months, and a knowing expression crossed his face. "It's him."

My head tipped to one side. "It's who?"

"The guy you hate to acknowledge."

"I don't—" He shot me a quelling look, and I slammed my mouth shut. "It's... complicated."

"It always is." He leaned forward, resting his elbows on the desk as he regarded me. "I want you to do whatever you think is best for you. If you change your mind, you will always have a place here. Deal?"

My eyes watered. "Deal."

"When are you leaving?"

I blinked my tears away. "I figured a week or two. Whatever gives you enough time to find a replacement."

He grinned. "We're not exactly slammed around here. I handled it by myself before you showed up; I can do that again."

"You're sure?"

"Absolutely. If you want to go with him, I wish you all the best."

A bittersweet longing tugged at my heart as I pushed out of my chair. There was nothing left for me here; it was time to move on. I just hoped I was doing the right thing. "Thank you again for everything."

He pulled me into a friendly hug. "You have my number. You need anything, you give me a call—no matter where you are or what time it is."

He pulled back and stared down at me, and I nodded. "I will."

"Good luck."

"Thanks." I tossed him a smile, then headed home.

Fox's wide eyes flicked to me as I walked through the door twenty minutes later. "You okay?"

"Fine." I shrugged. "I'm done."

He stood and slowly approached, stopping inches away. "You're sure?"

I nodded, and he kissed my forehead. "You won't regret this, angel, I promise."

I had my doubts.

EIGHT

FOX

The remainder of the day was spent packing Eva's things and getting everything in order. She refused to let me help —probably in a stubborn effort to drag things out as long as possible—so I spent a good portion of the afternoon on the phone finalizing our plans.

A quick glance at her closet revealed that she had nothing in the way of island wear, so I ordered a dozen outfits and swimsuits from a small local boutique to be delivered to the duplex. I briefly considered letting her choose her own things but immediately dismissed taking her out in public at the moment. The last thing I needed was for her to make a scene. Once we got to the island she could yell and scream at me all she wanted if she felt the need.

Eva tossed me a dark look when the clothes arrived but didn't say a single word. It irked the hell out of me, but I forced myself to remain calm as she disappeared into her room with the shopping bags and slammed the door.

Before staying with Eva I'd spent the previous several nights in a hotel downtown, and I'd arranged for my things to be sent back to Chicago so I wouldn't have to leave Eva alone. It left me with only one more change of clothes, but that didn't bother me in the least. I had plenty of clothing on the island.

Turning an eye to the clock, I realized that the day had quickly slipped away. I rooted through her drawers for takeout menus but came up empty, so I used Google to call in an order of Chinese food. Half an hour later, a delivery man knocked on the door and I paid him, then took the food. The exchange drew Eva's attention, and she finally exited her bedroom. I set the bag on the small, scarred kitchen table, then began to hunt around the open boxes for cutlery and plates. I heard her hovering in the doorway, but she remained silent as a mouse.

"Have a seat," I threw over my shoulder without looking at her.

"I'm not hungry."

Slowly, I turned toward her. "Remember what happens if you refuse to eat," I warned softly.

She glared at me and for a moment, I hoped with every fiber of my being that she would resist so I could spank her ass red. She'd been a brat all day and though I knew I was responsible for part of it, her behavior was grating on my nerves.

Locked in a silent battle of wills, I lifted a brow at her, and her eyes narrowed a fraction before she stomped forward, practically ripped the chair from under the table, and threw herself into it.

As soon as her ass hit the seat, I turned back to the box in front of me and a grin stretched over my face. God, I'd missed this woman. I loved her fiery personality as much as I loathed it, and I swore I would never get tired of being with her. Was I fucked in the head? Absolutely. Did I give a shit? Not a single one. Eva was the only thing that mattered, the only woman I wanted, and I was going to prove it to her, no matter what it took.

After dinner, Eva brought out the things we could ship back to Chicago. We made another pile of things to be donated and scheduled a pickup for the following day. The rest of her clothes were packed up for our trip to the island. We retired to bed, and I spent another frustrating night on my side of the mattress, feeling Eva toss and turn restlessly just a few inches away from me.

Though I wanted to roll over and pull her into my arms, I held myself back. I'd promised her that I would give her time and space, and I was determined to follow through with it. I knew Eva well enough by now to tell that she was just as bothered by the distance between us as I was, but she'd drawn the line in the sand—she would have to be the one to cross it first.

The following morning passed mostly in silence as we dressed and got ready to leave. Eva had promised to lock the apartment and leave the key under the mat, so she tucked it away as the hired driver pulled up to the curb.

"Ready?"

Keeping her gaze focused on the ground, she nodded and headed toward the car. I lugged our bags down the sidewalk where the driver took them from me and placed them in the trunk. Eva was already in the backseat, and I slid in behind her. Her gaze never moved from the window as we pulled away, leaving her new life behind.

Something similar to regret churned in my stomach as I studied her profile. Was she truly happy here? I didn't think so. Eva was a fighter, and if she'd truly wanted to stay, she would have. So why did I feel bad? I wasn't used to taking others' feelings into consideration, but Eva was different. I wanted her to be happy, but I also selfishly wanted her to find that happiness with me. As the miles bled away, I hoped like hell I wasn't making a huge mistake.

Eva remained quiet during the drive to the private airfield, and I watched her surreptitiously from the corner of my eyes. The tension in her muscles had exacerbated despite our tenuous truce. She seemed intent on punishing me, and though it irked me, I knew I deserved it. I was on a mission to win her trust, even if it killed me.

Her eyes widened a little bit as the driver pulled up next to a small, sleek black plane, the steps folded down and ready for us to board. She cocked a brow, and I found myself smiling. "Better than commercial," I said. "Besides, these guys come highly recommended."

She threw a challenging look my way. "You mean you don't have your own private plane? I'm shocked."

"Can't justify the expense," I returned. "Maybe if you start traveling with me more…" I allowed the sentence to trail off, and my unspoken words hung in the air between us. I wanted her with me all the time, everywhere I went.

Her eyes returned to the aircraft in front of us, but she didn't say a word. I knew she didn't believe things would actually be different this time, but I was determined to prove her wrong. Her edict that we not have sex had only strengthened my resolve. She was right; she was leaving this new life she'd created for me. Though I wanted to balk at the idea of not touching her, not kissing her, I would do it if only to show my sincerity.

"Come on," I said to her, gesturing toward the plane. "The faster we board, the faster you get to see your surprise."

"Fantastic," she returned with no small amount of sarcasm. "I still don't understand why you can't just tell me what it is.".

"Where would the fun be in that?" I asked, striving to keep my tone light.

Honestly, I was scared to death of what her reaction might be. She was already pissed at me, and this could push the delicate balance one way or the other. I was hoping that this would be a grand gesture of sorts to show her how much I cared for her.

Once Eva's meager belongings had been stored in the belly of the plane, we ascended the steps and were greeted by the pilot and his staff. Eva buckled herself in without looking at me, and I took a seat across the aisle from her. I caught her peeking out of the corner of her eye, and I reached over and lightly stroked the back of her hand with my fingertips. "I'd sit next to you, but the weight distribution is better this way for takeoff."

She nodded and shrugged like it didn't matter, but I saw the slight flicker of relief in her eyes. After ordering a glass of wine from the flight attendant, she settled into her seat, then tipped her head back and closed her eyes, effectively shutting me out. I would let her have a few more minutes to herself to come to terms with all the changes that had occurred over the past couple of days, but I knew better than to give her too much space.

Eva lost in her own mind was a dangerous place. For such a smart woman, she tended to overthink things, and for once, I wanted her to just feel. I wanted to show her that I meant every word, but I knew it was easier said than done. To hell with waiting for her to come to me. She was finally back in my life, and I wasn't about to let her get away again—not even for a second.

I waited until the plane reached altitude, then I unbuckled my seatbelt and moved over to the seat next to Eva. Even when I brushed her knee as I moved past, she continued to ignore me. Although her eyes were closed, I could tell from the tense set of her shoulders that she wasn't asleep. She was intent on punishing me, and that was fine. I would take her anger over her sadness any day. But one thing I wouldn't do was let her retreat back into her mind and fortify the wall she'd built up between us.

Picking up her hand, I laced our fingers tightly together, not relinquishing my hold when she tried to pull away. Her lashes fluttered, but she kept her eyes closed, and I tipped my head so my mouth was next to her ear. "You can be mad at me, that's fine. But you're going to be angry with me next to you. No matter what, I'm not leaving your side again."

There was a brief hesitation, then she lightly squeezed my hand. It was such a tiny gesture but for the first time in months, my world slowly began to shift back into place.

NINE

EVA

After another sleepless night, I was exhausted emotionally and physically. Fox's steady presence calmed me yet stoked my ire at the same time. I wanted so badly to believe him, but I was frustrated that he was still holding something back.

Why did he feel the need to hide things from me? Despite the fact that I'd asked several times, he refused to give me any indication of what awaited me at our destination. Things would be much less complicated if he would just be open with me. Still, he'd refused to say anything, and I stubbornly battled back with silence of my own.

Though I tried to sleep during the several hours we spent in the air, it was next to impossible. Curiosity kept me awake, ideas and speculation running rampant through my mind. If he thought some million-dollar beach house was going to win me over, he was dead wrong. It was going to take a hell of a lot more than a show of wealth to bring me back.

I knew he had money; that was well and good, but I wanted more. I wanted—needed—love. Respect. I wanted him to see me as an equal, not just a woman who lived with him. Much like the last two months, I'd spent the past few days replaying my time with Fox over and over in my mind. He'd pushed me out of my comfort zone in the bedroom yet protected me from harm.

For so long he'd been lost and alone. I wasn't sure he knew how to let anyone else in. I knew he cared for me—but would he ever be able to give me his heart?

Something flickered in the back of my mind. The night of the engagement party, he'd said something to me in a foreign language, but I'd run before he had a chance to explain what it meant. After we had sex four nights ago, I'd almost asked but chickened out at the last moment, afraid of the answer.

Another car was waiting for us when we landed on the island. Not wanting to appear too curious, I hadn't asked Fox many questions. I didn't want to admit it, but during the trip, my anger had begun to wane. We still had a long way to go, but I was tired of being unhappy, and a huge part of me wanted to wipe the slate clean.

He hadn't exactly given me a reason to trust him before, but I could tell he did truly care about me. I could either hold myself back and keep the walls between us to protect my heart, or I could decide to have faith in him and hope for the best.

The driver of the black car loaded my things, his dark

eyes studying me intently. He wore a kind of secret little smile, like he knew something I didn't, and it made me even more nervous. He was friendly enough during the drive through the winding hills, asking about our flight and making small talk with Fox. For the most part, I stared out the window, reveling in the rich and dense foliage and bright flowers that grew along the road.

The car slowed, then turned into a gated driveway. A few seconds later, the palms parted, revealing a huge stucco mansion the color of white sand.

"We're here," Fox said unnecessarily. I bit down on my tongue and schooled my expression into mild disinterest, but I knew I hadn't pulled it off when he chuckled a little. "So hard to please, Eva. Hopefully the next surprise will be better."

I couldn't honestly imagine anything better than this, but I didn't say as much. The driver opened my door, then held it for me as I slid out. A slight breeze ruffled my hair, kissing my skin with its gentle caress and bringing with it the scent of the ocean. Almost immediately, I began to relax. It was strange, but now that I was here, I had a sort of physical proof that Fox meant what he'd said.

The driver closed the door behind us, then gathered our bags and headed into the house. I stopped in the foyer, taking in the decor. For some reason I expected an island flare, but it was almost a mishmash of contemporary elegance mixed with the eclectic. As odd as it sounded, it just worked, and it appealed to me. It was exactly what I would've done with the place.

I glanced toward the stairs that led to the second floor. "Where will I be staying?" It was a sort of test, and I didn't realize how much I needed to hear the answer until Fox spoke.

Turning to face me fully, he met my gaze. "You can pick any room you'd like, but"—he drew a deep breath—"it would make me happy if you stayed with me."

I gave a little nod as relief filled me and lightened my heart. I didn't want it to look like I'd forgiven him just yet, so I kept quiet even though I was perilously close to throwing myself into his arms.

"You don't have to decide now," Fox continued, unaware of my train of thought. "Besides, there's something I would like to show you first."

Settling a hand on my lower back, he guided me further into the house. Ceiling fans whirled lazily overhead, gently stirring the air. The house was spacious and open, the rooms primarily divided by large arches and towering columns.

Toward the back of the house, we passed through a large, well-appointed kitchen, and though I was loath to admit it, it was one of the most beautiful places I'd ever seen. It wasn't as big as Fox's home in Chicago, but it was every bit as nice.

Windows lined the walls, allowing the natural light to spill in. We wound our way through a sitting room into a large, screened-in lanai full of potted plants and comfortable looking furniture. Pushing open the French doors, Fox allowed me to precede him onto a wide stone terrace. A large, crystal blue pool took up a good portion of the space, complete with a dozen chaise lounges and a small cabana that stood off to the side.

My eyes scanned the beautiful space, dotted with more

expensive looking patio furniture, a fire pit, and beautiful flowers, variations of which I'd never seen.

"Just a little farther," Fox said.

From what I could tell, the only other thing out here was a small building next to the pool where I assumed the pump and other necessary components were housed. Beyond that was a set of steps that led down to the beach. I was starting to get antsy, afraid that, after everything he'd said, he was going to let me down. I wasn't entirely sure what I was expecting, but this wasn't it.

I didn't care about a pool or a private beach. I wanted Fox, needed his love and devotion. I wanted to know that he was capable of opening up and inviting me into his world. "I've seen the ocean before," I said caustically.

Fox wrapped his fingers around my elbow and, using a slight pressure with the pads of his fingertips, turned me so I was facing him. I tipped my head up, shielding the sun from my eyes as he spoke. "I know I withheld information from you, and for that I was wrong. I want you to know everything—about me, about my life. I don't want any more secrets between us."

I let out an exasperated sigh. Why the elaborate ruse? Why couldn't he just open up and tell me instead of dragging this out? "You keep saying that, but…"

Motion from the corner of my eye drew my attention, and I trailed off as a figure emerged from the corner of the main house. Fox's hand dropped from my elbow, slipping lower to settle on my waist as I slowly turned toward the person. A blankness settled over my body as my heart stuttered to a halt.

My mouth opened as if trying to form words, then snapped shut again. Seconds felt like minutes, and I could practically feel the thrum of blood pulsing through my veins as I studied the woman who slowly approached, a tremulous smile on her face. Surely this was a mirage, a figment of my imagination.

I swallowed hard, fighting the tears that had gathered in my eyes. "Elle?"

TEN

EVA

"Surprise, angel," Fox whispered from just over my shoulder. He gave my waist a little squeeze, then released me. "Why don't you go say hello?"

Still frozen, I couldn't even look at him, my gaze still transfixed on my sister. I was dreaming; I had to be. There was no way…

"Eva."

That single word coming from my sister's mouth broke the moment, and I sprinted forward and launched myself into her arms. In a tangle of limbs, we held each other tight, and the tears fell unchecked. After what seemed like forever, I finally pulled back and framed her face in my hands. "It's really you. You're here. My God, I can't…" I still couldn't quite wrap my mind around the fact that this was real. She was here, alive.

"It's me," she whispered, tears sparkling in her pretty

blue eyes. "I thought I'd never see you again. I missed you so much."

"I missed you too," I managed to choke out. "How did you—" My mind spun then slammed to a halt as realization finally sank in. Fox had known about her all along. He'd been responsible for her disappearance, but contrary to what I'd been led to believe, he hadn't hurt her. I'd asked him once about my sister's death; all he'd told me was that she'd felt no pain. It was all so obvious now. But... "Why?"

She smiled, but there was a trace of sadness in her eyes. "It's a long story."

I'd almost forgotten that Fox was there until Elle lifted her gaze to him. She welcomed him with a hug, and I felt a slight twinge in the region of my heart as I watched them together. I could see his discomfort, and I knew how much it cost him to allow even that amount of intimacy from another person. There was so much more to him than met the eye, and I couldn't begin to reconcile every facet of his personality right now. It was just too much to comprehend.

The dark-eyed driver who'd dropped us off appeared at Elle's shoulder, and he wrapped one arm around her waist. My gaze bounced between all three of them, and I felt lightheaded as I swayed on my feet. "I think I need to sit down."

Almost immediately, Fox was there supporting me. "Come on, angel, it's been a rough couple of days. Let's go inside."

"No!" I threw a panicked look at Elle. "I—"

"Don't worry," he soothed. "She's not going anywhere. Let's get you two settled, then you can talk, okay?"

I nodded a little, and he kissed my temple before leading me into the sunroom that overlooked the pool. He guided me into a chair, then disappeared inside the house. I watched with a sense of disbelief as Elle and the other man entered the sunroom, and she dropped into the corner of the loveseat adjacent to me. Fox was back a minute later, pressing a bottle of water into my hand. "Drink."

Gratefully, I twisted off the top and took several healthy swallows. When the world no longer felt like it was spinning, I focused my attention on Elle and shook my head. "I just… God, this doesn't seem real."

My sister smiled softly then turned her gaze to the dark-skinned man who stood sentinel next to her. At her brief nod, he kissed the top of her head and moved away. Fox couldn't be so easily moved, though, and he continued to hover by my side. "You look pale."

I flicked a wry look his way. "More than normal?"

His teeth flashed in a grin before his expression turned serious once more. "You're sure you're feeling all right?"

I opened my mouth to speak, but Elle cut me off. "I'm sure she'll be fine as soon as the shock wears off."

Sending one more indecipherable look my way, Fox lifted my hand and squeezed my fingers. "I'll be right inside if you need anything."

I nodded, then watched him disappear into the kitchen. His gaze stayed glued to mine until the doors were firmly closed behind him.

"He's a good man."

I couldn't form words, so I just nodded. We sat in silence for a second, neither of us really knowing what to say. It all seemed so… surreal. My gaze roved over my sister. She looked healthy. Happy. I met her gaze. "How have you been?"

"Good." She smiled. "You look beautiful. How are you?"

Tears pricked my eyes again. "I missed you. So much."

"I missed you, too." Elle blinked away tears. She drew in a deep breath then let it out slowly, her blue eyes piercing into mine. "I'm sure you want to know what happened and why I'm here."

That was an understatement. "I thought… we all thought…" I couldn't even voice it. The hurt I'd felt at her absence radiated in a dull ache from my chest. I was grateful to see her, of course, but I couldn't help the tiny stab of resentment at the fact that she'd allowed us to believe she was dead.

"I know, and I'm sorry for that," she said, her tone drenched with sympathy. "But I had to completely disappear, and this was the best solution."

"But it's been months, Ellie," I argued. "Why didn't you have Fox at least let us know you were okay?"

"I didn't know you two"—she gestured toward the house with one hand—"knew each other. Besides, I couldn't risk Daddy or Spencer finding out."

Cold settled over me. "Did something happen?"

Her gaze dropped to the floor and stayed there. "Spencer is… charismatic. It's what makes him so good at his position in the Senate. He draws people in, makes them believe every word. It's the same thing that happened to me."

I remained silent, uneasy tingles stirring in my gut as she continued. "It started small, little things that didn't seem like such a big deal at the time. He wouldn't let me leave the house, took away all the credit cards. I knew he had the occasional drink, but then I found out he was using drugs. When I confronted him, he told me it was nothing—just a little something to help him relax. But then it got worse and worse. Hossam worked for him at the time, and he eventually helped me leave."

"Is that him?" I asked, thinking of the man I'd seen earlier. "Hossam?"

"That's him, although neither of us technically exist anymore." Her eyes met mine. "When we left the States, we had to change our names. Legally, Hossam is Miguel Kerik now, and I go by Claire when we're away from the house."

I stared at her, feeling cold and numb. "You changed your name?"

"It's safer this way." She lifted one shoulder. "It was better to leave everything in the past."

I gave my head a little shake. This was sounding worse by the minute. "Elle… Exactly how bad was it?"

Her mouth tightened. "It was bad," she said quietly.

How had we not known? "When did it start?"

Her lashes fluttered as she seemingly drew back to that moment in time. "Almost two years ago now."

I was floored. Judging from what Elle said, he must have flipped a switch right after they got married. A sick feeling took up residence in my stomach as she continued.

"You know what's crazy? I didn't even object to him making me stay at home unless he was with me. He told me it was for my safety, and I just… trusted him. Looking back, it was all so obvious."

She gave a little shake of her head, lost in thought. "He came home drunk one night, and we got into an argument over something stupid. I don't even remember what. He hit me, and afterward, he apologized over and over. I thought that was the end of it."

She let out a breath. "Turns out, it was just the beginning. The second time was even worse, and Hossam… helped me."

My stomach clenched. "Is that when you left?"

"I'd like to say yes, but…" She gave a sad little shake of her head. "Hossam wanted to take me to the hospital that night, but I couldn't risk Spencer finding out. That would have only made it worse. I didn't know what to do, and I didn't have anywhere else to go."

I swallowed down the emotion clogging my throat. "What happened?"

"There wasn't much Hossam could do, but he checked in with me later—asked if there was anything he could do to help. Nothing was ever supposed to happen between Hossam and me," she said. "But things with Spencer progressively got worse, and I didn't know who else to go to. Hossam helped me escape, made it look like I was killed. Fox used his contacts to brush any evidence under the rug, then helped us get new identities and put us up here."

God. I shook my head. I never would have pictured Spencer as a user, let alone abusive. But people surprised me all the time—our own father included. Which reminded me—Elle more than likely didn't know that story, either. "Daddy is in serious debt. He basically gave me to Fox."

Elle's eyes flashed with fire. "Are you kidding me?" Outrage poured from her. "What did Mom have to say?"

"I haven't spoken with her." This was all so messed up. "Did you even want to marry Spencer?"

She shrugged. "He didn't seem so bad at first. Besides, he was friends with Daddy. How bad could he be?"

A shiver rolled down my spine. He'd fooled every single one of us—except Fox. Elle's words from a few minutes earlier came back to me. *He wouldn't let me leave the house, took away all the credit cards. He told me it was for my safety, and I just... trusted him.* That was hauntingly familiar to what had happened between Fox and me, and I couldn't help the doubt creeping into the back of my mind, making me waver.

But then I met my sister's gaze, saw the glow in her eyes that had been missing for the past few years. Whatever had happened between her and Spencer was lightyears from what Fox and I had. I would never let him control me that way—never again.

ELEVEN

FOX

Seeing the women side by side was almost eerie. They looked so much alike I couldn't believe I hadn't noticed the resemblance immediately. Eva's eyes were the color of evergreens, while her sister's were blue. Elle's hair was a few shades darker, more of a rich honey than the pale gold of Eva's locks. Still, they shared the same nose, the same dark brows and high cheekbones.

I couldn't help but smile at Eva, her sweet laughter filling the air as she and Elle reminisced on some of their childhood antics.

"And the tree!" Eva said between giggles.

"Oh, my gosh… the tree!" Elle covered her mouth with one hand.

Eva caught my questioning look and explained, "When we were young, our mother bought this tree for the backyard. It was some special variation, and she paid a crazy amount of money for it. Anyway, one day Elle and I were outside playing, climbing on the branches"—she cut off again as she started to laugh—"and we snapped the top off the damn tree."

Hossam grinned at Elle, and she leaned into him, chuckling at the memory.

I draped an arm over the back of Eva's chair and lightly traced a pattern of circles on her shoulder. "What did you do?"

"Well," she threw a look my way before glancing across the table at Elle again. "We were terrified of what our mother would say, so Elle and I panicked. We had to fix the tree before she got home. We ran into the house and grabbed some tape—like the kind you wrap packages with. We taped the top of the tree back on and everything was fine—for a couple weeks."

Laughter bubbled up again, and she fought to control it. "Naturally, the part we broke off died, so while the rest of the tree was all green and full, the top was just this dead brown stick."

We all laughed, and Elle's face turned an even brighter red as she nearly doubled over.

"Did your mother figure out what you'd done?" Hossam asked.

Elle shook her head, a huge grin on her face. "To this day, she has no idea."

I laughed. "How did you hide it from her?"

Eva leaned slightly into me. "She demanded the gardener go up and find out what was wrong. Of course, he knew right away what had happened." She grinned. "But he kept our secret and told my mother the damage must have been caused by a storm. He rearranged some of the branches at the top to hide the bald spot, and we never got caught."

I loved seeing her like this, so open and uninhibited. I hadn't yet had a chance to talk with her as she'd spent all afternoon with Elle, but I loved that this had put a smile on her face. Even if she decided not to come back to Chicago with me, I would have brought her here a thousand times over just to see that look of pure elation.

For the next hour, Eva and Elle laughed and sipped wine until their cheeks were pink, their eyes sparkling. Elle leaned into Hossam, and he kissed her forehead. Eva watched them, a yearning expression on her face. Part of me wished she was comfortable enough to do the same with me. I wanted to pull her into my arms, prove to her that I could be her shoulder to lean on.

Instead, I sat silently. I'd pushed her enough over the past few days. Although she'd decided to come with me, she could still choose to walk away at any time. Now that she knew her sister was alive and well, she truly had no reason to need me anymore. She'd come to me to avenge her sister's death. Without that driving her, what would she do?

She'd told me before that she was with me because she wanted to be. But then she'd run without having all the facts. Would she do so again? I knew I was getting ahead of myself; I needed to give Eva some time to adjust and feel her way through it. I still hadn't told her everything—something I would have to do soon. I wasn't looking forward to that conversation, but I'd promised there would be no secrets between us.

Elle yawned. "Sorry. I'm exhausted."

The sun had dipped below the horizon hours ago, and

it had to be nearing midnight. I was hoping Eva was ready for bed, too, because I desperately wanted some time alone with her.

"It is getting late," Eva conceded, obviously disappointed. Instead of sulking, though, she stood and began to gather the dishes. I reached for my own, but she waved me off. "I've got it."

I watched Eva go, head dipped together with Elle's as they made their way toward the house.

"She's a wonderful girl."

I turned to face Hossam. "She is. Much like her sister."

He grinned. "Same temper, certainly."

At that, I laughed and lifted my glass in a mock toast. "Very true."

Hossam's eyes followed Elle, a soft look on his face. "I wouldn't have it any other way."

I knew exactly what he meant. I was so fucking thankful that Eva was back in my life. The months without her had felt like an eternity. I knew we still had unresolved issues to work through, but I was willing to do whatever it took as long as we could be together. I'd rather fight with her every day for the rest of my life than live without her.

For several moments we sat in comfortable silence, enjoying the cool night as the breeze swept over the ocean. Below us waves crashed softly against the shore, tossing the moonlight across the rippling surface.

"How have you been? No trouble, I presume?"

Hossam shook his head. "Everything has been quiet."

"Good."

"I owe you a thank you," he said quietly. "Without your help—"

I held up a hand. "You owe me nothing. I would do it

again, given the choice. Besides"—I bared my teeth in a feral smile—"you know how much I enjoy fucking with Masterson."

"That, I do." Hossam's expression turned deadly. "I should have killed him."

I'd asked him at the time what he wanted to do, leaving Masterson's fate up to Hossam. Because Spencer was fairly high profile, we'd decided it was in everyone's best interest to let him live. But what he'd done to Elle was inexcusable, and if Hossam wanted the man gone, I would find a way to make it happen. "Is that what you want?"

His shoulders rose and fell as he heaved a sigh. "Only on the bad days."

If there was anyone in this world who hated Spencer Masterson more than me, it was Hossam. He'd worked under the man for several years and had seen firsthand the damage Masterson had inflicted on Elle, both mentally and physically.

I remembered the day Hossam had requested a meeting at Noir. I'd assumed he needed a loan. But unlike most men of our acquaintance, Hossam didn't gamble or overindulge. Instead, he'd come for something far darker. He told me how Masterson's drug problem had worsened and how his wife, Elle, suffered because of it. Unable to step in to protect her himself, Hossam requested my help. It was evident to anyone with eyes that he cared deeply for Masterson's wife.

Naturally, I did what I did best. I'd read him and seen for myself just how cruel Masterson could be. No additional explanation needed, I had decided on the spot to help. Spencer Masterson had connections of his own— but mine were more widespread. To ensure their safety, I told Hossam that he and Elle would have to leave the country, at least until things had settled. He agreed, willing to do anything to help Elle.

The timing couldn't have been better. I had just purchased this home, and I offered to let them stay here under the stipulation that he work for me. Hossam was an incredibly hard worker and loyal as hell. That night at Noir, we worked out an elaborate plan to extricate Elle from Spencer's control. To make it believable, though, Hossam had to leave Masterson's employ.

Convincing him to do so wasn't easy, but I promised I would have someone watching over Elle in his absence. Hossam laid low for the next month until I was able to pull Elle from Masterson's clutches. Over the next month, I met with her once a week at Dr. Marlowe's office, where he drew a pint of her blood. When the time finally came, my men and I staged the crime scene using Elle's blood and trace DNA.

I would never forget Hossam's reaction when I finally brought Elle to the house where he'd been staying. I had never seen a man look happier in my entire life, and it was the same look he'd bestowed on her this evening. I was incredibly glad that things had worked out for them. I only wished that I could find the same happiness with Eva.

From my spot on the terrace, I could see through the windows into the kitchen. Eva stood next to the large island, and even from here I could see the joy radiating from her. My heart twisted in my chest. Would she ever forgive me? I sure as hell hoped so, because I had no idea how I would ever go on without her.

TWELVE

My head spun, and my heart felt like it hadn't slowed down all afternoon. Though I'd spent nearly the past six hours with my sister, it still didn't feel quite real. I was terrified that I would wake up tomorrow and find out it was all some horribly wonderful dream.

Standing next to Elle in the kitchen, I dragged out the process of cleaning the dishes, making small talk with my sister until Fox and Hossam finally came inside.

"Ready for bed, angel?"

I bit the inside of my lip and threw a surreptitious look at Elle, but she only had eyes for Hossam. Turning back to Fox, I pasted on a smile. "Sure."

He wrapped one arm around my shoulders and nodded to the other couple. "We'll see you in the morning."

"Good night." Elle gave a little wave, and I longed to throw my arms around her again and hold her close. I'd lost her once; I didn't want to let her out of my sight, even for a second.

"Come on. You've both had a long day." The firm but gentle pressure of Fox's fingers against my shoulder prompted me to move, and I gave a little wave of my own before turning and heading toward the stairs. He steered me into a room at the corner of the house with windows on two walls that overlooked the ocean. So preoccupied was I with my thoughts that I couldn't even appreciate the beautiful view.

Behind me, I heard Fox close and lock the door. I spun toward him and thumped him on the chest.

He let out a soft *oof*, and his eyes flared with surprise. "What the hell was that for?"

"That was for not telling me about Elle months ago." I flung myself into his arms, overjoyed by the revelations of the day. Looping my arms around his neck, I pulled him down for a kiss.

Nearly a minute later he lifted his head, breathing heavily, eyes glazed with lust. His voice was thick when he spoke. "And what was that for?"

"For being you." I lifted my hands to the thin straps of my sundress and shrugged them off my shoulders. The fabric fell to my waist, catching on my hips, and Fox's eyes lit with interest as they landed on my exposed breasts.

"Is this my reward?"

"Something like that," I teased, pressing my hands to his shoulders and jumping into his arms. He caught me, just as I knew he would, and spun so I was pinned to the wall. Strong fingers curled into my bottom, and I arched, rubbing myself against him. I needed to feel close to him again, and this was the best way I knew how.

Fox levered his weight against me, the hard ridge of his arousal expanding and pressing against my hot center, covered only by my thin cotton panties. "Are you drunk?"

I leaned in and bit his ear. "Why?"

He let out a little growl as he shifted me in his arms so there was barely a breath of space between us. "Because I don't want you to regret this in the morning."

Would I regret it? Maybe. I couldn't be sure. Confusion and lust and need ricocheted through my heart like pinballs, but I couldn't overlook the fact that he'd done this for me. The fact that he'd brought my sister back to me showed me exactly what kind of man he was. He wasn't perfect. Hell, he wasn't even good. He could have allowed me to live in ignorance, believing for the rest of my life that my sister was gone forever. Instead, he cared enough to bring me here and show me the truth.

"I won't regret it," I murmured as I wrapped my arms around his neck. "I want you—only you."

His head dipped, and he kissed the slope of my neck before sinking his teeth into the base of my throat. I jerked, my pelvis rubbing deliciously against his erection, and an involuntary moan filtered from my lips.

"God, Eva…"

Abruptly, Fox spun us away from the wall and strode toward the bed. My back hit the mattress a mere second later and I stared up at him, unable to move, as he grasped the hem of my dress and jerked it upward until my stomach was bared to him.

"So fucking gorgeous."

My hands sank into the short, coarse hair at the back of his head as his lips brushed across my navel. Feathering kisses lower, his fingers teased the waistband of my panties before tracing a line across my hip bone and down the crease between my torso and thigh. Deftly he slipped beneath the fabric, and I arched into him as he swept his thumb over my clit. "Fox!"

With his free hand he brushed the backs of his fingers over my nipple, sending a shiver down my spine. His kisses changed direction, taking the stiff peak between his lips and teasing it with a gentle scrape of his teeth. My hips jerked at the sensation, and I could feel the moisture pooling in my core, easing the way for Fox's questing fingers.

He lifted his head and smiled down at me. "I love that you're always so hot for me."

Part of me wanted to slap that smug grin off his face, but I couldn't summon the energy, dazed with pleasure as I was. The only sound that left my mouth was a little whimper of need as Fox pulled his fingers free and started to strip my panties down my legs. I lifted my hips, maneuvering my feet in an attempt to help. Once my feet were free of the material, I struggled out of the dress.

Fox towered over me, a little smile on his face as he stared down at me, his fingers dancing softly up and down my calf. "You were awfully mouthy these past couple of days."

A little thrill ran through me at his words. "What are you going to do about it?"

The corner of his mouth kicked up in a smirk and, quick as a flash, he grabbed my hips and flipped me over so my ass pointed up to the sky. A shiver of anticipation rolled down my spine as he ran his hand over the curve of my right cheek. I knew what was coming; I wanted it— needed it. Just like the other night, the first blow took my breath away. It was just hard enough to hurt, just powerful enough to make me jolt forward under the force of it.

He landed two more slaps in the exact same place, and I winced even as I felt the heat in my core flare outward, my arousal coating my lips and inner thighs. I loved giving myself over to him like this. I didn't have to think, didn't have to worry. I knew he would take care of me, give me everything I needed and then some. Handing him control over my body was an exercise in trust, and there was no one I wanted more than Fox.

A hard smack to my left cheek caught me off guard, and I jumped a little. The pain morphed into intense pleasure, causing my toes to curl. More playful than punishing, he delivered a dozen more stinging slaps. He massaged my cheeks, then spread them wide so I was completely exposed to him. "Fucking love this view. All wet and ready for me."

I shivered as he kissed one cheek, then moved lower. His tongue darted out, licking through my folds, and I clenched the bedspread to keep from crying out in sheer ecstasy. My legs trembled, and Fox chuckled. "You like that, angel?"

I couldn't find the breath to form words, and I jumped as a firm hand landed on my left cheek. "I asked you a question."

His mouth fastened onto my clit and he sucked hard, eliciting a wail from me. "Oh, God!"

"Was that a yes?"

My entire body shook from the effort of holding myself up, and Fox rolled me to my back before levering himself over me. I stared up into those intense dark eyes and said the only thing that came to mind. "I love everything you do to me."

His nostrils flared and some unnamed emotion glinted in his eyes. I sucked in a breath as his fingers curled into the flesh of my hips, and Fox jerked me toward the edge of the bed. My heart pounded with excitement as he spread my legs in a wide vee and ground his pelvis against mine, the soft fabric of his slacks brushing over my sensitive folds.

I bit my lower lip, choppy breaths escaping in shallow pants as I watched him drink in every inch of me. He took my feet in his huge hands, gently massaging the arches before sliding his palms over my ankles, up my calves. His hands hooked behind my knees and dragged me up his body until I rested on my shoulders on the bed, my pussy inches away from his face as my legs dangled over his back.

Holding my hips firmly, he met my gaze and dipped his head to my center. I nearly shot off the bed as his tongue speared into me, hot and insistent. I pressed my head into the mattress as he nipped my clit, curling my fingers into the fabric of the comforter to ground myself in the storm of violent emotions. He licked and teased and ate at me, drawing out the sensual torture until I was nearly mindless with need and crying out for release.

Fox lifted his head and smiled down at me, his lips shiny from my arousal. "You ready to come, angel?"

"God, yes, please!"

He chuckled and flicked his tongue over my clit once more before lowering me to the bed. "I want to be deep inside you when you come so I can feel every inch of you."

I watched as he stripped out of his shirt and pants,

discarding the expensive garments carelessly on the floor. Instead of waning, my desire ratcheted up with every second that passed. Things had never been easy between Fox and me—except in the bedroom. Here we spoke fluently, attuned to one another's needs. I'd gone months without him, and I needed to feel the connection we'd once had.

After the tumultuous events of the past few days, I needed to feel close to him. I needed the solace and strength that only he could offer. Never in the time I'd spent in Omaha had I considered sleeping with anyone else. Now Fox was back. I had no idea what would happen tomorrow or the next day, but I wanted this moment right here, right now.

"I need you." The words cracked as they left my throat, and Fox paused briefly as he stripped off his socks.

Propping a knee on the edge of the bed, he slowly climbed between my legs and caged me between his lean, muscular arms. "You have me, angel. I won't let you go."

THIRTEEN

FOX

Using my knee, I nudged her legs apart and settled between her thighs, every inch of her pressed against every inch of me. My erection prodded her wet, hot folds, and I slid one hand from her hip up to her breast. Her hands skimmed over my shoulders and across my back. I met her gaze and held as she splayed one hand over my scars, like she could take away the pain of the past.

And it was true. With Eva, I forgot about everything else. She was my whole world, the light that chased away the oppressive darkness. I let out a little growl then pushed forward, sinking into her. There was no resistance as she accepted me easily; she was always wet for me, always ready.

I pulled out until I was almost free of her then plunged back in. Reaching behind me, I captured first one hand then the other and pinned them to the bed over her head. I loved her like this. This position had always filled me with a sort of power, but seeing strong-willed Eva, breasts pushed forward in offering, completely and totally at my mercy, made me harder than I ever thought possible.

My dick throbbed as I thrust deep on slow, measured strokes. Our lovemaking the other night had been rough, fast, and raw, driven by mutual need. Tonight was different, more intense somehow, propelled by a multitude of emotions I couldn't begin to analyze. All I could focus on was how glad I was that she was back in my arms— hopefully for good—right where she belonged. The relief was almost palpable, and her presence calmed me, settled my heart.

I'd loved watching her reaction—the sheer disbelief, the pure joy—when she'd set eyes on her sister this afternoon. I wanted to put that same look on her face for the next fifty years. I had a kingdom to run, and I couldn't do it without my queen by my side. She made me better, stronger… more human. She belonged with me.

I set out to prove that very fact, using the slower, more tortuous pace to drive us both crazy until she was writhing beneath me. Her hips bucked upward to try to take me deeper, to push herself closer to the edge. With a little chuckle I pulled back, teasing her clit with the tip of my cock as I brushed it through her folds.

"Fox!" Her green eyes flashed up at me. "Please!"

"What do you need, angel? This?" I dipped my head and took the taut peak of one nipple in my mouth.

A little mewl broke free from her throat, and she wrapped her legs around the backs of my thighs, urging me to move. "Damn it, Fox! I need—Oh!"

Her body jerked as I lightly bit down on the tender tip, and her sexy little gasp filled the air. I rolled my hips, sinking an inch inside her sweetness. Christ, she felt so good. Releasing her wrists, I braced my hands on the mattress next to her shoulders for better leverage as I pulled out, then plunged back in, my cock bottoming out inside her. Her hands automatically moved to my biceps, her nails cutting into my skin as I withdrew then drove into her over and over.

Her tits bounced under the force of my thrusts, and I palmed one globe, digging my fingers into her flesh hard enough to leave bruises, holding her tightly in place as I pistoned in and out. Sex had never felt this good before. She gasped and clawed at me, searching for more. I gave her everything I had, pounding into her with everything I had.

Her pussy clenched tightly around me, and I knew she was close. Abandoning her breast, I slipped a hand between her legs to her distended clitoris. She bucked wildly as I fingered the sensitive bundle of nerves, and a keening cry ripped from her throat as she hurtled toward the edge of orgasm. Gripping her shoulder in one hand, teasing her clit with the other, I thrust into her, each stroke harder than the last. She shattered on a scream, her pussy flooding my cock with her juices.

I picked up the pace, and my muscles tensed as fire licked up my lower back. My mouth pulled into a grimace as my cock swelled with my release, and I emptied myself inside her on a groan.

I collapsed on top of her, trying to catch my breath as my exhausted muscles quivered under the strain of exertion. Our bodies were sealed together by sweat, but I didn't care. Keeping her clasped tightly to me, I rolled to my back and pulled her with me so she lay draped over my torso. Her head nestled into the crook of my neck, and I brushed a kiss over the top of her head as I held her close.

We didn't need words. We didn't need assurances. We needed nothing but each other.

FOURTEEN

EVA

I fingered the red silk scarf in front of the vendor's booth, lost in thought.

A firm hand landed on my hip and squeezed gently. "We could put that to use later if you'd like."

A tiny smile quirked my mouth, but I didn't meet his gaze. "We'll see."

I continued down the row of booths lining the street, falling into step next to Elle as she moved to the next street vendor. No matter how many times I tried to turn it off, the memory of last night—of yesterday in general— flashed to the forefront of my mind. Things between Fox and me had seemed… different. Or maybe it was just me. I was still just as in love with him as I was two months ago —maybe more so.

It was true that he'd withheld information about Elle, but even she herself had told me that it was for her own safety. Part of me was still disgruntled that Fox hadn't trusted me enough to understand, but I grudgingly knew why he didn't. If he had opened up to me, I could've slipped and said something to my father, and it would've jeopardized Elle's safety.

I respected him deeply for taking care of both Elle and Hossam. He could have merely sent them on their way as soon as he had secured their new identities. Instead, he had set them up in his own home based only on good faith. Granted, the situation was mutually beneficial, but it didn't change the intent behind his actions.

Elle and I walked in front, but the men remained close by, not letting either of us out of sight. Both Fox and Hossam were protective, but I assumed they knew best. I'd heard horror stories about tourists, primarily females, who were kidnapped and never seen again. With these two at our side, I knew no one would mess with us.

I knew from what Elle told me yesterday that Hossam had worked as a guard to Spencer before they ended up together. It was obvious to me that she cared for him, but I couldn't for the life of me figure out why he'd chosen Elle instead of remaining loyal to Spencer. I was eternally grateful that he'd helped her, but I was just suspicious enough to be wary of his intentions. Our family was well-off, and I didn't want him taking advantage of her if she was only a means to an end.

Elle and I perused the fruit at the stand before moving on. I kept my voice low as I leaned closer to her and spoke. "I still have trouble thinking of you as Claire."

She threw a smile my way. "Doesn't really fit me, does it?"

"It's not that. It's just..." I hesitated. "I think it's all of it. In my mind, you were gone for almost a year. And now you're here. But everything's so different."

She pulled me to the side and we took a seat on a small concrete bench. "I know it sounds weird, but I wouldn't have done this if I didn't want to."

That was true. Something had been bothering me, and her words stirred something in my mind. "Why don't you stay in the main house with us? There's plenty of room, and—"

Elle shook her head. "I like our house."

"I won't have my sister treated like a servant," I snapped. "If Fox thinks—"

Elle grabbed my hand. "It was our choice."

The wind immediately left my sails. "But why?"

"Fox has done so much for us. Hossam's pride wouldn't allow him to accept Fox's charity. We looked for another home on the island, but Fox finally managed to convince him to live in the servant's quarters in exchange for taking care of the main house."

I swallowed hard. There were so many facets to Fox I'd never seen, and each time a new one was revealed, I fell for him a little more.

From outward appearances, it seemed that Hossam truly loved my sister. Still, I couldn't stop the nagging need to keep asking, to make sure she hadn't been coerced. "As long as you're happy, that's all that matters. But don't you ever want to go home?"

She shook her head. "There's nothing for me there. I have everything I need right here. For the first time in years, I'm... happy."

"Good." I forced a smile to my lips. "I'm glad."

She seemed to sense there was more to my question,

because she tipped her head to one side as she studied me. "Something's bothering you."

"It's just…" I sighed. "Don't take this the wrong way, okay?"

She nodded, and I threw a quick look over her shoulder before meeting Elle's gaze again. "I know you love Hossam—but does he feel the same?"

"I think so." A tiny smile curled the corners of her mouth. "It seems strange to you, doesn't it?"

I couldn't lie. "I mean… He worked for Spencer. I don't want him using you or tossing you aside as soon as he thinks it's safe."

"I don't think he will." She gave her head a little shake. "You know… Hossam and I had kind of a rough beginning."

"What do you mean?" I tucked a strand of hair behind my ear and turned to face her more fully, pulling my knee up and resting it on the bench between us.

"Hossam and I didn't exactly get along when we first met."

"Really?" I'd assumed that they'd at least been friendly; why else stick up for her once he'd learned of her troubles?

Elle let out a little laugh. "Not at all. We butted heads constantly. He always seemed so hard and fierce. He was more like a jailer than a bodyguard."

It still struck me as a little strange that Spencer had needed bodyguards. Something Fox had said about him months ago came to mind, and I wondered if Fox was investigating him as a possible lead in the human trafficking ring. I made a mental note to ask him later as Elle continued.

"We pretty much despised each other. He thought I was high maintenance and snooty, and I called him a narcissistic, egotistical asshole."

I smothered a laugh. "How in the hell did you guys end up together, then?"

My heart clenched as Elle's expression turned serious, almost sad. "He overheard us arguing one night. Spencer lost his temper and slapped me right across the face, then stormed out of the house."

Her fingers curled around the seat of the stone bench as she spoke. "I was so embarrassed, you know? Part of me couldn't even believe it had really happened. I went into the kitchen and Hossam was already there. He didn't say a word, just handed me an ice pack from the freezer, then left."

"Spencer came home later and apologized, swore he'd never do it again. Said he was just stressed out." Elle blew out a breath. "Things were okay for a while and after a month or so, I thought he really meant what he'd said—that it was just an accident. But he started using more, and things got increasingly worse. One night we got into it and he cracked my ribs. That was when Hossam finally spoke up.

"I'll never forget that," Elle said softly. "He wanted to take me to the hospital, but I refused. He looked me dead in the eyes and said, "Don't you dare forgive him. You deserve better than this." He took care of me afterward, then asked me about leaving. I tried to talk to Daddy, but he didn't want me to come home. He said it would look bad."

Elle shook her head. "Hossam tried to keep me out of the way when Spencer was in a mood, but sometimes it couldn't be avoided. It escalated quickly over the next couple of months, but by then Hossam had contacted Fox about getting us out of there. He had to leave first so it wouldn't look suspicious when I disappeared. Those few weeks without him were… horrible."

"I'm so sorry," I whispered. "I had no idea."

"You couldn't have known." She lifted one shoulder. "I tried to hide it from everyone. It was strange how he and I went from almost enemies to friends, then… you know." She smiled a little. "It wasn't even a sexual attraction—not at first. But I knew there was more to him than met the eye, and he eventually admitted that he'd been attracted to me from the very beginning but couldn't say anything because of Spencer."

"I can understand that," I said. Fox was the same way.

"What about you?" she asked, studying me.

I shrugged. "I'm still processing everything, I think. It might take awhile for it to really feel real."

"What about Fox?" she prodded. "Is he good to you?"

I hesitated before speaking. "Yes, though I didn't know it at the time."

Confusion filled her eyes, and she turned to face me. "What do you mean?"

I recounted the events I'd glossed over before, telling her how I'd broken into his home to avenge her death, then was caught by the man himself. I told her how he'd kept me captive, refusing to allow me to speak to anyone from my old life.

Throughout my tale, her expression morphed from disbelief to concern to fury. "I hope you gave him hell for that."

"I may have…" I bit my lip. "Kind of… stabbed him." Her eyes widened, and her jaw went slack.

"With a fork," I added.

A muscle in her face twitched, then her composure cracked completely and Elle exploded into a fit of laughter. My cheeks burned as I met Fox's curious gaze over her head.

"It's not funny," I said caustically.

"No," she said between giggles. "It's hilarious. I'll bet he won't piss you off again."

I snorted. "He pisses me off all the time."

She used her thumb to wipe a tear from her cheek as she curbed her mirth. "Only because you two are so much alike. God, I swear you were made for each other."

It felt like a swarm of butterflies had taken up residence in my stomach, their wings battering my heart. Outwardly our situation seemed so strange. Most people would have thought the absolute worst—that he was preying on me, taking advantage of my naivete . But for Elle to see us as compatible meant the world.

My sister reached over and took my hand, leaning her head on my shoulder. I was aware of the men hovering several yards away, giving us our privacy but always keeping us in sight.

"You love him, don't you?"

Elle's words startled me. "Who?"

She lifted her head and gazed at me, the expression on her pretty face telling me she didn't believe my ignorance for a second. I sighed and dropped my eyes to the ground at my feet. "I… I don't know."

"He's a good man."

"I know." I lifted my eyes to hers. "But life with him will never be normal. Nothing with him will ever be easy."

Her gaze flitted over my shoulder before returning to me. "There's something to be said for easy things. Anyone can do something if it's easy. Fox will never be an easy man to love. It will take a strong woman to stand by his side and absorb the pain and hurt of others in order to help."

My eyes burned with tears. "But what if something happens to him?"

Elle's lips lifted into a tiny smile that almost immediately fell away. "People die every day. You could marry an accountant who lives a safe life and you could be happy. But he could die in a car accident on the drive to work one day, and you'd feel exactly the same."

I knew she was right, but it didn't ease the emotions roiling in my stomach. I still had so many concerns, not the least of which was the fact that I continued to fall into bed with him every chance I got. I couldn't tell if it was self-destructive behavior or if it was love. I'd fallen for him months ago, and the past few days had only served to reinforce those feelings. I knew he would keep me safe, do everything in his power to protect me.

Elle reached over and laid her hand over mine. "Men like Fox come around once in a lifetime. He has everything most men only dream of having—money, power, prestige. But not the thing he really needs. Love him, Eva. Love him the way he deserves."

Tears pricked my eyes. "When did you get so smart?"

She looped her arm around my shoulders and pulled me into a hug. "Since I met the love of my life."

In that moment, I knew exactly what I needed to do. Fox had left a mark on my heart that would stay with me forever, and no one else could ever fill that space.

FIFTEEN

FOX

I watched Eva where she sat on the edge of the bed, smoothing lotion into her skin. We'd retired to our room again after dinner, and Eva had taken her time showering —alone, much to my chagrin—before coming back into our room.

She'd pulled on a silky, semi-sheer nightie that I'd ordered from the boutique in Omaha. It clung to every soft curve, stopping mid-thigh so her lean legs were exposed to my view. Her hair was still damp, hanging in loose waves down her back, and she looked so goddamn pure and sweet that I wanted to strip her bare, take her over and over all night long.

But the change in her demeanor worried me intensely. Something with Eva had seemed off all day, ever since she and Elle had spoken earlier while we were at the market. "What's bothering you, angel?"

She offered me a small smile that didn't reach her eyes. "Nothing."

I shed my jacket, hanging it over the back of the chair before moving toward the bed. "Are you enjoying yourself so far?"

"I am. It's been wonderful to see my sister—like a dream come true."

She said it so wistfully that something tightened in my chest. "And that's a bad thing… why?"

She sighed. "Because it can't last."

"Why not?" I took a seat beside her.

"Because I have to go home eventually."

I shrugged. "Not unless you want to. You could stay here forever if you chose. "

Her misty green eyes met mine and held. "You would let me stay here?"

I tucked a strand of hair behind her ears. "Anything your heart desires is yours. You know that."

I found myself hoping that she would see the truth in my response, that she would choose to stay here—to stay with me.

A heavy breath left her lungs. "I can't. I need to go home and speak with my father."

At that, I stiffened. "I would prefer you not."

After everything that asshole had put her through, I didn't want her anywhere near him.

Her eyes hardened. "I have to. After everything he's done —to both Elle and me—I can't let him just get away with it."

Biting down on my tongue, I forced down the urge to forbid her from doing so. If I denied her outright, it would only push her to do the opposite out of spite. "We can do it together," I offered. "Or we can figure out some other way to make him accountable for his actions."

"I can't ask that of you." She shook her head. "You've done so much for me already."

Her words sent a pang of guilt through my heart. I'd held her captive and lied to her about my reason for doing so, yet she still viewed me as her savior. "I will always be here for you. You can speak with your father and clear the air once and for all. Then you can come back here and stay with Elle and Hossam if you'd like, or..."

I couldn't voice that last thought. The idea of letting her go again cut me like a knife. I wanted what was best for her, of course, but... I wanted her to choose me.

She was silent for a second, teeth cutting into her lower lip as she studied me. I could practically see the thoughts flitting through her brain as she undoubtedly tried to determine my sincerity. Finally, she spoke. "What about you?"

"I need to finish this. I need to find Araña and bring him to justice."

She nodded a little. "I want to help."

No way in hell. I never wanted to expose her to the things I'd heard and seen. I chose my words carefully, speaking with as much honesty as possible without telling her no outright. "We don't have to figure this out today. You can stay here as long as you like, take all the time you need. But for right now..." I lifted one hand and trailed my fingers beneath her chin. "I just want you to feel. We lost so much time, Eva. I want to make it up to you."

She looked like she wanted to argue, and I coasted my hand down her neck, teasing her collarbone with the tip of my fingers. "Close your eyes, angel."

She did as I bade, and I took my time touching her, lightly dragging my fingertips up and down her arms, over her shoulders, kneading the tight muscles there. Her lips parted slightly under my ministrations, and I just had to kiss her. Lightly at first, I took her mouth with mine, teasing her with my lips and tongue.

Eyes still closed, she looped her arms around my neck and threw herself into the kiss. Sliding my hands down her back and under her bottom, I pulled her over my lap so she was straddling me. I tore my mouth from hers and kissed my way across her jaw, down her neck, and over her shoulder to the spaghetti-thin strap that held her negligee up.

I slipped one finger beneath the material, licking along the edge of her collarbone as I worked it over her shoulder. The bodice of the nightie sagged, and I moved lower, dropping kisses over the swell of her breast before freeing it from its confines.

Eva made a little sound of pleasure deep in her throat and curled one hand into the back of my head, holding me close. I could have told her she had nothing to worry about; I wasn't going anywhere. But my mouth was preoccupied with much better things at the moment.

I worked down the bodice of her nightie until her torso was completely bared to me, and I plumped the mounds in my hands. "Fucking love your tits."

"I know."

I grinned at the breathless sound of her voice and brushed one pink tip with my thumb. "You like it when I play with them?"

She arched into my hand, giving silent confirmation. She was going to have to do better than that. I rolled her nipple between my thumb and forefinger, then tweaked it hard. I was rewarded when she let out a sharp hiss. "You like that, angel?"

"God, yes." She shifted on top of me, grinding her pussy against the swell of my erection, her body begging for release. Turning, I lay her on her back then kissed my way down her body as I slid from the bed. I grabbed the fabric pooled around her waist and worked it over her hips and down her legs, then dropped it to the floor.

Once she was completely bare, I shucked my own clothing before climbing back onto the bed. Eva watched me through hooded eyes as I moved up her body and straddled her chest, my dick only inches from her lips.

"Take it, angel." I fisted my cock and brushed the tip across her lips. "I want to fuck that pretty mouth of yours."

Her tongue darted out, wetting her lips, and I eased forward, sliding into the hot cavern of her mouth. Her arms were trapped down by her sides, but that didn't stop her. She grasped my hips, pulling me as far into her mouth as she could take me. I let out a little groan as her tongue swirled around the head, and my pelvis jerked at the sensation. Fuck, that felt so good. I reached between her legs and fingered her slit, fucking her mouth and pussy at the same time.

The angle wasn't ideal, but I didn't give a goddamn. The sight of my dick sliding between her shiny, saliva-slick lips, Eva completely at my mercy, was erotic as hell. I lifted myself off of her, replacing my cock with the fingers I'd had buried in her pussy. Eyes locked on mine, she licked my fingers, lapping up her own juices. "Such a dirty girl."

I leaned forward and captured her mouth with mine in

a hard kiss. My dick was rock hard, and I needed to be inside her. Rolling to the side, I pulled her with me and maneuvered to a sitting position against the headboard. "I want you on my cock."

One brow arched toward her hairline, and I lightly spanked her ass. "Now."

Taking her time, Eva arranged herself over my lap. My cock jutted up eagerly, just waiting to slide inside her, and it jumped when she took it in her hand. She pumped once, twice, then notched the tip just inside her entrance. The feel of her... It was like nirvana. A hundred years could pass and I would still recall in vivid detail exactly how she felt, how she tasted. I would never get enough.

SIXTEEN

EVA

Suspended over him, I rolled my hips once, delighting in the little hiss Fox let out. I loved teasing him. His hands slipped around to my bottom, and he squeezed my cheeks hard. "Woman, if you don't start moving…"

"You'll what?" I cocked a brow and grinned at him.

Fox let out a little growl, pulling me down at the same time he thrust up into me. The sensation of him filling me took my breath away, and I clung to his shoulders as he lifted me up and down. I finally caught the rhythm he'd set and began to move.

One hand curled into my ass cheek while the other tunneled into my hair as I rode him hard. He tightened his hold on my hair and yanked me down to him, fusing our mouths together in a hot, needy kiss. His tongue swept over mine, stealing my breath and making my heart race. His hand left my hair and trailed down my neck to my breast. He fondled it in his hand, teasing my nipple with a feather light touch. I ripped my mouth away from his with a groan and picked up my pace.

Seeming to sense my need for more, Fox dipped his head and took my nipple in his mouth. He sucked and nipped the tender flesh, and I felt the tell-tale tingles start low in my belly. Fox's hand crept lower on my bottom until his finger rubbed at my cleft from beneath, right where I rode his cock. He reversed directions and dragged his finger upward, through my cheeks until he reached the rosebud entrance of my ass. I sucked in a little breath and momentarily lost my rhythm as he circled it, gently probing the gathering of nerves there.

It was such a strange sensation, one I'd never felt before, and one I wasn't entirely sure I was comfortable with. "Fox..."

He released my nipple and kissed my jaw, then my lips, all the while teasing my back entrance. "Trust me, Eva." He nipped my chin. "Let go, angel. Just feel."

I was helpless to the myriad sensations streaming through my body, and I had no choice but to obey him. I rolled my hips, taking him deeper. His mouth moved to my nipple again as his finger pressed against my rosebud and gently breached the entrance.

I gasped at the fiery sensation that shot through my muscles. Just as quickly as it'd come, the shock of pain bled away, leaving only pleasure in its wake. I felt full, more aware of every movement as his cock sank into me, deeper and harder with every thrust. The added stimulation sent me spiraling over the edge, and a tiny scream ripped from my throat as I came.

Fox stayed with me the whole time, thrusting up into me as I rode out the longest orgasm of my life. I collapsed forward, wrapping my arms around his shoulders and hanging on for dear life. Fox looped an arm around my waist and rolled us so I was pinned to the bed. He caged me in his arms and stared down at me. "You feel so damn good."

"So do you." I curved one hand around the back of his neck as he pumped inside me with long, slow strokes.

He pulled out almost to the tip, then slammed back inside. My body jolted under the force of it, but I loved that tiny bite of pain. It was rough, raw, and perfect. Fox fucked me hard until he emptied himself inside me a couple minutes later, setting off a second release for me. Pulling out, he settled himself on his side next to me.

Just him and me, all my worries began to fade away. This was how we were meant to be. Fox was true to his word—he would take care of me, do whatever he had to make sure I was safe. It would never be a normal life, but who wanted ordinary when an extraordinary love lay in the balance? We'd been so close once. We could get back to that point. It would take time and trust, but there was no doubt in my mind that it could work.

Like this, with nothing between us, things felt so perfect. But would it be enough? I'd spent nearly two months with him, but I didn't really know him. He'd saved my sister—but he'd never explained why. There was no doubt in my mind that he wasn't a good man, despite the fact that he occasionally did good things. I couldn't quite reconcile it in my mind.

Knowledge was power and if I was truly going to be

with him, I needed to know everything. Once I knew what we were facing, I could begin to prepare mentally.

Stretching out one hand, he began to trace circles on my stomach. It was such a strangely tender gesture that my breath caught. I would have to do something about birth control soon if I was going to stay with Fox. We'd never used condoms, and I had a feeling the last thing he would want was a surprise pregnancy. What would he think about a baby? We never talked about the future and I found myself incredibly worried about his answer.

As the haze of pleasure wore off, I felt like I needed reassurance more than ever that he wasn't truly the monster he claimed to be. "I'm curious about something." He rolled his head toward me, one dark brow arched in silent question. "How did you end up doing, you know… what you do?"

He huffed a mirthless laugh as he rolled to a sitting position. "You have impeccable timing, you know that, angel?"

There was no mistaking the anger and hurt in his tone as he stood from the bed, stark naked, already swiping at the clothes he'd discarded several minutes earlier. I scrambled to my knees and reached for him, but he easily dodged my grasp. "I didn't mean anything by it," I insisted. "It's just… You show up out of the blue a week ago in my fucking apartment of all places, insist that I come to this island with you where I find out you've been stashing my sister away for God knows how long, and—"

He shoved one foot into his pants, then the other. "I thought you were happy about that."

"I was—I *am*," I corrected quickly when he threw a

dark look my way. "That's not what I meant. Please—just stop for a second!"

His hands stilled in the act of pulling up his zipper but he kept his gaze glued to the floor, every muscle in his body completely rigid as if bracing for an attack. "What?"

"I appreciate everything you've done—I do." I gentled my voice. "I only asked because I want to know more about you."

Slowly, his head swiveled my way, his eyes dark and unreadable. "Why?"

"Because…" I took a deep breath. "Because if we're going to be… together… I feel like I deserve to know."

"There are some things you don't need to know," he replied flatly.

He didn't move to leave, though, and that gave me confidence to continue. "I know I don't need to know—but I want to." I held his gaze for several seconds. "I know that your mission to bring down these men and women is personal. I've already seen your scars, but what I don't know is the story behind them."

I hesitated for a second, watching him intently. "From the moment we met, you let me—you let everyone—assume the worst about you. Why is that?"

"Angel…"

"I understood at the beginning when I meant nothing to you." His dark gaze shot upward, spearing into mine, and I released a shaky breath. "I would hope after everything that's happened that you don't see me as just a woman to take to bed, then forget about."

"You know you're more than that." His tone was fierce, and a tiny spark of hope flared to life.

"Then tell me. Please."

He sat heavily on the edge of the bed, his body turned partially away as if he couldn't quite bring himself to look at me, and a sigh filtered through his lips. "I told you I was adopted. I lied."

A shiver of foreboding stole down my spine at the sound of his dead, listless tone. I didn't dare speak, knowing instinctively if I did, he wouldn't continue.

"The orphanage back in Romania had a standing deal with a very powerful man. He would come to the orphanage and select children that were "ideal candidates," young and impressionable. He would take them back to the states and sell them to some of the most depraved individuals willing to pay. I was one of those children."

Tears sprang to my eyes, and I fought to keep them from falling as he continued.

"My master was… ruthless. Brutal. The scars I carry are the result of the weekly beatings I endured at his hands. I killed him when I was fourteen."

My eyes widened and my mouth fell open, but I couldn't seem to form words. Fox stared at me. "Aren't you going to ask me how?"

Oh, Jesus. I wasn't sure I wanted to know. "H-how?"

"A box cutter." The back of my throat burned with bile as I envisioned the gory scene. I'd heard horror stories about his ruthless nature but I'd never believed them, especially not after I'd gotten to know him. But to have him admit it… God. I couldn't imagine.

He paused, seemingly lost in the past. "Before I came to America, my name was Garridan Vulpe. My last name, translated literally, means fox in Romanian. I use the nickname in Chicago for my business dealings, but it started long before I moved to the city. My master… He liked to play a game."

He trailed off, and my heart slammed against my ribcage as dread mingled in my stomach. "What do you mean?"

His tone was flat, lifeless. "In his sick, twisted game… I *was* the fox."

SEVENTEEN

FOX

All the shame, all the insecurities came flooding back with impressive force despite the fact that I'd spent decades trying to push the darkness down. The intimacy of a few moments prior had dissipated into thin air, leaving me naked and feeling vulnerable, something I swore I'd never feel again. Dredging up those horrible memories just minutes after we'd had sex was too much.

A thick, heavy silence hung in the air as she processed my words. "I don't..."

Of course she didn't understand. Who could? I'd lashed out at Eva, but I wasn't truly upset with her. After all, she was only curious; she had no notion of my upbringing or what would cause me to react so violently. Things were still too precarious between us, and I really didn't want to push her further away. Worse, I didn't want to see the look of pity that would surely fill her pretty green eyes once she learned the truth.

"It doesn't matter anymore." Her eyes narrowed, and I sighed. "I'm not used to sharing with anyone. My past is…"

Horrific. Depraved. Unsuitable for someone as pure and perfect as Eva.

"But it's yours." She reached out and laid a gentle hand on my arm. "Haven't you figured it out yet? No matter how messy it is, I want to know about it—about you."

"I just…" I gave my head a little shake. "It's not pretty, Eva."

"You've told me that before." She shifted a little closer. "But it's just me."

I huffed a mirthless laugh. "That doesn't exactly make this easier. I don't want it to change things between us."

She lifted a brow. "You think it could get much worse?"

The thought of revealing every dirty detail of my past made me physically ill. What would she say when she finally saw the real me? I was terrified she would leave me, but I also knew I couldn't put off telling her any longer. I was only hurting her by holding back, and she deserved to know every ugly truth.

"He called me his fox." I closed my eyes and allowed the memories to wash over me. "My master owned a huge ranch out west. Every weekend, he would release me, give me a five-minute head start. Then he would come for me."

It was vile, and I watched it unfold in my mind as if it'd happened yesterday instead of more than twenty years ago. The first time, I was too young and naïve to truly understand Simon Hastings's depravity. He'd screamed at me, ordered me to run and hide, but all I could do was cry. The beating that night had been horrific, most of the scars on my back inflicted from that moment alone.

He allowed me a full week to heal. The following weekend when he'd turned me out again, I ran as fast and as far as I could. But it didn't matter how hard I tried, I couldn't escape. He'd tracked me down within an hour and dragged me back to the house, to a special place no one knew of.

"There was a room in the basement where he carried out my punishments. Sometimes it was a whipping." I reached over my shoulder and absently fingered one of the scars. "Other times he would use a cane. Once I was broken and bleeding, he would take me over and over until he was satisfied."

Week after week it was the same thing. Sometimes I managed to stay hidden for hours at a time. But that only increased his anticipation and his sexual appetite. Over the first few years I learned to shut down and not fight back. He loved the thrill of the hunt, and the more I fought back, the more pleasure he derived from it.

"I stayed with him for almost eight years. Over time, he began to drop his guard and while I'd once been locked up, he began to leave me free. He never expected me to fight back." I took a deep breath. "I found a discarded box cutter outside one day and hid it away where he would never find it. I spent weeks thinking about it. One night he came for me, and I... I couldn't take it anymore."

I remembered vividly the feel of the blade sinking into his flesh over and over. Driven by pure rage, I had nearly sawed his head off by the time I realized what I'd done. Knowing I had no choice but to leave, I scoured the house for money. Master Hastings had gotten lax, allowing me to be present in his office more and more often, and I'd memorized the code to the safe. Inside were stacks of bills, and I'd grabbed them all.

I started walking, not caring where I ended up as long as I was far, far away from that hell. I made it to Vegas first, where I met Admir. Old enough to be my grandfather, the Albanian crime boss took a liking to me after I nearly killed one of his men in the street. He'd seen the darkness inside me, but he also saw the potential to harness it.

He taught me how to read, not only letters and numbers, but people as well. He taught me how to hunt, how to kill without getting caught. Though I never told him my exact reasons for tracking down the people I did, I had a feeling he knew.

Admir also taught me the importance of financial security. When he pulled me into his office that first day, I hadn't been able to tell the difference between a five-dollar bill or a hundred-dollar bill. He taught me to invest, and by the time I was eighteen I'd purchased my first business, a self-serve car wash. A second one followed a year and a half later, and I gradually began to grow my business.

I was twenty-two when Admir passed, and I moved to Chicago to be closer to the border. There was a wide diversity of criminal organizations, and I fit right in. Maybe one day I would tell her all of that, but I'd revealed enough tonight.

I turned to meet Eva's gaze, and my heart clenched when I saw the tears sliding silently down her face. "Angel…"

She swiped them away, shaking her head. "I… I can't even imagine."

"It's in the past." I didn't dare move, afraid I would spook her and she would pull away from me.

"That's why—" Her eyes widened suddenly, and I could practically see the pieces of the puzzle connecting in her mind—my curiosity and sexual exploration at Noir. The fact that I hadn't slept with a woman until I was in my mid-twenties.

I'd never been attracted to men, especially after what had happened with Master Hastings, but I couldn't quite bring myself to seek out women's attention, either. It had taken me years to even consider having sex with a woman, and revealing the reasoning behind that to Eva physically hurt. "I'm sorry I didn't tell you sooner. I understand if you're disappointed or upset."

"Hell yes, I'm upset." Fire leaped in her eyes. "I'm furious. I wish he were still here. I could kill him for what he did to you."

Her words, full of vehemence and spoken in my defense, sparked something inside me that felt very much like absolution. I pulled her into my lap, entwining her body with mine so I could absorb her goodness, her innocence. This woman was so amazing, I swore I would never let her go.

"He's gone, and I don't want to waste my breath on him anymore." I buried my face in her hair, breathing in the sweet, calming scent of her. "But there are more men like this out there, and I vowed when I escaped to take down every single one of them."

Silence descended for several long minutes as we sat there, just holding one another. "I'm proud of you." Her words made everything inside me still, and I waited with bated breath as she continued. "You're not the monster you think you are. You've been through something horrible that no one—especially a child—should ever endure, but you've persevered."

It was like the last barrier between us had been ripped away. She'd seen all of me, accepted me—and I was never going to let her go. "Thank you, Eva."

Her head rolled on my shoulder, and I could feel her looking up at me. "For what?"

"For accepting me as I am."

"Nothing could change the way I feel about you." I was afraid to hope that there was any deeper meaning to her words. I wanted her to feel the same way about me that I did her, but I didn't want to push her. She fell silent for a moment, like she was lost in thought. Finally, she spoke up. "Remember the night of the engagement party?"

God, how could I forget? It was the last time I'd seen her right before she'd run from me. I swallowed hard at the memory and nodded. "I remember."

Those gorgeous green eyes met mine. "Those things you said to me in the closet—what did they mean?"

A ghost of a smile lifted my lips. "I was wondering how long it would take you to bring that up."

She stayed quiet, and I exhaled deeply as I tried to best put my feelings into words. "I've never met a woman like you—ever. I've never been able to just be myself around another human being. Before you, I was never able to touch another woman. I don't do well with emotions, but you've touched me, both physically and emotionally. What I said to you that night, it means that my heart, Eva— whatever I have to give—is yours."

Tears glistened in her pretty eyes. "Really?"

"Really." I turned slightly and kissed her forehead.

"What do we do now?" she whispered.

I shifted her in my arms so I could see her better. I wanted her to be able to read every emotion clearly in my eyes. "I want you, Eva. I've always wanted you. It's your turn to decide what you want."

God, I hoped she said yes, that she would stay with me.

"I'm scared," she admitted, looking incredibly torn.

"I don't blame you." I swept my thumb over her cheek. I couldn't reassure her that everything would be all right. These men and women were desperate to cover up their proclivities and they wouldn't hesitate to take out anyone in their way. "I'll do everything I can to keep you safe."

"I want to be with you," she finally said, her words low.

Thank God. I took her face in my hands. "Thank you, angel."

Her lips lifted into a sweet smile. "I love when you call me that."

I smiled. Four months ago, she had a very different outlook. "You'll always be my angel, but I'd rather call you something else."

Happiness sparkled in her eyes before she quickly schooled it and wariness took its place. "What's that?"

I watched her carefully as I spoke. "My wife."

Her mouth opened, but no sound came out. She blinked once. Twice. Her lower lip trembled, and I stroked one hand down her arm. The gentle touch seemed to jolt her from whatever internal debate she was hosting in her head, because her eyes cleared as she stared up at me. "Really?"

"There's no one I'd rather have by my side." I parroted the same words to her I'd said two months ago, and her eyes welled with tears as she threw her arms around my neck.

"Yes. Oh my God, yes."

I pulled her close and took her mouth in a hard kiss. I broke contact, then moved toward my bag and fished out a dark red box. Taking a knee before Eva, I flipped open the lid, watching in fascination as her eyes widened and her hands flew to her mouth. "What—Did—" Her gaze flicked from the box to the bag, then back again. "Wait. You had that with you the whole time?"

"Every single day since you left. It's been waiting for you."

"Every day?" Her words were soft, almost as if she couldn't quite comprehend them.

"Every day," I repeated. "I would have spent a lifetime tracking you down to give this to you. It's always been you, Evangelina."

Tears sparkled in her eyes, then spilled over onto her cheeks.

"Don't cry, angel." I stood and enfolded her in my arms. "We can take this as slow as you want. If—"

She shook her head against my chest, then gently pushed away. "No. This… It's perfect."

She held out her left hand and I slipped the ring onto her trembling finger. Tightening my hold on her waist, I dipped my head and kissed her hard. If there was such a thing as love, this was it.

EIGHTEEN

EVA

I woke up alone the following morning, and the cool sheets in the spot next to me told me that Fox was gone and had likely been up for several hours already. I had no idea how he functioned on so little sleep. We'd fallen into bed last night where I showed him my appreciation for the marriage proposal—twice.

I smiled at the feel of the band encircling my finger. Slipping my hand over the sheets, I watched the early morning sunshine filter into the diamond before scattering over the walls and ceiling of the room. Part of me still couldn't believe that this was real. Speaking with both Elle and Fox had helped to calm my fears, and I was now beginning to look forward to our life together with a nervous anticipation.

Happiness bubbled up inside me, and I bounded from the bed. After washing up and using the bathroom, I dressed and headed downstairs. Following the sounds from the kitchen, I practically skipped into the room. Elle turned at my presence and lifted one eyebrow when she saw the elated expression on my face. "Good morning?"

She said it like a question, and I couldn't help but grin. "It's a *very* good morning."

I bounced over to her and held out my hand. Her gaze dropped to my ring finger, and her eyes widened as her jaw dropped open. "Oh, my God!"

I let out a squeal as we threw our arms around each other, talking over one another. A deep chuckle came from the doorway, and I glanced over my shoulder at Fox. A sexy smile curved his face as he sauntered toward us, his gaze fixed on mine. "I assume you told her the good news?"

I grinned back. "I did."

Sliding one arm around my waist, he dipped his head and brushed a light kiss over my lips. "Good morning, angel. Sleep well?"

"Yes, thank you."

Elle watched our interaction, a soft smile on her face. "Why don't you two head outside? I'll finish up breakfast and be out in just a minute."

"Oh, you don't have to—" I started to say, but Elle placed a hand on my arm, effectively cutting me off.

"I'm almost done anyway." She gestured toward the patio doors. "I'm sure you two have a lot to talk about."

Fox settled his hand on my lower back and guided me outside, holding the door for me as we stepped onto the wide stone terrace. The sun shone brightly overhead, its rays catching and reflecting on the rippling surface of the pool. Fox took a seat next to me at the wrought iron table, then slid a pair of sunglasses my way. I smiled in thanks and shielded my eyes against the bright light.

I glanced over the table at him. "You must have been up early again."

He grimaced apologetically. "I was trying to get some work done before you woke up."

I loved that he thought of me, that he didn't want his work to take away from our time together. "I was kind of hoping to wake up next to my fiancé," I whispered.

His eyes turned dark with desire. "Tomorrow, angel. I promise."

I smiled. Was it healthy to love someone this much, to be so completely head over heels for them? Probably not, but I couldn't dredge up the effort to care. I was done fighting this feeling between us.

"Have you given any thought to what I said last night?"

I tipped my head in question. "About what kind of wedding we should have?" He nodded.

We'd spoken of it a little bit last night as we lay curled in each other's arms after we'd made love, but it'd been late, and I didn't have a specific vision in mind. As a child, I'd always imagined a large church wedding, the pews filled with family and friends, their eyes on me as I made my way down the aisle in an elaborate white gown. Lately though…

I turned to look out over the surface of the gulf. The only people worth having in my life at the moment were Elle and Fox, and now Hossam. I didn't need to put on a show for anyone else. I turned back to Fox. "What about here?"

Behind the dark frames of his sunglasses, one dark brow arched upward. "On the beach?"

The idea probably seemed quaint and immature to him. "It was just a thought. I'm sure you'd probably prefer to have something more extravagant, but—"

"Not at all. A beach wedding sounds nice." Fox reached over and laced his fingers with mine. "How soon were you thinking?"

Was there any real reason to put it off? I didn't think so. "What's the wait time down here?"

"To be honest, I don't really know," he replied. "I can look into it. Would you like to have the ceremony while we're here?"

"I think so."

The space between his brows wrinkled with concern. "Are you sure you don't want your family present? We can wait," he offered.

I shook my head. "Everyone I want by my side is already here."

Fox squeezed my fingers, an indulgent smile on his face. "Whatever you want is fine with me."

Noise from the doorway drew my attention to Elle, and she delivered a tray of fresh fruit and scones to our table, along with freshly squeezed orange juice and dark coffee a moment later. As she disappeared back into the house, my mind churned. I turned back to Fox. "Can I ask you a question?"

"Of course," he replied around a bite of melon.

"Elle and Hossam… They're technically married, aren't they?"

Fox dipped his chin. "When I had their new identities created, it made sense for them to be a couple."

I knew Elle was in love with Hossam, and she deserved a happy ending after everything she'd been through. I turned my gaze back to Fox. "Would you mind if I asked them to join us?"

"As attendants?" Confusion marred his handsome face, and I shook my head.

"No. I'd like them to have a real ceremony. I was wondering if we could… share?"

He stared at me for several seconds, then a slow smile spread over his face. "I think that's a great idea. Why don't you check with your sister?"

I smiled, pleased he'd accepted so easily. There seemed to have been a definite shift in our relationship, and I felt closer to him than ever. As Elle had said, there would always be doubts and troubles in every relationship, but it was a matter of how you resolved them. I would be missing out on the most amazing man I'd ever met if I let fear control me.

Once we'd finished breakfast, Fox turned to me. "I have some work I need to finish up and send back to my men. Will you be okay out here until I'm done?"

I smiled at his overprotective nature. "I'll be fine. Elle and I may go to the beach in a bit."

"Stay close to the house." He leaned down, and I tipped my head up for a kiss.

His lips brushed over mine in an achingly sweet gesture, and I felt my heart melt a little more. I was so incredibly in love with this man. He pulled back, sent me a wink, then headed into the house. Elle passed him, exiting onto the terrace as the door closed behind Fox, and I smiled up at her. "You don't need to wait on me hand and foot."

She sent a sisterly look my way. "Please. I didn't come out here to clean. You've got two good hands."

Laughing, I balled up a napkin and threw it at her. God, it felt so good to have her back. My chest tightened at the reminder of pain and loss I'd felt without her. My eyes clouded with tears, and Elle immediately reached for me, pulling me into a hug.

"Oh, honey."

A hiccupping sob left my mouth as I leaned into her. "I'm just… I'm so glad to see you again." I hadn't let myself dwell on it for the past couple of days, but now it hit me full force. "I missed you."

"I missed you, too." She pulled away, allowing me to dab at my eyes. "Now you know where I am, and you can come visit me anytime."

I smiled, vanquishing the last of my tears. "Fox offered to let me stay here with you guys."

Elle grinned. "You should. It's really wonderful here."

"I'm sure it is." I glanced out at the ocean, drawing in a deep breath of the salty air. "But I have to go back. I want to be with him."

"I understand." She studied me for a minute. "I'm really happy for you. I'm so glad you found someone who can make you happy."

It was almost unbelievable. Just a few months ago, I never would have envisioned myself in this position. I shook my head. "He really does."

"He loves you." I turned to meet my sister's eyes, and she nodded. "Even Hossam says he's never seen Fox like this."

"Really?" I was intrigued. "How long has he known Fox?"

"A few years, I think, at least in passing. Although Hossam worked for Spencer, they all kind of ran in the same circles. From what I understand, Hossam went to Fox's club several times when Spencer was gambling."

Fox's illicit business didn't seem to faze Elle, which surprised the hell out of me. She'd always been the good girl, the one who always did the right thing. I knew she felt she owed him in part for saving her from Spencer, but even I worried that his troubles would come knocking one day. "Do you feel safe here?"

"Very." Her pretty eyes filled with warmth. "Hossam would protect me with his life."

I smiled, thinking of the two alpha men who would burn down the world and everyone in it to protect the women they loved—us. Once, I'd felt disdain for men like that who felt they were exempt from the rules of the law. Now that I'd experienced it for myself, I was incredibly grateful that Fox was as strong and determined as he was. I knew he would do anything for me.

"I have a question for you." Her brows lifted in question, and I continued. "Fox and I have decided to get married on the beach while we're here."

A huge smile wreathed my sister's face. "That's amazing! I'm so glad I'll get to see you two tie the knot."

"Well, that's what I wanted to talk to you about." I rearranged myself in the chair so I faced her. "I know you didn't get much of a choice when you had to leave the States. Fox told me that your identities are of a married couple out of ease."

"Basically." She lifted a shoulder. "We knew we wanted to be together, so it just made sense."

I smiled at the way she phrased it, just as Fox had said.

"I know you love each other. But you never had a chance to actually say your vows." Elle stared at me intently, trying to figure out where exactly I was going with this. "If you—both of you—are interested, I thought we might have a double ceremony."

Elle's eyes widened, and her mouth dropped into a small 'O' of surprise. "I... I don't know what to say. That's..." She shook her head a little. "Are you sure? I wouldn't want—"

"Trust me, it's fine with us. Talk it over with Hossam and let me know."

Elle leaned in and hugged me hard. She and Hossam could have technically had a ceremony anytime they wanted. But all of us sharing that special moment was priceless.

NINETEEN

FOX

I lifted my head at the knock on the door, and my eyes collided with Hossam's dark gaze. "Back already?"

"Yes, sir. The women are out by the pool."

"Thank you." Eva and Elle had wanted to visit the market again this morning for fresh fruits and vegetables, and they needed someone with them at all times for protection. With their fair skin and pale hair, they stuck out down here like sore thumbs. Though not as dark as me, Hossam's Egyptian heritage allowed him to better blend in with the natives and secure the women's safety.

As much as I wanted to join them, I had a few pressing needs to take care of first. I hated that this was taking time away from Eva, but I hoped she would appreciate my efforts in the end. Though we had filed the paperwork with the city earlier in the week, it would be another couple of days until we could have the ceremony.

I had reached out to a contact and scheduled an

appointment for Friday. The pastor worked in the local village, but he assured me that he would meet me at the villa after work in time for an evening wedding.

Eva, being Eva, had requested nothing, but I wanted to make the day unique—something she would never forget. I wasn't the romantic sort, but Eva brought out a tender side of me, and I wanted our wedding to represent the beginning of our life together. While she had spent the morning shopping, I'd been on the phone with a local event planner, contracting strands of lights to be brought in along with an archway and miscellaneous other decor.

Although the stretch of beach behind the house was relatively secluded, we'd decided to hold the ceremony on the terrace instead, to cut down on the number of possible distractions. I'd contacted a caterer as well, wanting the women to not have to worry about organizing food on their wedding day. Part of me felt foolish for putting so much thought and effort into it, but she never asked for a single thing. She, just like Elle, deserved the absolute best, and I planned to give it to her.

"Sir, may I speak with you for a moment?"

"Of course." I waved Hossam into the office and gestured for him to close the door for privacy. Turning my body slightly, I looked out the east window to ensure that the women were still safe by the pool. They lounged in chairs side-by-side, looking almost like identical twins from this far away. A smile curled my mouth as I directed my attention back to Hossam. "What do you need?"

"First, I wanted to congratulate you on your nuptials," he stated.

I dipped my head in acknowledgment. "Thank you. I believe I could say the same to you."

"That's what I wanted to speak to you about," he began. "Elle asked me about having a double ceremony. This is a special day for you and Eva. If you would rather it just be the two of you, we would be more than happy to stand up for you. Elle and I are already technically married."

Absorbing his words, I tossed another look out the window at the women below. I watched them as I spoke. "Do you love her?"

"I do."

I turned back to him. "It would please both of us if you would share our wedding day."

He inclined his head. "Thank you, sir. We appreciate it."

"Before you go, I have a question for you," I said. "Did Elle ever mention anything about Spencer's business affairs, or did you ever overhear anything?"

Hossam shook his head. "He hired me on for security, but I was kept out of the loop for the most part. Why do you ask?"

"I was wondering how well Spencer Masterson and Sebastian Moreau know each other."

"Aside from being acquaintances, I'm not aware of any joint ventures or business dealings. Moreau never came to the house, so if they were working on anything, it was probably conducted either at Spencer's office or in private somewhere."

That was what bothered me. I needed to find a solid connection that tied them together, otherwise this was all just conjecture. I suspected that both Sebastian and Spencer were involved in the human trafficking ring, but I wasn't quite sure how.

A trend had begun to emerge over the past eight months, and four shipments that we knew of had come across the Canadian border. Sebastian had money and friends in all the right places, and Spencer had plenty of connections politically. Even if they were involved, I seriously doubted they were the ones in charge. They were lackeys—not the person pulling the strings.

That didn't change the fact, though, that there would be dozens if not hundreds of people below them—handlers, transporters, people at airports and shipping ports to assist in the transfer.

Twice recently Masterson and Moreau had contracted a private plane and flown into North Dakota. The trips had only lasted a few days each. There was no reason that the men couldn't have just been on a trip to the mountains—but why? It had struck me as strange at the time, and I voiced my question to Hossam, who shrugged. "Masterson does not hunt. In fact, he's vehemently opposed to it."

Hossam had more than proved his loyalty to both myself and Elle, and I knew I could trust him. I explained to him what I had learned about Araña and his operations. "It's interesting that both Spencer and Sebastian made two separate trips to North Dakota only a couple of months apart. With his connections as senator, I believe he may be greasing the hands of the port authority or border patrol in order to smuggle the children across. Possibly both."

Hossam's eyes darkened. "That wouldn't surprise me. Especially if someone was controlling him. He would do anything to get his next fix as long as it didn't become public knowledge."

I'd had the same thought, but Hossam's words

confirmed my suspicions. "I have my men back home running background on both of them to see if anything jumps out."

Hossam's gaze sharpened. "You think they're running this together?"

"No." I shook my head. "That would make it too obvious if anyone else stumbled onto their recent activity. This has been going on for more than thirty years, and Masterson is only thirty-six. Moreau is in his early forties. Though I can't rule out the possibility that he took over for someone else, I get the feeling that they're pawns in a much larger game."

"So we need to figure out how Spencer and Sebastian are connected, and that will lead us to Araña."

I nodded. "It would be someone close to them—a friend or relative, someone they could easily pay off or pull the wool over their eyes. I'll have my men back home look into them further, see what they can come up with. Until then, we need to keep a close eye on the women. I am trying to convince Eva to stay on the island until this is all settled. Maybe Elle can give her some incentive."

Hossam nodded in agreement. "I'll see what I can do."

"I appreciate it. And if you think of anything in the meantime, please let me know."

He nodded slowly, seeming to think it over. "I seem to remember Masterson being particularly stressed right about the same time I left his employ."

I tipped my head. "What are you thinking?"

"I'm not sure." He gave his head a little shake, like he was trying to draw back on his memory of that time. "Things had gotten progressively worse for Elle, which is the only reason I remember. Masterson was pushing particularly hard to have a bill passed around that same time. I don't remember exactly what it was for—some green initiative, maybe? Maybe there is some correlation."

It was entirely possible that he was indebted to someone. Or, more likely, the proposal was a form of quid pro quo. Perhaps Spencer had greased the way for the bill to be passed in exchange for leniency when the shipments crossed the border.

"Do you remember who he was working with?"

"I do not." He grimaced a little in apology. "I would assume it's someone in his circle of friends, someone he owes or who owes him a favor."

"Thank you, Hossam."

He dipped his head, then retreated from the room, leaving me with my thoughts. As of right now we hadn't been able to determine exactly how both men were involved. Aside from the fact that they'd traveled together twice last year, there was no outward sign of them being accomplices or partners in any way.

There were no joint ventures between the two, no familial relations. I'd begun to suspect that Sebastian and Spencer were connected indirectly through some third-party entity. Hopefully whatever information we turned up would tell us exactly what we'd been looking for.

I emailed the information off to my men back in Chicago and asked them to research the bills that had been passed through the Senate around that time last year, then closed up my laptop. One thread at a time, Araña's web was slowly beginning to unravel. One of these days I would find him. But not today. My gaze snagged on Eva as I stood and rounded the desk. Today I had more important things to do.

TWENTY

My anxiety ratcheted up with each passing minute, and the bubbly champagne I sipped turned to acid in my stomach.

Earlier this afternoon, Fox had insisted we stay in the house and get ready. Elle and I had selected dresses from a boutique in town a couple of days ago, and the seamstress had finished alterations just this morning. He had brought someone in from the village to do our hair and makeup, and we spent several hours sipping champagne as we were pampered and dressed for the evening ahead. To say I was nervous was an understatement.

The glass of champagne trembled in my hand, and all I wanted to do was run to Fox. For some reason I couldn't explain, I was terrified he wouldn't be waiting at the end of the aisle for me. The sitting room we were currently ensconced in faced out the front of the house, and the cosmetologist chattered away with Elle as she packed up her things and got ready to leave.

Unable to stand it for another second, I set my flute down with the clink on the end table and escaped from the room, a swarm of butterflies battering my stomach. I picked up my skirt and headed up the stairs, intent on catching Fox alone. I passed Hossam on the landing, and his eyes widened as they fell on me.

"What are you doing, Miss Eva?"

My eyes darted toward the bedroom door at the end of the hall. "I need to speak with Fox."

One dark eyebrow lifted, and his large hand moved to my bicep. "It is bad luck for the groom to see the bride before the wedding."

I knew all about that superstition, but I couldn't bring myself to care. "Please," I implored. "I just need two minutes with him."

His eyes softened as he noted my expression. "Okay."

He opened the door, emitting me into Fox's domain. The man in question turned to me, shirt unbuttoned, like he was in the middle of getting dressed. "Angel." His expression turned wary as I crossed the room. "Is everything okay?"

"Fine." I waved one hand in the air. "I just… I needed to talk to you for a second."

"Okay?"

I could hear the thread of tension in his voice, and I felt terrible for worrying him. "I needed to see you before we went down there. I wanted—" I gestured out the window and froze as I caught sight of the people down below. "What… What's this?"

Fox's hands landed on my hips, and his familiar weight

pressed against my back as he dipped his head close to my ear. "Do you like it?"

I tossed a look over my shoulder at him. "You did this for me?"

He tipped his head slightly. "Both of you, yes, but mostly for you, angel."

The white fabric of the arches billowed in the gentle ocean breeze, and the sight brought tears to my eyes. "I..." My attention was drawn back to the men and women who had strung lights over the terrace and were putting final touches on the several dozen arrangements of fresh flowers that had been brought in. "It's beautiful."

"I'm glad you like it." He turned me in his arms. "God, you're stunning."

His eyes swept over me from head to toe, sending fire sparking along my nerve endings. "Thank you."

"Welcome." We were silent for a second before he spoke again. "You said you needed something."

"Right." I couldn't steady my nerves. I wasn't getting cold feet, exactly, I just needed the reassurance that Fox wanted this as much as I did. After our tumultuous beginning and everything that had happened since, we'd really only been a couple for a short amount of time, and never during a calm period of our lives. Everything had always been in upheaval, marred by betrayal and distrust. "I just... What if people find out?"

He lifted a brow. "I was counting on the fact that they would, unless you prefer to keep our marriage a secret."

His expression was guarded, and I lifted my hands to his chest. "That's not what I meant. But you told me a long time ago that anyone serious in your life could be viewed as a weakness. I don't want to be the one responsible for that. This doesn't have to be the next logical step if you don't want it to. We could just—"

Fox lifted a hand and pressed a single finger to my lips to silence me. "I'm not good with emotions, angel, and I'm even worse at putting them into words, but let me tell you this."

He hesitated for a long moment before continuing. "You are the only woman I have ever wanted this way. This is not a business transaction, nor is it an excuse to keep you safe. I want all of you—your gorgeous body, your agile mind, your beautiful heart. I belong to you, and you belong to me."

The honesty ringing in his words made my heart swell almost to the point of pain. I blinked rapidly, sniffing away the burning sensation rippling across the bridge of my nose. I didn't want to cry and ruin my makeup, so I tried to deflect by cracking a joke. "Is this where you tell me I have to obey you 'til death do us part?"

A broad grin transformed his face, lighting his eyes. "Obey? I didn't know that word existed in your vocabulary."

I grinned, glad that the tears had passed. "First time for everything."

"Give me your hand." I placed my palm in his, and he crossed my middle finger over my index finger. "Just like this. That way, when you recite your vows, we'll both know you didn't mean it."

I sputtered with laughter and smacked his chest with my free hand. "I can't believe I'm willingly signing up for a lifetime of this."

Although I joked about it, I knew in my heart that I wanted this more than anything.

"There's still time to back out," Fox countered, his words teeming with seriousness.

I shook my head. "Someone has to take care of your stubborn ass."

"Only because you do it so well. I would never let another person order me around the way you do."

And that admission right there solidified my thoughts. What he said was the truth; in the beginning, he had refused my help, shunned my presence. But now we'd found common ground with each other. He would always take care of me, and I would always take care of him. Though we were both strong, confident individuals, we had both learned over the course of the relationship that we could retain our independence yet lean on each other in our times of need.

"What do you think, angel?" His dark eyes bore into mine. "Are you ready for this—for a lifetime with me?"

"More than ready," I replied.

"Good." Fox dropped a kiss on my lips, then smacked my bottom. "Now go before that dress ends up on the ground."

Feeling much better about everything, I headed back to the sitting room. Elle glanced up at me as I entered. "Is everything okay?"

"Perfect." I smiled. "Are you about ready?"

"I hope so." She shook her hands nervously. "I swear, I wasn't half this nervous when I married Spencer."

I threw a look her way. "There's more at stake now that you've found someone you really love."

Just like Fox and me. I loved him so much, and I hoped one day he would feel the same about me.

"True." Elle stood, and I linked my arm through hers. "It's going to be perfect."

Together, we left the room and headed toward the back of the house. The men stood beneath the archway that had been set up on the terrace, and my heart gave a little thump in my chest. Fox's dark gaze moved to mine, almost as if he could sense the emotions roiling inside me. A small smile lifted the corner of his mouth, and he held up his hand, fingers crossed.

I couldn't help the grin that overtook my face.

Beside me, Elle leaned in close. "You good?"

"Perfect." I couldn't tear my gaze from Fox.

Fox had hired a photographer, and the man captured our movements as we crossed the terrace under the glowing lights as the sun began to dip below the horizon. Since it was just the four of us, we decided to have the man marry us all at once, rather than having to do two ceremonies.

Elle broke away, moving toward Hossam, and I stepped into Fox's arms. He wore a suit similar to the ones he wore every day for business, and I couldn't help but smile. "Nice of you to dress up for the occasion."

He let out a low growl, and his hand slipped down my back to pinch my bottom. "You'll pay for that later."

I grinned back at him. "I hope so."

The reverend greeted us warmly, then launched into his liturgy. Standing there, looking up at Fox, my hands in his, the moment was absolutely perfect. I loved him more than anything, and I couldn't wait to spend the rest of my life with him.

TWENTY-ONE

FOX

From my spot on the chaise lounge, I swiveled my head to look at Eva, acutely aware of the asinine smile that had taken up residence on my face. I couldn't stop looking at her—couldn't believe she was mine. Forever.

As if feeling my gaze on her, Eva rolled her head toward me. "What are you looking at?"

"You."

One eyebrow arched upward behind the rim of her oversized sunglasses. "I can't be that fascinating."

"Oh, but you are."

"Hmm…"

She said nothing and instead sat up to liberally apply more of the SPF 25 we'd found in town. The people in the village looked at her like she was crazy when she'd asked if they had anything more potent. "I never knew they made SPF 50 until you asked for it."

She snorted as she applied more of the lotion on her

arms. "Yeah, well, I can thank my European ancestors for my fair complexion."

My gaze roved over her once more, and my grin grew. "You're so white, I swear I can see the blood pumping through your veins."

"Hey!" She reached over to slap my chest, but I caught her hand with a laugh and laced our fingers together.

Yanking on her hand, I pulled her close enough to kiss. She melted into me as she always did, and I slid my hands under her thighs, then lifted her onto my lap.

She pulled away, scowling at me. "You're such a jerk."

I grinned. "You know you like it."

Here we could be free to just be ourselves, another pair of newlyweds. There were no witnesses, no one who could use her against me. I could hold her all night and all day, kiss her whenever the hell I wanted. Even Hossam and Elle had made themselves scarce over the past couple of days, joining us for dinner before retreating to their cottage no doubt to celebrate their own nuptials.

It felt so good to be able to lower my guard and just be happy. And it was all due to her. She was everything I'd ever wanted and then some. My captive. My lover. My wife. Every day with her was better than the last.

Unfortunately, it couldn't last. We'd already been here for twelve days. Soon we would need to go home so I could pick up the reins where I'd left off. I wanted to track down Araña and rid the world of him once and for all. But after that… I wanted this. Quiet days on the beach. Eva at my side. Elle and Hossam next door.

I wasn't nearly ready to broach the subject of me returning to Chicago, but it was a discussion I couldn't put off any longer. "Can you believe we've been here for almost two weeks already?"

"I know." She let out a contented little sigh and snuggled deeper into my arms despite the heat of the day. "I feel like so much has happened in such a short period of time. It's like I got caught up in a whirlwind that just won't stop."

Several long tendrils of hair had come loose from the knot secured at the top of her head, and I brushed one behind her ear. "My offer still stands. You're more than welcome to stay here, angel. Spend time with Elle."

She glanced over her shoulder at me and held my gaze through the darkened lens of her sunglasses. "What about you?"

I trailed my fingers up and down her arm as I spoke. "I have to go back. I can't leave this unfinished. But if you stay here, I'll know you're safe. I'll return to you soon as I can."

Her hand moved to my bare chest and traced small circles over the space above my heart for what seemed like several minutes before she spoke. "I don't want to be away from you. I'm coming with you."

Of its own volition, my head began to shake before I caught myself. I knew all too well how this would play out. "Are you sure? Elle has missed you so much. I know she'd love to have you here with her," I coaxed.

Her head tipped slightly to one side, and her lips pressed into a thin line as she studied me through narrowed eyes. "I know what you're doing."

"What am I doing?" I asked innocently.

She let out a soft snort. "If this is your backhanded way of thinking you're protecting me, you can drop the idea right now. We both know how well it worked out for you last time."

The memory of her running because of my stupidity flared in my gut, and I tightened my hold a fraction. I felt anger at her for throwing it back in my face, but most of it was reserved for me, for my own ignorance. "I thought we were past that," I said, trying to keep my emotions in check.

"We are past it," she soothed. "Whatever happened, happened. But you can't continue to make choices for me just because you think it's the right thing to do."

Stubborn woman. I drew in a deep breath. "Can't you just make my life easy for once and do what I say?"

A little spurt of laughter burst from her throat. "I knew you were out of your mind, but I didn't think you were senile already."

I smacked her ass cheek, loving the way she jumped and dragged in a stilted breath. But her smile didn't diminish. "Is that any way to talk to your husband?"

"You'll have to forgive me," she purred. "I'm new to this whole marriage thing."

It was my turn to scoff. "Still just as much a smart ass as ever."

Her arms curled around my neck, and her lips moved to my jaw. "Don't pretend you don't love it."

It was a valid point, except... "I couldn't bear it if anything ever happened to you."

Suddenly serious, she drew back and looked at me, her hands curled around my shoulders. "We can live in Chicago, or we can live here," she said. "But I need to go back home, at least for a little bit. I need to see my parents."

Now that I was going to have a problem with. How could she even think of defending her father after what he'd done? "Your father practically sold you to me."

"Which is precisely why I need to go home, just this once." Her eyes were sharp and clear. "I need the closure. I want him to see that he didn't break me—that despite what he did, everything turned out for the best."

It could have been so much worse. William had pawned her off on me without a second thought. What if I'd sold her off to Nikolai to recoup my losses? What would have happened to her then? Just the thought made my blood run cold. I fucking hated the idea of Eva even being in the same state as that asshole who called himself her father, but I would give my angel whatever she needed —within reason.

"If you go to him"—and that was still a big if—"I want myself or one of my men with you."

"I can do that. How long do you expect to be back in Chicago?"

"There's no telling." I lifted one shoulder. "I would like to say no more than a few months, but sometimes these things can drag out. I've been hunting this ghost for decades."

There was a trace of sympathy in her eyes though she tried to school it. "You can take as long as you need. After that, we can come back here and stay forever for all I care."

That sounded like absolute perfection. "You would be okay with that?"

She lifted one shoulder in a tiny shrug. "Why not? As long as I have you…"

"Always."

I didn't tell her as much, but after this was all over I

planned to hang up my white hat permanently. I'd already started the process of aligning operations with Johnson so that he could keep an eye on the gambling ring while I was away. While I would have to make occasional trips back to Chicago, he would be able to take care of the day-to-day activity.

We'd agreed to sit down and draw up the final plans once I returned home, and I found myself anticipating it more so now that Eva was back by my side. I couldn't wait until I could be with her every single day just like this.

Sliding my hand under her jaw, I tipped her chin up and covered her mouth with mine. Her bottom shifted in my lap, and my cock leaped at the feel of her. It didn't matter how many times I had her; I would never get tired of being inside Eva.

I pulled away. "Let's take this inside."

A slow smile spread over Eva's pretty lips, and she slipped her hand into mine as we headed inside. Nothing else mattered but her.

TWENTY-TWO

EVA

Rodrigo had looked less than thrilled to see me when we arrived home. He looked even more surprised when Fox introduced me as his wife. While the other men took it in stride, Rodrigo had given me a tight nod, his fathomless eyes as dark and cold as usual.

I'd tried not to focus on it, but the scar on his face hadn't been there when I left, and I wondered how he'd gotten it. Ice slid down my spine as the most likely reason occurred to me. I was sure Fox had something to do with it.

Despite the tension between us, I needed to seek Rodrigo out. Regardless of whether he chose to accept me or not, I wasn't going anywhere. I wanted to put everything behind us and move on—hopefully in a positive manner this time.

Striding down the hall, I was gratified when I saw him move from a darkened doorway, and I called out to him.

His back stiffened, and he hesitated at the sound of his name before finally turning to me. His face was expressionless, his hands hooked together at his lower back as he regarded me impassively.

Still incredibly wary of him, I stopped several feet away. Neither of us said anything for several seconds, and I saw the faint flicker of irritation in his eyes as he finally broke the silence. "How can I help you, Mrs. Vulpe?"

I blinked at the sound of my new name, then gave my head a little shake. "I just… I want to settle things between us."

He stared at me. "I assure you, there is nothing to settle."

That was a lie if I'd ever heard one. "Please, Rodrigo. Be straight with me."

That got his attention, and he startled slightly. "I'm not going to fight with you. I understand you want him to finish this, and so do I. For his sake, we need to get along. I only want the best for Fox, just like you do," I added softly.

Rodrigo tensed, a myriad of emotions crossing his face before sliding back into the stoic mask he typically wore. "I understand."

"Do you?" I persisted. "Because I'm not going anywhere. I'm going to do what's best for him. I'm sorry I ran and put you in this position."

He gave a tiny nod of acknowledgment. "To suggest you leave him was selfish, but I thought it best at the time."

"I know." I smiled. "I know you care about him, too."

His mouth opened, then closed, his gaze sliding away before meeting mine again. "I am indebted to him."

A million thoughts swirled through my mind. I wasn't even sure how to phrase my next question. "Were you... Did he...?"

Rodrigo nodded. "Most of us are the same. We all have a personal interest in wanting this to end."

My heart broke for the man standing before me, for whatever horrors he'd endured. "I understand," I said. "I know you'll find him."

With that, Rodrigo offered a tight smile, friendlier than the last, and turned on a heel to leave. Feeling like a huge weight had been lifted off my chest, I moved into the sitting room across from Fox's office. Spring had turned to early summer here, and the backyard bloomed beautifully with bright, colorful blossoms and vibrant shrubs.

"I should have known I would find you here."

I turned at the sound of Fox's voice, unable to keep my smile at bay. "Hey."

He moved forward, and I automatically slipped my hands around his shoulders as he pulled me into him for a kiss. Though I'd seen him hours earlier, it felt much too long.

Fox pulled back and lifted a package I hadn't realized he'd been holding. "This is for you, angel."

I opened the lid to reveal a shiny black cell phone. "What is this for?"

"In case you need to go somewhere, I want to be able to reach you."

"Oh?" I threw him a look full of challenge. "I don't have to escape this time?"

"Smart ass." He lightly swatted my bottom. "No escaping. But I do have a stipulation."

I opened my mouth, but he quickly pressed a finger to

my lips, silencing me. "No arguments. If you leave this house, you have one of my men with you at all times. They drive, and they act as your guard and shadow."

I was faintly irritated at the thought that he still didn't trust me. Almost immediately, it dissipated and the truth stood out, stark and bright. "Araña."

"Yes." His dark eyes were serious. "I'd like you to stay inside as much as possible and let my men handle everything. If you need anything to be delivered to the house, let my men check it first to make sure it's safe. If you have special requests for food, let Carmen know and she'll acquire it for you."

"I understand." I nodded. "Thank you."

"You're welcome. Now"—he cupped my face in his palms—"I unfortunately have some work to do."

I leaned into him as he dropped a kiss on my forehead. "That's fine. I'm sure I can find a way to entertain myself."

He pulled back and stared down at me, a wry smile on his face. "One last thing." He pulled a flat, dark object from his back pocket and passed it to me.

My eyes widened as I automatically reached out to accept the credit card. "Is this for me?"

"Yes. Anything you need, put it on there."

"Oh, good," I smiled wickedly as I slipped it into my pocket. "Think of all the shoes and purses and clothes I could put on this baby." We both knew I was teasing. In truth, there was nothing I wanted or needed, but I appreciated the gesture.

He gripped my chin between his thumb and forefinger, tipping me up for another kiss. "Whatever you want, angel, it's yours."

"Thank you." I kissed him one last time, then let him

go, patting the lapel of his dark jacket and smoothing the creases. "Is there anything I can help with?"

"Most of it is research, building dossiers on the men and women we know are involved and trying to find that connection that will lead us to Araña. You can sit with one of my men and learn the databases if you'd like."

I was glad he hadn't immediately written me off. I thought about it but quickly discarded the idea. "I'll only slow them down."

"I can find something else—"

"It's fine." I stretched up on my toes and kissed him. "It's more important for you to do this quickly, and I don't want to jeopardize anything. I'll find a way to entertain myself today. Really, it's fine," I said when he raised a dark brow my direction. "I do have this shiny new credit card burning a hole in my pocket…"

A smile tipped the corners of his lips. "I sense I made a mistake already."

We both knew I was kidding, and he caressed my cheek with one finger before stepping away. "You know where I'll be if you need anything."

I watched him go, feeling that same fluttery sensation in my chest, and I rubbed one hand over my heart. Would that feeling ever go away? I hoped not.

TWENTY-THREE

FOX

I blinked my eyes open, and the first rosy streaks of dawn lighting the sky greeted me. Sprawled on my stomach, I rolled my head to the left and smiled when I saw Eva curled up just inches from me. My movements must have disturbed her, because her hand swept over the sheet, fingers twitching, almost like she was searching for me in her sleep.

She let out a sweet little sigh as I slipped my fingers into hers, and my heart swelled. I'd never known a woman like Eva, so full of devotion. She wanted—needed—me, yet also took care of me in return. It scared me sometimes, how much I cared for her. My heart beat too fast, and it felt like every nerve ending in my body crackled like a live wire in her presence. She was everything I never knew I wanted, and I couldn't believe sometimes that she was actually mine.

I couldn't help the smile that curved my mouth as I

drank in every inch of her beautiful face. Despite the fact that we'd spent nearly two weeks in the Caribbean sun, her skin was still so fair I could see the spidery blue veins on her eyelids. My gaze lifted to her dark brows, such a stark contrast to her long, pale locks. My fingers itched with the need to trace the contours of her face and commit every single inch to memory.

Not wanting to wake her, I released her fingers then eased from under the covers and sat up. I was exhausted physically, but mentally—emotionally—I'd never felt better. We'd been back home for less than a week, and everything so far had been… perfect. I had no idea how long I sat there lost in thoughts of my wife, dreading leaving our room, when Eva's soft touch startled me out of my reverie. Her fingers traced the lines etched into my back.

I threw a look at her over my shoulder. "Don't like my scars, angel?"

She didn't even look at me as the pads of her fingers coasted over every imperfection. "I don't like the story they tell."

Twisting toward her, I caught her hand in mine and lifted it to my chest. "Being with you makes it feel like it was a lifetime ago."

Her eyes darkened. "I hate him."

This woman. God, I had no idea what I'd ever done to deserve her. My hand tightened around hers as a fierce possessiveness welled up inside me. I would spend every day protecting her, caring for her, until the day I died. "Don't be angry, angel. I'm filled with enough hate for both of us."

She closed her eyes briefly, then looked up at me. "I wish I could take it all away."

"You do." I brushed a kiss across her forehead. "More than you'll ever know."

There was nothing I wanted more than to put all of this behind us and move on. My men and I had been hard at work since my return, pulling strings that would hopefully lead us to the one man I needed to kill. I'd spent nearly three decades waiting for this moment. It was all I'd thought about, everything that had driven me. But now that it was here, I felt nothing. There was so much more to life than revenge. Now I had Eva.

After I'd taken care of Araña, I planned to keep investing in ways to stop human trafficking and continue to advocate for the victims. But I could pay people to take care of that. I wanted a life with Eva. I wanted the family I'd never thought possible. As each day passed, I yearned for it more and more. I couldn't wait for that day to finally come when I could move on in peace.

"I have to get some work done." I kissed her once more, then stood. "Plans for today?"

Propping herself on one elbow, she shrugged. "Not particularly. I've been thinking…"

She trailed off, and I paused in the act of pulling on my pants, then turned to face her. "What's that, angel?"

She bit her lip, her gaze darting away for a moment before returning to mine. "I was thinking of going back to school."

My brows lifted at that revelation. I had no objection to it, of course, but there was still the matter of her safety. She seemed to understand the direction of my thoughts, because she pushed to a sitting position and peered at me.

"I could check the requirements, find an online program. I already have my associates degree... Maybe I can find something to build on that."

I settled back on the edge of the bed. "Would you continue your criminal justice studies?"

She quirked a sassy little grin. "I think you've taught me more about crime than I'll ever need to know."

"Smart ass." Grabbing her ankle, I tugged her toward me. Her yelp of surprise dissolved into laughter as I climbed over her, using my weight to press her into the mattress.

She looped her arms around my shoulders. "I don't think that would be very practical if we don't stay here in Chicago. It was just a thought, something to occupy my time while you're busy."

"I can find a way to keep you busy." I slid my hand from her hip along the dip of her waist until I cupped one breast in my hand.

Her eyes fell closed as she arched into me. "Are you trying to distract me?"

I grinned and brushed my thumb over her nipple, making it stand at attention. "Never."

"Mmm..." She wiggled in my lap, and my dick hardened. "Feels like you could use a distraction, too. Might want to tell your men you'll be running late."

Scooping her up, I lay her back on the bed and kissed my way down her stomach to her sweet, tender folds. "They'll figure it out."

Nearly forty-five minutes later, I finally entered my office. They knew better than to say anything to my face, but I saw the knowing looks on their faces. I focused on Rodrigo. "What do we have so far?"

His bland eyes met mine. "There's chatter of another shipment coming up, but something is different with this one."

"How so?"

"I'm not entirely sure, exactly. Like the past few, there are specific code words that we're not sure how to interpret."

"What's the context?"

"Appears to be either a person or a location. Xavier is trying to break it, but so far we haven't been able to pinpoint an exact correlation."

"I see." I steepled my fingers against my chin. "And what have our friends been up to?"

"Moreau spent the past two weeks in Napa, and according to the guy I have watching Masterson, he's been lying low."

I crossed one leg over the other. "Where are we on the information we received from Hossam? Have we narrowed down whatever Spencer was working on last year?"

"I believe so." Xavier stepped forward and passed me a sheaf of papers. "Remember when they had that massive push for electric vehicles last year and installed several hundred charging stations all across the county?"

I riffled through the pages, skimming the document. "Waste of money."

"Not to Nathaniel Thurston."

"Let me guess," I drawled. "He has shares in the electric plant?"

"Better." Xavier quirked a smile. "His wife's family owns the coal plant that produces the electricity."

Fucking figured. I rolled my eyes, though I truly

expected nothing less. "So he's making a fuck ton of money from this "green" initiative. Any relation between Thurston and either Masterson or Moreau? Do they have a stake in this, too?"

"Not that I was able to find. However"—Xavier met my gaze—"Thurston happens to have a second cousin who works in customs at the port. Ted Pattinson."

Now we were getting somewhere. I flipped through the papers until I came to the information I was looking for. An employee for the past four years, Pattinson could approve the manifests of the shipping containers that came in, then look the other way when the transfer was made. Spencer could have pushed the bill to be approved in exchange for Thurston and Pattinson's silence. It also allowed Spencer to hold a good amount of blackmail over the men.

"Also," Xavier continued, "if our math is correct, he was on duty the night each shipment came in."

I lifted my brows at that little tidbit of good news. "I think we need to have a chat with Mr. Pattinson."

TWENTY-FOUR

EVA

I lay in bed long after Fox went downstairs, thinking about the changes that had occurred over the past few weeks. It boggled the mind how far we had come. Just a little over three weeks ago, I was alone and unhappy in my tiny condo in Omaha. Now I was married to the man I loved more than anything, my sister was safe and happily wiling away the days in the sunshine with her husband, and I was back in my hometown where this all had started.

I couldn't get Elle's situation out of my mind. I would never look at Spencer Masterson the same way. Hopefully, I wouldn't have to see him ever again. I wanted Fox to finish up his business here quickly so we could go back to the island.

The idea of him putting himself in danger was terrifying. He was strong and sure, but he wasn't invincible. Three months ago, I had stood in the *en suite* bathroom just a few feet from the bed and stitched up a bullet wound inflicted by the very same people he was now hunting.

I knew this was something that he had to do, a personal mission he began as a young boy. I recalled the day Elle and I had spoken as we perused the farmer's market. She was right. I never would have been happy with a man who wasn't as domineering and forceful as Fox. Not because he overshadowed me in any way, but because he pushed me, made me stronger. We were better together, no matter the situation. He was shrewd and cunning, and he hired only the best men to fight by his side. I trusted that they would do everything in their power to keep him safe.

I truly admired his dedication to his cause. Some men would've given up—but not Fox. He would never rest until the man responsible for so much destruction had paid for his sins. I wasn't naïve. I knew other factions existed for the same purpose, and many more would probably sprout up as long as men like Araña were allowed to get away with the things they did. I wanted Fox to make an example out of him.

It was funny how my view had changed over just a few short months. I had called Fox a monster when I was held captive in the panic room, but I knew now that was the furthest thing from the truth. He had always done his best to take care of me despite the circumstances. That knowledge only dug the memory of my father's betrayal deeper into my chest. A few weeks ago I'd told Fox that I needed the closure, that I needed to speak with him and get it off my chest. Now I wasn't so sure.

A huge part of me wanted to demand answers for why he'd done what he had. But I also trusted that what Fox told me was the truth. If he believed that my father couldn't pay back the debt, then I believed him.

It was no secret that my mother was the breadwinner in the family. My grandparents were incredibly wealthy, and they left everything to her in a trust when they passed. She was incredibly dedicated to her career and would let nothing stand in the way—especially not my father. I was certain that they had only married because of my dad's family connections.

Although he had inherited his father's business, my dad wasn't particularly driven. He wasn't business minded, so he relied heavily on others to make decisions for him. I had never before questioned his work ethic or his inability to manage money, but I couldn't say his incompetence surprised me.

He, like my mother, had come from a trust fund. While she has done everything in her power to make her life better, my father steered in the opposite direction, leaning heavily on the resources he'd inherited instead of forging his own way through life. I knew my mother kept my father on a tight leash, but I wondered if even she knew of his gambling debts. I seriously doubted it. If she had, she probably would have cut him off years ago.

Her goal was to work her way up through the political ranks with the prospect of being the first female president of the United States. It was a lofty aspiration, even for her. Though she was incredibly smart, she wasn't particularly personable or charismatic. Still, she was my mother, and I missed her. Even if I never spoke with my father again, I wanted to see my mother if only to see how she had fared over the past few months. What had he told her about my disappearance?

I looked at the phone Fox had purchased for me. I could call or text my father right now, but something stopped me. There was no point in dredging up the past if I planned to move forward. There was nothing else that he could tell me at this point that would make it better.

It hurt my heart to think of what he'd done, but maybe it was best to leave sleeping dogs lie. Everything worked out for the best, and that was all that mattered. Though I might never forgive him, I found a measure of peace in knowing that his actions had brought me to Fox. And that was worth everything.

Fox spent most of the day holed up in his office, no doubt still working on tracking down Araña. I knocked just after dinner time, and his men scattered as he welcomed me in.

He remained seated, waiting until we were alone to speak. "How was your day, angel?"

"Fine." I moved around the desk and he pulled me into his lap, then kissed me long and slow. "Getting any closer?"

He gestured to the stacks of papers cluttering the surface of his desk. "Yes and no. It's a process."

Though I had offered to help, I didn't have the necessary stealth or skill set to go about gathering intel on the multitude of people involved. From what Fox had told me, it was an intricate process of digging up dirt and paying off informants. Although I'd studied Criminal Justice in school, I'd never spent a day in the field. I knew Feds paid their CIs all the time to pass along vital information, but I'd never seen anything to this scale.

"I'm sorry."

"We'll find him." His voice was full of confidence, but I knew it was wearing on him.

I idly ran my fingers along the back of his neck, gently kneading the tight cords of muscle, and his eyelids fell closed. "Are you hungry?"

Those dark eyes opened, boring into mine, and his hand slipped up the curve of my waist. "Not particularly, not for food."

I smiled. "I can help with that."

"Good." He squeezed gently. "One stipulation—a game first."

I cocked my head. "A game?"

He smiled, revealing a row of shiny white teeth. "Whoever wins gets to be in charge."

Now that I could get onboard with. "You're on."

We moved to the den down the hall where we'd played previously, and I settled into my seat. "I'm rusty," I warned. "You better take it easy on me."

His grin turned feral. "When have I ever been easy with you?"

Never, thank God, because I loved him rough and raw. He swooped in for a swift, hard kiss, then took a seat across from me and began to arrange his pieces on the board. Several moves in, he flicked a glance at me. "Ironic, isn't it, that the entire point of the game is to protect the king, yet the queen has the most power?"

"Just like real life," I quipped with a smile as I moved my rook.

His eyes captured mine. "A king would be lost without his queen."

And suddenly we were no longer speaking of the game. His words sent heat curling through me, and I made several careless moves, no longer invested in trying to win. All I wanted was him.

"Did you throw that game intentionally?" he asked later as he snapped one cuff around my wrist, securing me to the bed.

"I have no idea what you're talking about."

I let out a little hiss as he sucked my nipple into his mouth, arching at the sensation. His hard weight settled over me. "I may be the king." He teased my lips with soft kisses. "But you, angel, will always be my queen."

TWENTY-FIVE

FOX

The man's terrified brown eyes stared up at me. "Please, I'll tell you anything."

"I'm sure you will," I agreed. "Do you know a man by the name of Spencer Masterson?"

His eyes widened a fraction at the mention of Masterson's name, but he quickly blinked away his fear. "N-no. Never heard of him."

"Are you certain?" His eyes flickered again but he nodded his head. I studied him from where I stood several feet away. "You know what they say about climbing into bed with the devil?"

"I—"

"It was a fucking rhetorical question," I snapped, cutting him off. "It means that you had better be damn certain whatever you're getting out of this will be worth it. Masterson doesn't give a damn about you. When this whole operation comes crumbling down around his ears, who the fuck do you think they're going to look at?"

I stepped forward. "Sure as hell won't be him. He's a senator. Respected. Well-liked." Just not by me. Or anyone else I knew. "You'll be facing felony charges for approving these shipments without checking the manifests."

His eyes widened. "B-but—"

"But you won't even make it to jail." I closed the distance between us and dropped my face close to his. "They'll kill you first, because you're disposable. You're just one in a long line of handlers and transporters. People like you are a dime a dozen and unless you open your mouth and tell me the fucking truth, I may as well just put you out of your misery and kill you right now."

"Oh, God." Pattinson's entire body shook. "I have a family. They threatened my wife, my girls. You don't understand—I had to!"

I understood desperate measures. "That's precisely why we need to stop them. They can't be allowed to hurt anyone else. But I need your full cooperation, and I need everything you know—the sooner the better."

"I—I promise." He nodded frantically. I gestured for him to begin, and he darted a quick look at Rodrigo before meeting my gaze again. "It was only supposed to be one time. I needed the money, and Spencer paid me in cash. I thought it was over."

"Until they came knocking again."

He nodded. "I didn't want to do it, but... they wouldn't let me out. Threatened to kill my girls."

I moved closer. "Did you know what was being moved?"

He shook his head. "I never asked, and he never said."

Not surprising. "There were dozens of children inside those containers." I watched as his eyes widened and his face paled. "They were brought into the States, purchased by sick fucks who use and abuse them. Make them wish they were dead. And you helped them."

"Oh, God—I—" He looked positively ill.

"You're responsible for that."

He shook his head emphatically. "N-no, I swear. I had no idea. I—"

"You helped them," I said forcefully as I braced my hands on the arms of the chair and leaned in close. "Now help me. I need to know everything that happened."

Half an hour later, Callum and Rodrigo escorted Rhys Pattinson from the building. After checking with Miranda to make sure everything was running smoothly, Xavier and I headed home. Who was Spencer working for? I knew he was just a pawn in a much larger game, but each breadcrumb led me closer and closer to the man in charge. I couldn't forget that Sebastian had been in the mountains, too. Was he the man I'd been searching for?

There was one question that resounded in my mind over and over. Using cash was an easy way to avoid detection. Businesses loved cash because they could cook their books, profit the difference with no one the wiser. But these would be incredibly large sums of money; an American child could sell for upwards of thirty thousand dollars on the market.

"Spencer paid Pattinson in cash for each shipment. Assuming Spencer and Sebastian are high up in the organization, they would be making a significant amount of money. How are they being paid? And what about the buyers? Not only would they need to have large sums of liquid cash, but would they risk being seen?"

"Wouldn't necessarily have to be face-to-face," Xavier said. "Could be a drop somewhere."

"Again with the risk if someone were to intercept it." I thought about it. There had to be a middle man—or a third-party organization that kept both the buyers' and sellers' identities concealed. "It would have to be somewhere safe and controlled if they were to make a drop somewhere. If it were me… I'd launder it through an established corporation. Let's cross-check Masterson and Moreau and see where they're involved, whether it's the same tennis club or investment firm."

Two days later, Xavier stepped into my office and passed a packet of paper to me. "Both men are involved with a number of organizations."

I glanced at the affiliations listed on the top sheet of paper. There were more than a dozen company names, each of which had a concise report printed beneath. "Assuming we're looking for a way to funnel money, let's exclude the clubs for the time being."

I began to mentally cross them off, focusing on corporations or larger scale companies that could handle transactions of substantial size without raising questions. "Let's focus on these for the time being." I ticked eight organizations that seemed most likely. "See what you can find."

We were getting closer—I could feel it. The idea of taking down those two alone filled me with feral satisfaction. I wanted them gone if for no other reason than the fact that they'd hurt the women they were supposed to care for. Sebastian Moreau was a cheating prick to his long-time girlfriend Marcella, and Spencer... Well, that fucker had it coming the second he laid a hand on Elle.

The following evening Callum and Xavier were gathered around my desk, poring over the information they'd been able to dig up over the past twenty-four hours. Rodrigo was currently taking my wife to meet with her friend Rose from school.

Neither had looked particularly thrilled to hear that I was sending Rodrigo along to watch over her, but they had to get over their issues—preferably sooner rather than later. I hoped they would survive the evening without killing each other.

Callum lifted his head. "What about William Jennings' business?"

"William's a terrible businessman." I shook my head. "He runs a software company that was basically handed to him by his father, but it's taken quite a hit recently."

"He's looking to sell." Xavier flicked pages until he reached a report at the back of the file and handed it to me. "Here are the last quarter's numbers."

Jesus. I knew things were bad for Jennings, but this? He'd hemorrhaged so much money that it'd left him in almost dire straits. I shouldn't have been as surprised as I was. The fact that he'd run his business into the ground, coupled with his penchant for gambling, was precisely the reason he'd approached me for a loan in the first place.

Subsequently, it was why Eva was now with me—a fact I would never take for granted. William was an idiot, and it didn't shock me that he was now forced to sell or declare bankruptcy. Idiot.

"What about this?" Callum passed me a multi-page dossier. "A foundation here in the states. Four other individuals appeared on this list several times, as well."

I skimmed the list of names that he passed to me. Marcella Levieva, Marcus Townsend, Kip Bernhart, and William Jennings. I immediately discounted Sebastian's girlfriend, Marcella. She was as innocent as they came. William Jennings—Eva's father—was an interesting one, but not completely unexpected. He and Spencer were good friends, after all, and I'd heard recently that Spencer was helping Eva's mother, Lillian, to gather support in her campaign to run for governor.

"Let's see what we were able to gather on Townsend and Bernhart." Xavier had included a brief background on each person, and my brows lifted when I read the details. "Interesting. Marcus Townsend owns a bank in Sweden."

"He could easily be paving the way for them to transfer money into account, and I would bet that he was getting a decent cut himself," Callum replied.

"Entirely possible," I agreed.

I flipped the page, and a cold chill slithered down my spine as I read the name of the organization. Helping Hand. I could feel the men's eyes on me as I read, and I cleared my throat before reading the name aloud. "According to this, the foundation was started several decades ago in an attempt to help women and children in unfortunate situations."

And that motherfucker Masterson was taking advantage of the very people it was designed to protect.

Xavier threw a look my way. "How would that work?"

"From what I remember, there are fairly strict regulations for foundations." That being said, I was certain that, with the above men involved, they would find a way around them. I couldn't begin to imagine the amount of money the foundation would bring in if they were using it as a front for their trafficking business. And it would certainly be easy enough.

"If the money is actually coming through here, I would imagine that the buyers could be making payments in the form of donations through Helping Hand to secure a child."

Xavier looked as furious as I felt. "We need financial reports."

I nodded, mind whirling with possibilities—none of them good. "Find everything you can."

TWENTY-SIX

EVA

My knee jumped impatiently, and my heart raced with anticipation. I couldn't wait to see Rose. It had been almost three months since I'd last seen her, and I was dying to talk to her. A huge smile split my face when Rodrigo pulled up to the curb, and I saw Rose standing outside next to the frosted glass doors of the bar. It took every ounce of patience not to just barrel from the car as I waited for Rodrigo to park, then come around and let me out.

As much as I wanted to just throw open the door and run to my best friend, I knew Fox would have a conniption fit if I did. He was 100% focused on my safety, and if I didn't follow his every request, he would probably never let me out of his sight again. Rodrigo finally opened the door with a little nod of his head, and I practically threw myself onto the sidewalk.

Rose caught sight of me, and her eyes widened as she

flung her arms wide open for a hug. "It's been forever," she exclaimed as she squeezed me tight. "How are you?"

She set me away from her, her gaze sweeping from the top of my head all the way down to my toes and back up again. "You look amazing."

"So do you," I said, linking my arm through hers. "It's been so crazy. I can't wait to tell you all about it."

The hostess inside showed us to a quiet booth, and Rose's bright blue gaze followed Rodrigo's movement as he took a seat close by where he could keep a close eye on me. Rose's eyes slid back to mine. "Is he with you?"

"For protection." I nodded. I opened my mouth to say more but was cut off when the server arrived at our table to take our drink orders. "Cosmopolitan, please."

Rose ordered a strawberry daiquiri, then turned back to me. "Okay, spill. Why do you have a bodyguard? I heard your mom is running for governor—is that why he's here? God, I've been dying to know what you've been up to."

I laughed at her enthusiasm. "Nothing that dramatic, I promise. And, yes, Mom is running for governor." Last I'd heard, anyway, considering I hadn't spoken with her in months. The reminder sent a little pang through my heart, but I shoved it down and focused on the happier, more recent events.

"But that's not why I have protection now." I folded my hands on the table, and the motion drew Rose's attention.

"Oh, my God! Are you engaged?"

I smiled. "Married, actually."

Her mouth formed an 'O' of surprise, then her eyes

leveled on me. "Start from the beginning and don't leave anything out," she ordered.

I let out a little laugh. "Remember when we talked a couple months ago, right after I took a break from school?"

"Well, I did some soul-searching." I couldn't hold back the smile at my words. The only searching I had planned to do was to raid Fox's house in order to blackmail him. Instead, I'd ended up with the man himself. "I met this guy—"

"Where?" she cut in.

"He's actually acquaintances with my father, but I had never met him before then. We kind of started… dating." I wasn't nearly ready to describe the dynamics of my relationship with anyone, not even my best friend. "Unfortunately, my mind was still kind of a mess after, you know… everything. Anyway, I broke things off and traveled for a bit."

That was an understatement if there ever was one. Fortunately, Rose didn't question it, only nodded for me to go on. "So, I headed out west for a couple months, worked in a bar out there for a little while. It was nice, but it wasn't home. I missed everyone like crazy, and I thought all the time about coming back.

"All of a sudden, Fox showed up out of the blue one day to surprise me. He convinced me to go on vacation with him to his home down in the Caribbean. He proposed while we were down there, and…" I lifted my hands in a little shrug. "I accepted."

Her head tipped slightly to one side as she inspected me. "Do you love him?"

I was fully aware of Rodrigo's attention on me from

several feet away, and I shifted uncomfortably. "More than anything," I admitted quietly.

"That's so sweet." A huge smile lit her face, and Rose let out a little squeal. "Just like a fairytale!"

I managed to hold back my laughter. On the surface, it probably looked that way. Fox was kind of like my dark prince; he achieved goodness through questionable motives, but I wouldn't have it any other way.

"So," I said, turning the focus back to Rose, "tell me how you've been."

She and I sat and chatted for another two hours until I finally smothered a yawn. She had to be up early for work the next morning, and I was eager to get home to Fox. Back in the car, I turned to Rodrigo. "Did that sound okay?"

He hesitated so long I wasn't sure he heard me. "Sounded real enough to me."

I wasn't sure if he meant the story I'd conjured for Rose or the fact that I said I loved him. My cheeks flared and I settled into silence. As soon as we arrived home, I immediately headed to Fox's office. Rodrigo followed just behind, and the others offered small smiles as I entered.

I headed directly to Fox as he stood and moved around the desk to intercept me. I tilted my head up for a kiss as his men made themselves scarce. I gestured to the papers scattered across the desk. "How's it coming?"

Something flickered in his eyes. "I'm not sure yet. I think I have a new lead, but… only time will tell."

I wanted more than anything to take that look from his face—the one that spoke of a tiredness both deep. He'd been fighting these demons for decades. I wanted him to forget them, if only for a few minutes.

I slid my arms around his shoulders. "Come to bed."

TWENTY-SEVEN

FOX

I should have known that everything was too good to be true. For the past six days, my men and I had been busy trying to dig up every scrap of information we could find on Helping Hand. Xavier had pulled the history of transactions dating back a full year and found that payments had been made to a shelf corporation under the name of Mercer and Melvin.

The name was similar to Moreau and Masterson, and Xavier was currently working on obtaining information on the company and any transfer of funds to the persons we expected were involved. I assumed the shelf corporation would lead directly to Sebastian and Spencer.

We'd also found a number of high-profile benefactors who'd made several large donations around the same time as the shipments, and Rodrigo and Callum were pulling background on them. One such donor was Marcus Townsend, a childhood friend of Moreau's. He came from a wealthy family who, among dozens of other holdings, owned a bank in Sweden.

Townsend had taken over operations a few years ago after his father retired. We suspected that, once the money left the foundation and went to Mercer and Melvin that it would then be rerouted out of the country and into Townsend's bank. It would be easy enough to manage, and I was certain that Townsend would be getting a nice little slice of the profits for easing the way.

Xavier strode into the room, an unreadable expression on his face as he stepped in front of my desk. "Mercer and Melvin is very well constructed, and it appears legitimate to the average consumer. Their website is updated regularly, and they even have a phone service."

I lifted my brows in silent question, and he continued. "I verified the transactions that went through and we were correct—several payments have been made to both Masterson and Moreau."

He hesitated, and I studied him. "And?"

"On a whim, I checked another name. I..." He paused, then extended a folder across the desk to me. "This may be the man you've been looking for."

My hand shook as I reached for the file, and I forced myself to steady. God. I'd been waiting for this moment for decades. We were so close... Would the information inside truly end this? A combination of relief and disappointment welled up inside me. I steeled my spine and flipped open the financial reports, then skimmed the first few pages outlining Masterson and Moreau's accounts.

I wasn't at all prepared for the next name on the list.

My entire body stilled, and I read it again—twice—just to make sure my eyes weren't deceiving me.

I lifted a brow at Xavier. "Are you sure?"

"Positive." He looked regretful, but not nearly as much as I felt. My stomach twisted as the full implication sank in at the sight of William Jennings's names and the corresponding account information. The numbers on the page floored me. The man was stockpiling money in a European bank. But why pretend that he couldn't afford to pay back the loan? "Are we sure this is the same man?"

William Jennings was a multi-millionaire—and completely full of shit. I'd written the fucker off because of his financial situation. Hell, he'd convinced me that he was so deep in the hole he had to pawn off his daughter in exchange for wiping out his debts. Christ. Looking back, it was all so clear. He'd readily given her up so I wouldn't look too closely. And Elle—he'd practically given her to Spencer, his little lap dog, in exchange for a job well done.

William was the right age. He had all the right connections. Jesus. How in the hell was I going to explain this to my wife? I closed the folder and set it on my desk.

Silence fell heavily over the room, and after a full minute I lifted my gaze to my men. "Thank you. Take the evening off. I need to speak with my wife."

Xavier sent a sympathetic look my way, then exited the office, followed closely by Callum. Rodrigo watched me intently as I slowly pushed out of my chair. "Sir?"

"Yes?"

His dark gaze seared into mine, and he tipped his head toward the folder on my desk. "I'd like to request your permission to check into Jennings."

I knew he didn't doubt Xavier's work, but in a

situation like this, we needed to be absolutely certain the man was responsible before making our next move. "I appreciate that, but tomorrow will be soon enough."

He looked like he wanted to say something else, but dipped his head and left the office. I followed suit, locking up behind me before heading up the back staircase to the second floor. My feet felt heavy as I trudged down the hall toward our bedroom. I hesitated just outside, wondering how in the hell I was going to tell Eva.

I stepped inside then closed the door behind me, my ears perking up at the sound of the shower running in the adjoining bathroom. I closed the door and leaned against it for a minute, staring at the ceiling. Despite everything, William was still her father. This would break her heart.

Pushing off the door, I stripped out of my jacket, then tossed it aside before sinking into a chair in front of the fireplace. I tipped my head back and closed my eyes, bracing myself for the conversation ahead. I tensed as the water cut off, and the familiar sounds of Eva rummaging around met my ears. I could practically see her brushing out her long golden locks, applying various creams to that beautiful fair skin of hers.

Just the thought brought a smile to my lips. There wasn't a single thing in this world that meant more to me than that woman. I would literally do anything in my power to protect her. Just as quickly, the smile slipped away. In the other room she went about with her life, completely unaware that her entire world was about to change.

Less than two minutes later, she left the bathroom. Though my eyes were still closed, I heard her pause in the doorway as she became aware of my presence. "Hey."

Her voice was soft and tentative, and I forced a smile to my lips as I rolled my head toward her. "Hi, angel."

"You look exhausted." An expression of concern settled over her pretty features as she circled to stand behind the chair and rested her hands on my shoulders, gently kneading my muscles. "Is everything okay?"

I could lie to her. I could brush it off as if everything was perfectly fine; but it wasn't. Things would never be okay again. I settled one hand over hers where it rested on my shoulder. "Come here."

Not relinquishing my hold on her, I guided her until she was in front of me, then pulled her onto my lap.

She gnawed on her lower lip as she studied me. "You're worrying me."

"I know, angel. I'm sorry."

From her position perched on my knee, she stared at me, those pretty green eyes searching mine. "Tell me."

There was no use trying to hide it from her. I let out a little sigh. "I need to ask you a question."

Immediately, the look in her eyes turned guarded. "Okay?"

"Your mother runs a foundation, is that correct?"

"Yes…" She drew out the word. "To enrich the lives of the less fortunate or something to that effect," she replied.

"How much do you know about the inner workings?"

"I attend the annual dinner, but other than that…" She lifted her hands. "I don't have anything to do with it. Mother wanted me to get involved, but it's really not my thing."

A smile lifted my lips as I sifted a lock of her long pale hair in my fingers. "I'm glad." Her brow furrowed. "Why?"

I let out the breath I'd been holding. "Because I believe they're involved in illegal activity."

Her eyes widened, and her mouth dropped into a little 'O' of surprise. "Are you sure? But—"

I shook my head, cutting her off. "Do you remember I told you about the shipments that came in across the border?" She nodded, and I continued. "We found evidence of payments to men who work at an airfield where we suspect they were flown in, as well as to a man who works for border patrol."

Dread filled her eyes. "Are you sure it wasn't for something else?"

"Unfortunately, no." I sighed. "The foundation has also made payments to Sebastian Moreau and Spencer."

Her head shook slightly, but she couldn't seem to form words. "There's more. Substantial sums of money have been transferred to an offshore account, and I believe from the amount stashed away, that the man in charge is Araña, the man I've been tracking for decades."

"Who?" Her voice was little more than a whisper.

"Your father."

TWENTY-EIGHT

EVA

No, it couldn't be true. There was no way my father could be involved in such an elaborate and nefarious scheme. But the look on Fox's face told me everything I needed to know.

"H-how?" I couldn't think straight, let alone form words. "Why?"

He shrugged helplessly. "Money? I'm not sure. I'm so sorry, Angel."

"Oh, God. You don't think...?" Was he using the foundation to select his victims? It made me sick to my stomach. He was heartless enough; the things he'd done to Elle and me proved that. I just... God, I didn't want to believe it.

"We're going to find out for sure."

"What then?"

He leveled a stare at me. "We take care of him."

He enfolded me in his arms and tucked my head into the crook of his neck. I was stunned by the information Fox had just imparted, but surprisingly, the tears I expected never came. In a way, it made sense. Daddy knew everyone on the board without being directly involved. Even after Elle's supposed death, he and Spencer had remained extremely close. Now it seemed they were working together while pulling the wool over everyone's eyes.

I clenched my teeth together as anger simmered in my blood. He'd fooled everyone, but especially me. I had defended him, and all the while he was responsible for the deaths of hundreds, if not thousands, of women and children. In a way, he was even responsible for the things Fox had endured as a child. It made me hate him all the more.

Again, the idea of contacting him flitted through my mind. No. I gave myself a mental shake. If he truly was responsible for this, he needed to pay for his crimes. I couldn't begin to imagine what Fox had in store for him, and my heart clenched at the thought. Still, I knew he couldn't be allowed to escape unscathed.

"I need you to be sure," I said softly.

Fox tipped my chin up so he could look me squarely in the eyes. "We're double checking everything to make sure. If he's Araña…"

Fox didn't need to continue. "I know."

Fox squeezed me more tightly to him and we sat there for what felt like forever, holding on to each other, lost in the memories of our past.

Fox found me in the kitchen cutting up an apple for an afternoon snack. An indulgent smile curled his mouth. "Carmen would have a fit if she could see you right now," he said in reference to the cook he employed. "I pay her a salary more than most people make in a year for the sole purpose of creating elaborate dishes, yet my wife grazes on snacks intended for toddlers."

I shrugged, still crunching on one of my apple slices. "I told you before—I don't need all that fancy food. Sometimes the basics are best."

"That, angel, is just one more thing that amazes me about you." He picked up the knife I'd been using and twirled it thoughtfully between his fingers before stepping up behind me, pinning me between his huge body and the unforgiving granite counter that cut into my waist. I tensed when he settled the flat edge of the blade against the curve of my shoulder, and a shiver rolled down my spine as he drew it down my bicep, the stainless steel scraping lightly over my skin.

In Fox's hands, the blade could either be incredibly deadly or incredibly arousing. I knew he would never hurt me, and his gesture was intended more to tease than intimidate. Still, the idea of knife play was faintly unsettling, and I couldn't help the rapid tempo of my pulse as it kicked up, bringing my breath faster and faster.

Fox must've seen my reaction, because he returned the knife to the cutting board before pulling me into his arms. "Most women would have thrown themselves into spending money—redecorating, buying purses and shoes and clothes. But not you, angel. Is there nothing you need? Nothing your heart desires?"

I turned to look at him over my shoulder. "Only you."

He spun me in his arms, then grasped my hips and plunked me down on the counter. His hands slid up my thighs and under the hem of my dress before reversing and coasting back down to my knees. As he spoke, he caressed my thighs in long, firm strokes, his thumbs brushing closer and closer to my core with each pass. "There's a game tonight that I have to attend."

"Somebody important?"

"Several somebodies," he confirmed. His huge hands held my hips in place and his thumbs moved inward.

"Mmm…" I closed my eyes as he drew slow circles over my clit through the thin fabric of my panties.

His lips landed on my collarbone, kissing lower until he reached the bodice of my dress. I fell back to my elbows and dropped my head back, lost in the hazy pleasure that had descended over me.

"They expect me there, and I can't afford to disappoint them," he continued between kisses. He used his mouth and teeth to work the fabric of my top down, and I arched into him as his fingers sank deep inside me at the same time his hot mouth closed over my nipple.

"Can't have that."

My words were low and breathy, and Fox chuckled, sending a faint tingle of vibration through my body. "So needy, angel. I have to go… but I think you need to come."

I let out a little whimper as he bit down lightly on my nipple before flicking his tongue over the sensitive flesh. My stomach muscles ached from the strain of holding myself up, and I collapsed to my back. I moved my hands to Fox's head, sinking my fingers into the short strands of hair there.

His fingers teased my slit, slowly dipping in and out,

and I writhed beneath him. I swore the man could turn me on with a single touch. He grasped the fabric of my panties, then slid them down my legs, baring me completely. He released my nipple and moved downward, dipping his tongue through my drenched folds. He attacked me until I slapped one hand over my mouth to stifle my scream as I came, my chest heaving with ragged pants.

When it was over, Fox eased me to a sitting position, then retrieved my underwear from the floor. Flashing me a grin, he opened the flap of his jacket and tucked them into an inner pocket. "So I can think of you all evening while I'm gone."

A sated sort of exhaustion pulled at me, and I smiled back, unable to dredge up a smidge of embarrassment at the thought. "I'll wait up for you."

Fox glanced at his watch, then kissed me. "I have to go. See you tonight, angel."

He turned around, and a strange sensation seized my chest. I grabbed his arm, forcing him to turn back to me. I couldn't explain why, but the sudden urge to tell him I loved him sprang to the tip of my tongue. Fox's brows lifted in silent question, and I swallowed the words.

He needed a woman who was as strong and independent as himself, and I wouldn't disappoint him by saying something so romantic. Unable to speak the words in my heart, I wrapped my arms around his shoulders, hoping he would understand.

A long second passed before one hand went to the back of my head, the other wrapping around my waist, clutching me to him in a fierce hug. Fox pulled back and framed my face with both hands, his dark eyes boring into mine.

He petted my hair away from my face, stroking and touching like he never wanted to let me go—like he couldn't bear to tear himself away. The gesture was so tender that it filled my heart to bursting. I heard more emotion in the silence hanging between us than I'd ever heard in the words he spoke.

After what felt like forever, he leaned in and brushed a kiss over my forehead. I closed my eyes at the sweetness of it. He was all I'd ever wanted—and I would never let him go. "I'll miss you," I admitted on a whisper.

He kissed me once more. "Until tonight, angel."

With that last promise, Fox slipped from the kitchen and I practically melted into a puddle right there on the counter. God, I swear I fell more in love with him every day. Pressing my hands into the granite, I slid from the counter, steeling my shaky leg muscles as I hopped to my feet.

My mind and body were still hazy with pleasure, and I moved slowly upstairs to our room where I could enjoy some solitude for a bit. I was tempted to stay bare under my dress until Fox got home so we could pick up where we'd left off, but it felt awkward with the guards around. I pulled on a fresh pair of underwear then settled onto the bed and pulled a blanket over my lap, allowing my thoughts free rein.

Since Fox had revealed the news of my father's involvement in the human trafficking ring two nights ago, we hadn't spoken of it again. I couldn't help but wonder exactly where things stood. It still didn't seem quite real.

Never in a million years would I have ever guessed my father was involved. But Fox would never lie to me—not about that. He'd promised to do a full investigation, make sure that every single scrap of evidence pointed to him before making any moves.

The thought made me sick, because I knew what had to happen. He was my father, after all, and even after everything, I hated the idea of him dying. I'd tried not to think too heavily on it until we knew more. My stomach clenched tightly. What about my mother? God, what would she think? Part of me wanted her to hear the news from me.

I stowed my phone in my skirt pocket and went to look for a guard. Fox had increased security, and Xavier and Callum had accompanied him to Noir tonight while another dozen men stayed at the house. Though Rodrigo was the highest-ranking guard here, I had no intention of asking him. It would be much easier to sway one of the other men to do my bidding.

I headed out of the den and, as if luck was smiling down on me, a big, burly man named Antoine stepped right into my path. I flashed him a bright smile. "Hello."

He dipped his head politely. "Good evening, miss."

He started to move past me, but I lifted my hand to stop him. "I was hoping you could help me with something."

"Sure thing."

"I'd like to head into town to go shopping. It shouldn't take long, and I really want to surprise Fox," I said. "It's our two-week wedding anniversary, and I wanted to get something he won't forget. Not for him, but for me. For me to wear for him," I clarified, watching Antoine's cheeks turn red with embarrassment.

"Anything you want," he quickly agreed, probably to shut me up.

Either way, I wasn't going to look a gift horse in the mouth. "Perfect. I'll—"

"Can I help you with something?"

My heart sank as Rodrigo's voice pierced the air over my left shoulder, and I tensed before turning toward him with a smile fixed in place. "We're good. Antoine is just going to take me into town for something real quick."

His dark eyes bore into mine before flitting to Antoine. "I'll take care of Mrs. Vulpe. Continue your rounds." His gaze returned to me. "I'll get the car and meet you out front."

I bit my tongue against the urge to tell him no. Doing so would only make him more suspicious. "Thanks."

I ran upstairs and grabbed my purse, then headed toward the front door. One of the other, newer guys, Oscar, met me there and escorted me to the car after surveying our surroundings.

Rodrigo met my gaze in the rearview mirror. "Where to?"

"Sunbelt," I replied, giving him the name of a small shopping strip near my father's office.

He blinked once, those cold, dark eyes seeming to read into my soul, and I shifted uncomfortably. Without another word, he returned his eyes to the driveway and eased the car forward.

I stared out the window, my heart racing in my chest. I had no idea how this was going to play out, but I had to go along with it now. There was no backing out. Besides, I needed to see my mother.

In the back of my mind a red warning flag waved wildly, but I dismissed it. I was his daughter; even if he was home, he wouldn't hurt me. The emotional damage he could potentially inflict, though, was another matter entirely, and one I wasn't quite sure I was ready to handle.

TWENTY-NINE

FOX

I made my way around the room, smiling and speaking with the high rollers who'd decided to join us tonight. I made small talk and offered them drinks on the house, but all I could think about was Eva. The way she felt. The way she tasted. The way she'd hugged me before I'd walked out the door.

It'd taken every ounce of willpower to walk away from her. I sensed there was something on her mind, something she wanted to say, but she'd held back. It'd been bothering me for the past couple of hours, and all I wanted to do was go back home and find my wife.

My wife. God, that sounded so damn good. Eva was everything I'd ever wanted and more, everything I'd never dared to dream of having. She was my life and my future, the living embodiment of perfection. She was the yin to my yang, my opposite and my equal in every single way. Our strengths and weaknesses created the perfect balance.

I loved her. There was no other explanation for the perpetual achy sensation that had taken up residence in my chest when I thought of her. I was certain she felt the same, but suddenly, I needed to know. I couldn't wait for this night to end so I could see her.

I stopped next to a table set up for blackjack. "How are we doing, gentlemen?"

"Damn good whiskey," said an older man to my right, holding up a tumbler of amber liquid.

The Booker's was a nice touch. Smooth and with a higher proof, it tended to encourage my players to loosen their pockets and drop a bit more cash than they might have otherwise. "I'm glad you like it. If you need a refill, just let one of the staff know."

A couple of the men didn't even spare me a glance, so engrossed were they in the game in front of them. I wondered if either were counting cards, and I flicked a look at my dealer. She met my gaze and gave a subtle shake of her head. She hadn't noticed anything yet, and that was good enough for me.

I moved away from the table, counting down the minutes until I could escape when a waitress wearing a concerned expression appeared at my side. "Sir, we have visitors."

Shit. The police. "Is the staff aware?"

"Yes, sir. They've begun to evacuate."

Glancing around, I noticed that a soft buzz of conversation was rising around the room as word spread. "Thank you."

I gestured to the dealers at the tables close to me, and they immediately began to gather their things. The men at the tables scooped up their chips, and we ushered everyone out the back door. The employees and I moved quickly, stowing the tables and chairs in a well-hidden room off to the side while the police cleared and searched the rooms of the club upstairs.

Anger threatened, but I forced it down. A raid was terrible for business—both of them—and I paid the local officials well enough to not have to deal with this. What the hell had prompted it? Most of the time we flew under the radar, drew no attention to ourselves. Either a member had spoken with the wrong person or some well-meaning official had caught wind of it and decided he wanted a feather in his cap. Either way I was going to figure out who was responsible and put an end to it.

When everything was concealed, we made our way up a set of stairs that led up into the back of the bar area. I headed straight for my office where I heard Miranda speaking loudly with someone—probably whichever figure of authority had decided to drop in.

I rested my shoulder on the door jamb, expression fixed in place. Miranda glared at the man, then her gaze slid over his shoulder to me. She gestured my way. "I told you he would be back in a minute."

The man in a sport coat and khakis turned to look at me, his gaze speculative. "Are you the owner?"

"I am. Vincent Kelly." I introduced myself using the alias I'd used to purchase the building as I extended my hand.

He shook, that wary look still in his eyes. "Detective Kiehl."

I flicked a look Miranda's way. "Thank you. You may return to your duties."

She nodded once, then escaped after throwing one last

dark look the man's way. I turned my attention back to the detective. "How may I help you?"

"As I'm sure you're aware, my men have infiltrated your club."

A tiny smile touched my mouth. "See anything they like?"

"This is a very serious matter," he insisted.

"Oh, it absolutely is," I agreed. "You're interfering in my business, but you've yet to explain why. My members pay an exorbitant fee to ensure their privacy."

His eyes hardened. "We received a tip that this is a front for an underground gambling ring?"

"Is that so?" I lifted a brow. "And did you see anything to that effect while you searched?"

"My men are currently in the main room with the employees and members," he stumbled a bit as he explained. "They're questioning and releasing, but I'd like to take a look around."

"By all means." I held out a hand. "Follow me."

Forcing myself to keep calm, I led him from room to room. He and a second officer checked each closet, every nook and cranny. Finally, I led him into the bar where I knew I'd have to explain the door that led into the basement. Almost immediately, Kiehl was drawn to the plain door in the wall. "What's here?"

"The basement." I retrieved my key ring and found the correct key, then unlocked the door and flipped on the lights. I entered the stairwell first, hoping to God we hadn't missed anything during our rushed clean up.

Once downstairs, I flipped on the several rows of overhead lights, illuminating the plain space. Detective Kiehl looked around. "What do you do down here?"

"Nothing yet. The extra space allows us the potential to expand, perhaps add a second stage in the future, maybe another designated room or two."

Kiehl's cheeks burned with a combination of anger and embarrassment at being thwarted. There was nothing to indicate several dozen prominent men and women had been here barely half an hour ago. He threw a grudging look the officer's way before meeting my gaze again. "Thanks."

The man looked less than willing to offer the single word, but I nodded regardless. "Sorry I couldn't be of more help."

They returned upstairs, gathered the rest of their men and left. Once the doors had closed behind them, I turned to face my customers, gathered along the side of the room. "I sincerely apologize for tonight's interruption."

I spent the next two hours soothing ruffled feathers, assuring each and every customer that we wouldn't have a repeat in the future. Each minute I spent here was time I was missing with my wife, and I was more than a little furious by the end of the night. Someone owed me one hell of an explanation—and it'd better be damn good.

THIRTY

EVA

"Ready to tell me the truth?"

I bit my lip and shook my head, not bothering to tear my gaze from the buildings whizzing past. Rodrigo never would have dared ask Fox a question like that, but he was right not to trust me.

"You have to tell me," he said softly. "I made a promise to Fox that I would take care of you, and—"

"Please don't say anything to him," I pleaded. "I just… I wanted to talk to my mother."

He met my gaze in the mirror. "I can't let you go to their house, not after what we suspect about your father." He shook his head. "Besides, there's no guarantee that your mother will even be there."

"It's Sunday, she'll be home." His brow lifted a fraction, prompting me to explain. "Sundays are her tea days. She plays golf in the morning with her country club friends, then has a handful of them over for afternoon tea at the house."

For as long as I could remember, her schedule had remained the same. As long as she wasn't out on the campaign trail or traveling, Sundays were the one day I could count on her to actually be present in the house. By now, they would be wrapping up the luncheon and her friends should be on their way home.

"And your father?"

"As far away as possible." He couldn't stand being in the same house as my mother, let alone a dozen country club snobs.

I could practically feel the displeasure emanating from Rodrigo. "I don't like this."

Desperation propelled me forward, and I leaned between the front seats. "I know we haven't always gotten along, and I'm sorry for that. But I haven't seen my mother in almost six months. My father is terrified to come within ten miles of Fox, and I can't even reach out to my friends for fear of putting them in jeopardy. I know it's a lot to ask," I said, infusing my voice with sympathy, "but I would really appreciate it if you would just do this one thing for me."

He was silent for so long that I thought for sure he would deny my request. Finally, he gave a terse nod. "They're over in Hargrove Estates, correct?"

Relief streamed through my body. "Yes. Thank you so much."

I settled back against the soft leather seats and watched the scenery change from stark, gray cityscape to the lush green lawns of the suburban community. A few miles outside of town, Rodrigo made a left turn, and my pulse kicked up as the familiar homes came into sight.

Following my instructions, Rodrigo parked in the driveway of my parents' house, and my fingers were already wrapped around the door handle before Rodrigo threw a look over his shoulder at me. "Stay in the car until I make sure it's safe to get out."

I released my hold and nodded, waiting impatiently as he slid from the driver seat, then quickly scanned our surroundings before moving around and opening my door. His eyes moved constantly, sweeping over the wealthy homes of the middle-upper-class community, as he escorted me up the pathway to the front door.

I punched the doorbell, and the familiar peal of tones from inside tugged at my heartstrings. Though I'd never been particularly close to either of my parents, this was still home, and it held precious memories.

The door swung open, and I was temporarily stunned by the sight of a tall, broad man in a dark navy suit. "Is my mother home?"

The bodyguard's assessing gaze swept first over me, then Rodrigo before he gave a single clipped nod and stepped back, opening the door wide for us to enter. Once inside, the man locked the door and led us to the formal living room where my mother entertained all of her guests. I could see that the furniture was still slightly out of place from this afternoon's luncheon, the depressions from where it had been moved still visible in the plush, expensive rug.

The tap of heels against the hardwood floor brought a smile to my face, and I stood as my mother entered the room.

"Eva," she greeted in her well-modulated voice, "I'm so glad you're here."

I didn't dare hug her and risk rumpling the expensive suit she still wore, but I crossed the room and took her hands, then gave an air kiss to each cheek. "Hi, mom."

Still holding my hands, she stepped back to survey me. Apparently deciding that I was sufficiently healthy, she finally released me. "How are you, darling?" she asked. Her eyes drifted briefly to Rodrigo who remained standing silently but imposingly in the corner, before her gaze returned to mine. "Your father said you were living with someone. Is this the lucky man?"

So that's what my father had told her—that I was living with a man. I'd wondered how he'd explained my absence for the past several months.

Her question drew a startled laugh from my mouth. "No, no. This is my guard, Rodrigo."

My mother nodded sagely, and lifted one hand toward the doorway. "As you can tell, we've had to increase security as well. So much unrest."

I wondered if she knew what had brought that on. I nodded sympathetically and took a seat on the edge of the couch.

"So," my mother said brightly. "Tell me everything. It's been an age since I've seen you."

"Well," I started shyly, "I'm not just living with someone. We're married."

Her eyes widened dramatically. "You eloped?"

In my parents' eyes it was practically a sin to not hold a huge, lavish wedding where all the prominent members of society could see and be seen. "We did. It was a... spur of the moment thing."

"I see." Her lips pressed into a thin line, and I spoke quickly to avoid her censure.

"It was a beautiful beach wedding on this little island in the middle of nowhere." I chose my words carefully, specifically avoiding telling her the name for Fox's sake. "It was... perfect."

My mother made a little sound in her throat but forced a smile, that hard look still hovering around her eyes. "You've always been the headstrong one, determined to rebel and do things your own way. I suppose I should have expected it from you."

The words stung, but I forced myself to focus on the result—I was Fox's wife, and I wouldn't change that for the world.

"Do I know this man?" she asked curiously.

"I'm not sure," I replied honestly. "But he's a friend of Daddy's." A slight blurring of the truth, but it directed the conversation where I'd intended. "Speaking of, he's not here today?"

She waved one hand. "You know he avoids my teas at all costs."

I smiled. "I think most men would. Has he been acting... different lately?"

My mother's eyes bore into me. "I don't believe so. Why do you ask?"

I bit the inside of my lip, wondering how to ask the question I needed answered without giving too much away. "He just seemed stressed the last time we spoke," I said vaguely. "Like he was worried about something."

My mother's gaze slid over my shoulder to the guard who stood in the doorway, and I watched curiously as they seemed to communicate silently for a moment before her eyes returned to me. "I couldn't tell you," she said breezily. "You know how absent-minded your father can be."

For some reason, her answer didn't sit well with me. "Mom." I waited until I had her full attention. "I think he's involved in something bad."

Her gaze sharpened. "Such as?"

"I…" I threw a look at the tall guard before returning my gaze to my mother. "I know it sounds crazy, but… I think he and Spencer might be involved in human trafficking."

My mother just stared at me. She didn't laugh at the ridiculousness of the suggestion, didn't recoil in horror. Her face never even changed. There wasn't a flicker of emotion in her eyes—not surprise, not worry. Nothing.

My mother leaned back in her chair, seemingly lost in thought as she twisted her wedding band around her finger. She'd never been the most demonstrative person, and I could only imagine what was going through her head right now. Was she analyzing my father's actions over the past few years, breaking down every situation that had seemed so normal at the time?

She regarded me for nearly a full minute before speaking. "When you told us you wanted to study criminal justice, I thought it was the most ridiculous thing ever. I mean…" She gave a half-laugh. "My own daughter tracking down criminals. You were always so willful, too smart for your own good. You could have been such an asset to us," she said softly as she rose from her chair.

A blur of motion from my right caught my eye, but surprise and confusion rendered me frozen, unable to react. The tall guard in the doorway drew his weapon and lifted it in my direction. A scream caught in my throat, and I threw myself forward as the report of the pistol resounded in the room. A second discharge followed the first and I suddenly realized he wasn't shooting at me, but at Rodrigo.

Fox's man reached for me with one hand, thrusting me behind him as he continued to fire at the guard. One round penetrated the guard's chest and he staggered backward under the force of it but didn't go down. He lifted his hand, and the long black pistol bucked as he pulled the trigger once more. Rodrigo's grip on my arm loosened, and he pitched forward.

I did scream then, long and loud, as I threw myself at him. "Rodrigo!" My breath sawed in and out of my lungs in rapid pants. "Oh God! No, no, no, no, no."

I tried to roll him to his back, but he was too heavy. Suddenly, a pair of strong hands grabbed me from behind. I bucked and kicked and writhed, screaming at whoever had a hold on me.

"Mom!" I let out another shriek as the man forced me to the floor. "Help!"

The last thing I saw was my mother standing across the room, an impassive expression on her face as she watched me struggle with the guard holding my arms at my sides. A dark hood was pulled over my face, obscuring my view, and I cried out as something pinched my shoulder.

"I swear to God," I screamed, "when he finds you…"

My voice trailed off as the drug coursed through my system and took over, dimming my world to black.

THIRTY-ONE

FOX

Raking one hand through my hair, I fished my phone from my back pocket and dialed Eva to let her know I would be running late. Even on nights like this, she tended to wait up for me. The phone rang nearly a dozen times before rolling over to her voicemail.

I glanced at the clock, wondering if she was busy, maybe getting a shower, or if she just hadn't heard her phone. I waited a minute, then tried again. After another dozen rings, the automated message of her voice mailbox filled the line.

Already aggravated, I stabbed the end button on the screen and pulled up Rodrigo's number instead. My anxiety increased with each ring that went unanswered. His voicemail picked up, and I lurched to my feet as I frantically dialed him again, with the same result. Concern replaced my initial anger, and I called one of the other men stationed at the house.

He picked up mid-ring. "Boss?"

"I need to speak with my wife."

"She's not here, sir."

"Where the hell is she?"

"Rodrigo took her into town for something."

Without responding, I ended the call and was already out of my office searching for Xavier and Callum. I found Callum first loitering right outside the door. "We need to run GPS on Rodrigo. He and Eva both seem to be MIA. Get Xavier and meet me at the car."

As I made my way to the back of the building and into the parking lot, I pulled up the tracking app on my phone, my heart beating anxiously in my chest as I waited for it to pinpoint Rodrigo's current location. When the pulsing red dot finally appeared, I zoomed in, and dread settled low in my stomach.

If this was correct, then Eva had somehow managed to convince Rodrigo to take her to her parents' house. To meet with William? The thought made my blood boil in my veins. What other explanation could there possibly be?

I swore to God, that woman would be the death of me. It wasn't even a surprise that she'd gone to see him. After what I'd told her the other night, I was sure she went to confront him. Damn it, didn't she realize how dangerous this was? Regardless that she was his daughter, he was the foulest sort of human. He'd sold her to me to settle a loan, and I guaranteed he would do far worse if she jeopardized his organization.

Why the hell hadn't she said anything this afternoon? And what the hell was Rodrigo thinking, taking her there? I was going to murder the son of a bitch the second I saw him for putting her in harm's way—again.

Xavier and Callum met me at the car less than ten seconds later, and we all piled in. "Head toward the Jennings' residence," I instructed.

My knee jumped restlessly, and my hand clenched and unclenched, seemingly of its own volition, as the next seventeen minutes passed like molasses in wintertime. By the time we pulled up to the gated entrance of the housing allotment where the Jenningses lived, I was ready to throw myself from the vehicle and track her down on foot.

Callum rolled down the window to speak with the guard. "We're here to see Mr. Jennings."

"Name?" Callum rattled off my name and the heavyset guard shook his head as he scanned the computer, checking for approved visitors. "Name's not on the list," he said apologetically.

I rolled down my own window and pulled several hundreds from my wallet, then thrust it out the window. "My wife—Eva Jennings—is here, and I think she's in trouble. I need to find her. Call the Chief of Police—he'll vouch for me."

I hoped. After the raid earlier tonight, I wasn't one hundred percent certain, but I would use every weapon in my arsenal to make sure my girl was okay.

The guard studied me for a long minute before his gaze dropped to the cash in his hands. Finally, after what seemed like forever, he nodded. "Go ahead."

"Thank you."

The gate lifted, and my pulse kicked up as we drove underneath, then headed deeper into the community. Unlike a typical subdivision, the lawns here were vast, at least an acre each, perfectly manicured and bright green.

My heart raced as Callum pulled up to the curb in front of a stately brick home.

"This is it," he said unnecessarily.

My stomach clenched into a tight knot as my gaze swept over every feature. The driveway was empty—not a good sign. This was the last place Eva and Rodrigo's phone had pinged off the local towers. They'd certainly driven here—but where was the car?

In the front seat, both men were silent as I worked through my raging emotions. I swallowed hard over the impotence clogging my throat. "Let's sweep the grounds, just in case."

I knew we wouldn't find anything, but that fact held little reassurance fifteen minutes later as we piled back into the car and turned around to head back into town. There was no trace of the car ever being here. It, like Eva and Rodrigo's cell phones, seemed to have vanished into thin air. An old feeling crept in, one I hadn't felt in years. *Fear.* If something had happened to Eva, if William had hurt her…

Callum steered the car onto the main drag as I dialed the man in question, my patience dwindling with each second that passed. Five rings later, Eva's father answered warily. "Hello?"

Just the sound of his voice made me want to reach through the phone and rip him to shreds. "Where the hell are you?"

There was a brief hesitation, then—"Who is this?"

"Don't play stupid." I let out a low growl. "You know who this is."

"Fox?"

"You're not at home." I figured I would give him one last chance to come clean before I killed him.

He hesitated for a second, probably wondering how I knew. "N-no," he stammered. "I haven't been home all day."

Of course he wouldn't have been home; he would need an alibi. Cold settled over me and my tone dropped. "Where the fuck are you?"

"H-Houlihan's, why?"

I knew exactly where the upscale restaurant was. "Meet me at your office building. You have five minutes."

I hung up without another word, a hundred different scenarios—all of them bad—flitting through my mind. I checked the GPS locator again, and my stomach dropped sickeningly when nothing showed up. It was as if they'd just… disappeared. Either they'd turned their phones off for some reason, or… I didn't want to contemplate the alternative. By the time we pulled up in front of the elegant, soaring office building, I was ready to tear something—or someone—apart.

Callum pulled into a parking space, and I glanced around at the empty lot. Less than two minutes later, a white Mercedes turned in and parked in the next space over. I was out of the backseat and approaching William before I even thought about what I was doing. His eyes were wide as he climbed out, watching warily as I approached.

"Where the hell is she?" I demanded.

His eyes widened dramatically under the glow of the street lamps. "Who?"

The hold I had on my temper was rapidly fraying, and my body vibrated with tension. "Eva!"

"Eva?" He looked absolutely bewildered. "How would I know—"

I was running short on time, and I needed answers. I took another step toward him, pinning him between myself and the car. "Where the fuck is my wife?"

His mouth dropped open like a fish. "Your… Your wife?"

He practically choked on the word, and his reaction would have been gratifying except for the severity of the situation. "So help me God," I said with a low growl, "I will gut you right here if anything happened to her."

"I—" He shook his head. "I don't know what you're talking about."

I was done playing his games. I grabbed William around his neck and slammed him against the car, already bracing myself for the volley of images assaulting my brain. I saw snippets of conversation between William and Spencer as well as the deal he'd made with me when he approached me for a loan. The images came rapidly, but none of them were what I was looking for. I forced my hand to relax and stumbled away from him. He wasn't Araña. And if he wasn't, then who was?

"Where the fuck were you an hour ago?"

He grasped at his throat, gasping for breath. "Pine Shadows," he said, referencing his golf club. "Then I went to Houlihan's." He coughed raggedly.

Fuck. "I can't get a hold of Eva. GPS last shows her and my man at your house, but there's not a single trace of them there. I need to know where she is."

He shook his head, brows drawn together. "My wife has her friends over on Sundays, so I make sure to stay the hell away."

I arched a brow, a thousand thoughts flitting through my brain. "Your wife's not home."

It took a second for the implication to sink in, and his face paled. "You're not saying… No." He shook his head. "Maybe they went somewhere together. I—I'll call Lillian."

He dug through his pockets to find his cell phone, and his hands trembled visibly as he dialed and held the phone to his ear. The seconds ticked by, and William looked ready to puke by the time he hung up. His green gaze, so much like Eva's, lifted to mine. "She's not answering."

"She has to know where Eva is." I tried to push down my fear, but I couldn't help the waver in my voice. "We need to find her."

"Why would anyone want to hurt Eva?" His eyes widened slightly. "Oh, God. You did this. They took her to get back at you!"

I growled but couldn't stem the guilt I felt at the truth of his words. "You're right," I snapped. "It's my fault. Which is why I have to find her. I'd rather die than have her hurt."

William glared at me. "What have you done now?"

I quickly summed up my search for Araña and how they targeted first me, then Eva. "Do you know anyone who would do something like this?"

William looked ready to throw up all over the sidewalk. "S-Spencer," he managed to stammer out. "He was supposed to meet me at Houlihan's, but he called to say something came up and he couldn't make it. If he…"

William didn't have to finish. I knew exactly what he was capable of. "Where would he go?"

"I… I don't know."

The private airfield Spencer had used several months ago came to mind. "What's in North Dakota?"

William blinked once as he processed the question, then slowly nodded. "There—There's a cabin. Somebody has a cabin up there off the books that they use once in a while."

"You been there?"

"Once." He nodded furiously.

"Good. Get in the fucking car. You're gonna give me directions. And I swear on her life…" I fisted my hand in the front of his shirt. "If anything happens to her, I'm going to kill you for putting her in harm's way and bringing that miserable piece of shit into our lives."

THIRTY-TWO

I came awake slowly, a strange buzzing sensation filling my ears. I felt cold all over, and my eyes felt heavy, my mind foggy. My entire body felt exhausted, and my eyes didn't want to stay open. I tried to rub the sleep away, but my arms wouldn't cooperate.

I sat up a little straighter in my seat and tried to move my arms again. I felt a resistance tugging at my skin, and the sensation sent a chill skittering down my spine. My breath came faster, and my heart raced as I realized my hands were bound behind me.

Frantically, I took in my surroundings, praying that I was wrong—that this was just a bad dream. My gaze focused on the tan leather seats in front of me and to my right. To my left was a small oval window and, beyond that, pitch blackness. I studied the white walls that curved slightly over my head, the thick bolts that ran up the panels. My stomach pitched as I realized the sound filling the air was coming from the plane's engines.

Oh, God. Where was I? And with who? Everything came flooding back in rapid succession. Going to my parents' house. Telling my mother my suspicions. Bile rose up my throat when I recalled her blank expression and cold words. I remembered being frozen in place at the sight of the pistol swinging my way, then—

Oh, God. Rodrigo. My stomach plunged at the memory of him trying to pull me out of harm's way, shoving me behind him for protection. In my mind's eye I watched as he let loose with a volley of rounds, the loud reports filling the air before he jerked and fell forward.

I threw a quick look around but no one was with me. Anxiety raced through me. Where was he? Was he okay, or was he…?

God, I couldn't bear to think of it. My brain skipped forward to a pair of strong arms pulling me away from Rodrigo's still form, yanking a dark cloth over my head. And the way my mother looked at me, so cold and unfeeling, right before darkness closed over my head and I was dragged away. She'd chosen greed and money over her own daughter. I shouldn't be surprised after what happened to Elle, but the betrayal stung.

I wanted to cry at the injustice of it all. I'd gone to her with the intention of telling her I thought my father was involved in trafficking. Instead, I'd discovered that she was involved, too. Why hadn't I seen it sooner? She'd coerced Elle into marrying Spencer and solidifying the bond between them.

What the hell was I going to do? There wasn't much I could do with the plane in the air. I couldn't even appeal to the pilot or flight crew. Chances were, if they'd seen me brought aboard in restraints, they'd probably been paid off by my mother's people. I would have to wait until we could deplane and try to escape.

A combination of fatigue and anxiety pulled at me, and my lashes fluttered. I needed to stay awake—figure out how the hell I was going to get out of here. Of their own volition, my lids closed again and I forcefully blinked them open wide, snapping to attention. I needed to focus. I needed to…

Exhaustion hovered over me, settling deep into my bones. I allowed my eyes to drift closed, and the heavy darkness of unconsciousness wrapped around me like a cloak. I had to fight back—and I would. Soon…

My eyes flew open a scant second before my body was thrown forward, and a sound of surprise lodged in my throat as I was tossed to the floor like a ragdoll. I landed face-first with a hard jolt, and a horrific roaring sound from all around me filled my ears.

Stars danced in front of my eyes; it felt like my brain was rattling around my brain inside my skull as I rolled awkwardly to my back. The light strips lining the cabin overhead flickered to life, and I blinked at the sudden brightness.

It took me a minute to figure out what had happened as the airplane began to slow to a halt. We were here— wherever here was—and I must have slipped from the seat when the pilot hit the brakes. My arms were still strapped behind my back, and I rolled to my left hip to take the pressure off my shoulders. I scooted my feet beneath me and awkwardly pushed up on one elbow until I could lever myself up into a sitting position.

I staggered to my feet, then slid back into my seat all the way at the back of the plane, taking a minute to get my bearings. The aircraft was small, separated into just a handful of seats, but I couldn't see who was in front of me, and I didn't hear anyone speaking or moving around. No one had seemed at all concerned about my fall, which was disconcerting but not necessarily surprising.

All of a sudden, a figure rose from the front row, and my breath caught in my chest as the man turned toward me. My stomach clenched, and a surge of hatred rose up as Spencer met my gaze. His eyes were cold, devoid of emotion.

"I should have guessed you would be involved," I said as he stopped next to my seat.

Spencer didn't say a word, just wrapped one hand around my arm and pulled me from my seat. "Let's go."

"I'm not going anywhere with you," I snapped.

I resisted, pulling against him, and he leaned forward, his face close to mine. "You don't understand how this works. They give the instructions, and we follow them. You need to cooperate before they kill both of us."

Dread curdling in my stomach, I reluctantly allowed him to pull me to my feet and guide me from the plane. Two large black SUVs waited on the tarmac, and a handful of men, dressed in black and armed to the teeth, surrounded the vehicles.

Another man slid from the backseat of the SUV in front and sent a cold smile Spencer's way. "You were due in half an hour ago."

I recognized the face from the dossiers Fox had been working through. It was something fancy and pretentious. *Sebastian.*

"Yeah, well, they had an issue with the first plane and it pushed us behind schedule."

Sebastian shrugged, and his gaze landed on me. I repressed a shudder at the way his dark eyes slid over me from head to toe. "Looks like your wife," the man remarked.

"I'm his sister-in-law," I spat.

Spencer squeezed my arm. "Shut up, Eva."

I watched as the flicker of surprise crossed Sebastian's face. Yeah, I hadn't expected my mother to sell me out, either.

"Big plans for me?" I taunted. "I hope you know what you're doing. You won't live to see the morning if you touch me."

Spencer gave me a little shove. "Just get in the fucking car."

"Push me around some more, you abusive prick," I threw back at him. "We all know what you did to Elle."

Even with only the glow of headlights, I could see the tinge of anger sweeping up Spencer's face, and a muscle ticked in his jaw. "Shut your mouth."

"You're worthless," I spat. "No wonder she wanted to divorce you."

The words had barely left my mouth when his palm connected with the side of my face. I stumbled backward under the force of the blow, and my feet, still unsteady from the combination of the drugs coursing through my system and the flight, got tangled up beneath me. I toppled backward, and pain exploded across the back of my scalp as my head connected with something hard.

The breath left my lungs when I dropped to the pavement, flat on my back, everything spinning in a vicious circle around me. Light danced before my eyes, mingling with the stars dotting the vast navy expanse overhead.

Every cell of my body ached, but I didn't have time to recover as a hand latched onto my arm and yanked me to my feet. Spencer grabbed my hands where they were bound behind my back and jerked them upward. I let out a stifled shriek as my shoulders protested the unnatural angle, and my knees buckled, sending me hurtling face-forward toward the pavement again.

Thank God Spencer still held my wrists, saving me from more damage to my face as he caught me and dragged me back up. I could taste blood, and I swept my tongue over my lips, wincing when I found the sensitive spot that had been split open. As my vision began to clear, I shot a quick glance at the guards standing around in a semicircle. All wore identical expressions of disinterest, as if this was something they encountered every day. They would be no help, then.

My cheek stung and my head throbbed, but I dredged up the effort to pull back my shoulders and face them head-on. "Disgusting, all of you. And you call yourselves men."

Although I was expecting it, the blow to my ribs took my breath away and I crumpled to the ground. Spencer loomed over me, his handsome face twisted into a sneer. "Just don't know when to quit, do you?"

My insides seized and I curled into myself, trying to

ward off the pain radiating through my body. I knew talking back would only make things worse, but I refused to go down without a fight. "Fuck you."

From somewhere behind me, a smooth, cultured voice that I was beginning to recognize as Sebastian's chuckled. "I like this one. She'll be fun to break in."

The implication made my blood run cold. Fox had told me something similar once, but there was a world of difference between the two men. While Fox banished every insecurity, every reservation I'd ever had, he'd broken down the old shell I'd been living in. He'd made me stronger, better. Sebastian and Spencer were depraved; they thrived on pain and misery, and I didn't doubt Sebastian for a second. He would derive great pleasure in trying to break me.

"Shame we couldn't have just killed you." Spencer leaned down and fisted one hand in my hair. I grimaced as tears sprang to my eyes, but I refused to let them out as he pulled me to my feet. "You're even more obnoxious than your sister. I thought Fox would have straightened you out, but you're a crafty little bitch, aren't you? You may have escaped him, but I guarantee you won't be so lucky this time."

The way he said it stirred something in my mind. Did he know that Fox and I were together—that we were married? Though I was tempted to scream it aloud, I clamped down on the urge, holding the information close to my chest. It could be my salvation—or my death sentence. Until I had a better grip on the situation, I would just keep quiet.

I was acutely aware of how much Fox despised Spencer—he wouldn't hesitate to kill him, especially after what Spencer had done to me tonight. What would Spencer do if he knew I was married? Would he convince the others to let me go? Or would they kill me and risk his vengeance? It was worth a try. Maybe I could get Spencer alone, explain to him that Fox was my husband.

"No smart remark to that?"

I met Spencer's antagonistic gaze and forced myself to play along, acting the subservient captive. "No."

His eyes narrowed suspiciously, and he grabbed the back of my neck, then marched me toward the first SUV. "Let's go. You've wasted enough of my time tonight."

Spencer forced me into the backseat, shoving me into the middle. He climbed in behind me, while a guard slid into the seat beside the window. It was a smart tactic, trapping me in the middle so I couldn't escape. I stared out the windshield, seething with anger as two more men climbed into the front. Having my hands tied behind my back limited my options to fight back. Being surrounded by armed guards narrowed those possibilities to almost nonexistent.

Sebastian and the remaining guards piled into the other SUV, and we pulled out of the tiny airfield. I wondered if anyone had been there watching. Wasn't that some kind of regulation—that they had to be manned any time a plane came in? The better question was—would anyone report the things they'd seen? Spencer and Sebastian obviously had the means to pay people to turn their heads, especially if my mother was truly the one pulling the strings.

The thought made me sick all over again. My father was crooked, but my mother was… evil. I couldn't believe she'd sacrificed me knowing full well the ramifications. If these men had their way tonight, I wouldn't see the light of another day.

I prayed with every fiber of my being that Fox would already be looking for me. Although I wasn't certain of the exact time, I was sure that by now, he had to know that something was wrong. I'd been kidnapped, and I feared that Rodrigo was dead. I refused to focus on him right now; I needed to think about how to escape or at least draw this out until Fox found me.

My cell phone had been taken, so there was no way to track me that way. I cursed myself for not telling him I was going to visit my mother—at least then he would have had a lead.

We drove for what felt like hours, winding through the dark, rugged wilderness. We passed through one small town, then turned off, heading deeper and deeper into the woods. All semblance of life disappeared. There were no houses, no lights… no one to run to for help. We bumped along over ruts and tree roots, and gravel pinged softly against the undercarriage as we climbed northward.

We finally crested a hill, and the house came into view in the bright moonlight. The SUVs parked in front of the house and Spencer grabbed my arm, then dragged me from the vehicle. My arms ached from being bound behind me, but the pain was no match for the fear coursing through my veins. One of the men moved ahead of us through the dark and unlocked the door. The night was cold, and I shivered, goosebumps spreading over my arms and legs.

Spencer's fingers dug into my skin as he shoved me up the two wide steps and into the cabin. The guards moved efficiently, turning on lights and building the fire. I glanced around, taking in everything as Spencer led me through a large living room, past a set of stairs that led to the second floor, then down a short hallway. There were several doors on each side, and he pushed me through the last one on the left before flipping on the overhead light.

"Make yourself comfortable," he said as he turned and walked out.

Once he was gone, I moved toward the window, inspecting every inch of the room.

"Planning your escape?" My heart stuttered as Sebastian appeared in the doorway, his dark eyes locked on mine. "You can try to run. You can try to hide. But you won't leave this house."

I steeled my spine as I stared back at him. "Killing me would be a mistake."

A slow smile lifted his mouth, making the hairs on the back of my neck stand on end. "And why is that?"

"My mother is the mayor of Chicago. What do you think the media will say when both of her daughters disappear?"

He stepped closer and shrugged. "No one has to find out. A picture could appear on your social media from time to time, showing you flitting around Europe. No one would ever be the wiser."

It was on the tip of my tongue to tell him about Fox, but I still wasn't sure that he wouldn't just kill me quicker and get rid of the evidence that I'd ever been with them. "If you think you'll get away with this, you're wrong. They're already on to you. Your time's running out."

"We'll see about that." A cold smile curved his mouth as he closed the distance between us. One hand trailed up my thigh, and I sucked in a breath as he delved beneath the hem of my skirt.

I shifted to move away from him but his forearm was suddenly across my throat, pinning me to the wall. I jerked as he forced his knee between both of mine, forcing my legs open and shoving his hand between my legs. I couldn't stop the tears that sprang to my eyes as he pushed my panties aside and cupped my center.

His fingers slid between my folds, and I clenched my eyes closed at the harsh intrusion, unwilling to let him see me cry. My stomach roiled and I gagged as bile rose up, threatening to send my lunch splattering all over his expensive suit. I let out a stifled shriek as his hand moved to my clit then pinched—hard.

Sebastian released me and I slumped back against the wall, terror streaming through my veins as he leaned close. "That's just a taste of things to come. And trust me—by the time we're done with you, Eva, you'll wish you were dead."

THIRTY-THREE

FOX

We arrived in the wee hours of the morning while the moon was still high in the sky. As I had requested, someone had procured a vehicle, and it sat in the corner of the lot. With a nod, I sent Xavier and Callum ahead, and they looked over every inch of it. William watched on curiously as Xavier dropped to the pavement and swept the light of his flashlight over the undercarriage.

"What's he doing?"

I threw a look his way, marveling at how he could be so naïve. "Looking for GPS devices, bombs, anything that could delay us."

His eyes widened at the mention of bombs, as if the possibility had never even occurred to him. While Xavier checked underneath, Callum retrieved the key from the back tire and opened the cab. He popped the hood and checked inside the engine compartment before signaling that it was all clear. Xavier followed with a similar motion, and I jerked my head at William. "Let's go."

He and I climbed into the back, while Callum slid into the driver seat, Xavier on the passenger side.

I looked at William. "Where do we go from here?"

"Turn right out of the lot." William pointed off to the side. "There's a two-lane highway a few miles up that will take you most of the way there."

For the next hour, we drove in near silence, all of us tense and worried. Every second that ticked by increased my irritation. William stared out the window, watching for familiar roads and landmarks. Finally, he pointed off to the left. "I think it's this road."

Callum made the turn, and headlights swept over the pitted country road, lined with trees on both sides. We drove for several more miles, William glancing side to side in agitation. "I know it's here somewhere," he murmured.

"You better not be leading us on some wild goose chase," I warned.

He threw me a dark look. "I want to help her as much as you do."

"Coming from you, that doesn't mean much," I snapped. "Six months ago you traded her to absolve your debts."

"I told you before—" he started.

"Your word means nothing to me," I cut him off. "You have two choices: either find my wife, or I gut you and leave you in the woods for the animals."

"I don't know!" he cried out. "I was only here once, and everything looks different in the dark."

I pulled my knife from the sheath inside my shin. "Think harder!"

William jumped, his eyes flashing with fear as they landed on the sharp blade. "Jesus, Fox, please!"

I pressed the blade to his throat. "Last chance."

"I'm trying! I... Wait!" His gaze sharpened as he stared out the windshield, then pointed. "Take a right up there!"

Callum flicked a look in the rearview mirror before turning down a narrow dirt and gravel road. Dust kicked up behind the car, and the moon overhead was obscured by the canopy of trees. We hadn't passed a single house— not even another car—in the entire time we'd been on the road. If they wanted privacy, they'd certainly found it out here. Instead of reassuring me, it only made me more anxious.

Privacy meant no one to overhear screams for help. The thought sent ice sluicing through my veins, and I looked at William. "Look familiar yet?"

"I-I think so," he nodded, and his Adam's apple bobbed when the blade of the knife scraped his skin.

My lip curled into a sneer as I studied him. "Better hope Callum's a good driver, otherwise..."

Another minute passed before William nodded frantically. "This—this is it. The cabin should be just a few miles up."

"Good." Callum steered the SUV off the road, concealing it as best he could behind some dense foliage that grew along the side of the road. Xavier looped a zip tie into a large circle, then passed it between the seats to me.

"No, please, I—" William was already shaking his head, but he stopped abruptly when I pressed the knife deeper into the flesh of his throat.

"Hands behind your back." He did as I asked, slowly

maneuvering both hands to his lower back where I looped the tie over his wrists and secured them together.

As I worked, I spoke to my men. "Find our coordinates and check his information."

Up front, Xavier pulled out a tablet, checking our current coordinates against any known residences listed.

"Boss." He passed the tablet over the seat to me. "Looks to be about a mile and half northeast. All wooded, and the terrain's about a forty-degree incline."

I quickly scanned the screen, then nodded. "Let's go."

I turned back to William and delivered a final warning. "Don't do anything stupid. You try to run, you call for help, you even fucking breathe wrong and I will kill you."

With a flick of my wrist, the blade of the knife I still held slashed through his shirt, and blood welled along the shallow cut.

"Son of a bitch!"

"That's for Eva," I said as I stepped from the car. "If anything happens to her, you can expect far worse than that."

Leaving William alone and cuffed in the backseat, Xavier, Callum, and I moved ahead on foot. We were woefully under-armed, considering the circumstances. I had no idea how many people would be at the cabin, but I was betting we'd be grossly outnumbered. The pilot was one I knew and we'd at least been able to pay him off so we could smuggle our firearms aboard.

Xavier had been correct; the terrain was difficult, with a fairly steep incline. It was made worse by the fact that it had rained fairly recently, making the ground spongy and wet. It slowed us down, and we skidded from time to time on the slippery leaves littering the ground. After thirty minutes of walking, Xavier spoke up. "About another half-mile to the north."

I was trying not to let it show, but the closer we got, the more worried I became. I knew what men like Spencer were capable of—I'd seen the damage Spencer had inflicted firsthand, and Elle was his wife. He would have no compunction hurting Eva, who was no longer any relation to him. And God only knew who was with him. If anything happened to her...

My entire body went hot with rage, and I forced myself to take a deep breath. Callum and Xavier had remained completely silent as well, both comprehending the gravity of the situation. This was our one chance to find Eva; if she wasn't here or if she was...

I immediately cut the thought short. God, I didn't even want to consider any possible outcomes other than finding her here and bringing her home safely. As much as I despised William, I had to rely on his information—there was no other option. We didn't have time to do a full recon as we normally would have. This had to pan out—it just had to.

Almost as soon as the thought crossed my mind, the sound of a large engine rose on the night air, and the three of us stilled. The yellowish glow of headlamps grew stronger as the vehicle made its way up the old gravel road toward the cabin. Fuck. Dread twisted my stomach into knots as we silently watched the SUV pass.

I didn't know if it was a good sign or not. My gut told me that we were headed to the right place and that Eva would be here. The arrival of the SUV solidified my suspicions and sent my pulse racing. Was she in the truck with them? Or was she already at the cabin, awaiting whoever was inside the vehicle? Either way, the sight of the vehicle crawling closer to the cabin meant that Eva was in grave danger. We needed to get there ASAP.

The men seemed to read my thoughts, and Callum gave a quick jerk of his head. "We'll intercept them as soon as they get inside."

Throat clogged with an emotion I didn't want to name, I quickened my pace as we covered the next half, driven by desperation and worry. A faint glow appeared through the dense forest as we crested the hill. This was it. I closed my eyes and pulled Eva's face into my mind. My heart gave a hard thump and I inhaled deeply, then exhaled and shut off all of my emotions. I opened my eyes, mind cleared, focused only on the mission now.

We approached quietly, slipping through the trees that surrounded the property. We split up fifty yards from the tree line, fanning outward so we could come at the cabin from different directions. Illuminated by the moon overhead, I counted four men outside, walking the perimeter in front of the cabin. All were dressed in dark clothing and armed with rifles. I watched for several minutes, but they never deviated from their patterns. Incompetent idiots.

I crept closer, taking care to stay concealed in the shadows as I moved silently from tree to tree. I peered around the trunk of the huge Oak tree, counting down the seconds until the guard would pass by again. Ten seconds. Five, four, three... I waited until he was a few steps past the tree so his back was to me, then I made my move.

Quickly covering the fifteen feet between us, I stole up behind him. Wrapping one arm around his neck, I arched my back, constricting his throat so he couldn't yell out.

With my free hand, I sank the blade between his ribs and into his heart as I dragged him backward into the shadows of the forest.

His muscles went lax as the life drained from his body, and I pulled the blade free as I lowered him to the ground, concealing him behind the wide trunk of the tree.

A soft grunt rose from the east, and I knew that Callum had just taken down another guard. I peered around the tree again and did another quick scan of the yard. The two remaining guards stood close together, speaking in hushed tones. By now, they sensed something was wrong.

Rifles raised, they cautiously approached the trees, sweeping side to side as they moved. Their movements were nervous, jerky, and I shook my head. One of them would probably spook and shoot the other before we even had a chance to take them out.

Xavier must have read my mind, because the call of an owl filtered from the forest to the west. Both men immediately spun in that direction, leaving their backs wide open. I was moving a split second later, and I was on the first guard before he could even react.

I drew my blade across his throat, catching the weight of his body just as Callum moved into my peripheral vision and took out the second man. But the last guard put up more of a fight than his comrade. His finger curled around the trigger of the gun, and a shot fired up into the trees.

I swore silently as I dropped the guard I held to the ground. It was something I'd been trying to avoid, because that sound would alert the men inside the cabin to our presence. Now we would have to move quickly to minimize damage. If they knew we were here, they wouldn't hesitate to kill Eva if they hadn't already. Callum and I stayed low as we crossed the yard to the cabin. At the corner, we split off again and Callum silently moved around to the back of the house.

I flattened my back against the roughhewn log exterior of the cabin and drew my pistol from my waistband. The time for stealth was over. A figure skulked around the corner to my left, and I lifted my pistol before Xavier's face was revealed in the silvery moonlight.

I lowered my weapon, and he nodded to let me know that his side was clear. I didn't have sights on Callum, but I trusted that he'd made his way around to secure the back of the cabin. Taking a deep breath, I prepared myself for whatever I might find in the cabin. I could only hope that Eva was inside—and safe.

Dark curtains covered the windows, obscuring the people inside. I had no headcount, no idea where they were. While a huge part of me wanted to go in hot, I forced myself to calm. Eva could be anywhere, and I couldn't risk her getting caught in the crosshairs.

I met Xavier's dark gaze, and together we moved toward the door.

I'm coming for you, angel.

THIRTY-FOUR

EVA

I huddled in the corner of the room, glaring at Spencer where he lounged in the armchair next to the door. Though it was the middle of the night, the lights in the cabin blazed brightly. I wasn't sure how many hours had passed since we'd arrived, but the minutes dragged on in agonizing torture.

The chill that had descended over my body at Sebastian's parting words hadn't abated. I wasn't sure exactly what he meant—but I knew for certain I didn't want to find out. Sebastian and Spencer appeared to be waiting on someone—or multiple people. I would be damned if I would just sit here and wait to die.

There was a window situated in the middle of the wall to my left, but any escape route was eliminated by the guard patrolling outside. The armed man passed the window once every minute or so, and I knew there was no way I could get past him without being seen. Spencer had been positioned by the door since we arrived, blocking my way out of the room.

I needed to find a way out of here, and fast. I wasn't sure exactly what would happen when the other members arrived, but I knew it couldn't be good. Whatever they had planned didn't bode well for me. I would rather risk being shot trying to escape than endure whatever they had in store for me.

"I need to use the bathroom."

Spencer, who'd been staring at the floor by his shoes, flicked an emotionless look my way. "I don't know if I can do that."

It was obvious that Spencer was the low man on the totem pole. "It's either the toilet or I make a mess on somebody's hardwood floors," I retorted.

His gaze swept the room like he was searching for answers before it finally returned to me. "Okay," he said as he stood. "But don't do anything stupid."

I climbed unsteadily to my feet, wrists still bound behind my back. I had a sick feeling that they had removed the hood so I could see everything around me, my mouth unimpeded to scream and beg for mercy. Unfortunately for them, I didn't plan to be there much longer and give them the pleasure.

Spencer warily watched me approach, and I fought to control the urge to kick out at him and dart past. The only thing stopping me was that I didn't know how many more were out there. Sebastian, obviously, and probably a couple of guards. I'd seen only the one passing back and forth in front of my window, but the others had to be patrolling the property, too.

I might be able to make it past Spencer alone, but I

wouldn't be able to escape the house with my hands still bound. Spencer gripped my bicep, then guided me across the hall to the bathroom. He closed the door to give me a modicum of privacy, leaving it cracked a couple inches so he could still keep an eye on me.

I stepped into the bathroom, already scanning the walls, but there were no windows to speak of. I glanced in the mirror as I passed, and my anger renewed. Dark circles ringed my eyes, and the side of my face was already starting to bruise from the earlier altercation in the parking lot of the airfield. My lip was split, and blood had trickled down my chin and dried in a jagged maroon line. Fuckers. I swore Spencer would pay for this if I had to kill him myself.

I used the toilet then flushed, all the while working on loosening my bonds. If I had any chance of escaping, I needed to get my hands in front of me. I'd been inconspicuously trying to work them looser over the last couple of hours. It was slow going, trying to keep my movements contained so I wouldn't alert Spencer to my actions. As the sound of rushing water filled the air, I took a seat on the hard tile floor, praying that Spencer wouldn't immediately come barging in.

I dipped one shoulder and pulled on the ties as hard as I could, trying to stretch them as far as they would go. My muscles ached as they stretched farther than they were designed to, all the while trying to maneuver them low enough to clear my hips. My heart jumped as the material finally gave enough to the point that I could wiggle them under my bottom.

Fierce satisfaction flowed through me as, inch by inch, I

got closer to being free. I contorted my body, bending my knees and angling them through the odd-shaped space my arms and torso created. I stepped free and climbed to my feet just as a commotion rose from the living room.

"Masterson!" An unfamiliar voice echoed down the hallway. Oh, God. That wasn't good. New voices meant more people were here—the people Sebastian and Spencer had been waiting for. Which meant I was out of time.

I froze, every instinct on alert as I listened intently. "Bring the girl out!"

Hell no. My stomach lurched, and my heart thumped erratically as the door swung inward. Immediately, I went on the offensive and rushed toward Spencer. He threw up his arms to fend me off, but he couldn't stop my momentum as I slammed into him. He stumbled, and we crashed into the wall behind him.

With my hands now in front of me, I swung wildly at him, aiming for anything I could reach—his nose, his eyes. Spencer let out a grunt as my fist connected with his face, and I felt a moment's satisfaction at my direct hit. It evaporated a second later when his hand connected with my cheek, then he threw me to the floor.

My gaze fixed on Spencer, I saw the shadow looming behind me too late. I screeched as a hand fisted roughly in my hair and jerked me backwards. I kicked out wildly as the man dragged me down the hall toward the living room. Laughter and jeers surrounded me, echoing in my ears, but none of the words penetrated the pain exploding across my scalp and over my eyes.

Suddenly the man let go, and I collapsed into a heap on the floor. I blinked against the spots clouding my vision and tried to roll to my feet. Before I could even get my hands under me for balance, a foot landed hard in my ribs, knocking the air from my lungs and rolling me to my back.

Agony ripped through my chest as I tried to draw in a breath and stars danced in front of me as black clouded the corners of my eyes before receding. When my vision finally cleared, I saw Spencer standing over me, an uncertain expression on his face. In my peripheral vision, I saw what I guessed to be another half dozen men seated sporadically around the room. Unwilling to look away, my gaze stayed locked on Spencer's face.

Vile taunts met my ears, turning my cheeks red with embarrassment and sending fury rippling through my veins. Spencer glared down at me, every muscle taut with tension. A small trickle of blood dripped from his nose where I'd landed a solid punch earlier, and I longed to unleash my rage on him.

"Look at her face," one laughed. "Had to put her in her place already, eh, Masterson?"

A voice I recognized as Sebastian's spoke up. "Gave us some trouble getting off the plane. Can't imagine why."

A muscle next to Spencer's eye ticked, and I saw the first sign of unease as he stood motionless, just staring at me. It occurred to me that, though he was an abusive asshole, maybe he didn't have it in him to take advantage of a defenseless woman.

"Looks like your wife," one of the men commented, parroting a remark from earlier.

"That's his sister-in-law," Sebastian's helpful voice cut in.

I didn't dare take my eyes off Spencer.

"Keepin' it in the family, huh?" Men's laughter filled

the air, and I watched his Adam's apple bob as Spencer swallowed hard.

"Don't blame you," the same man said. "She's a pretty little thing."

"But feisty," Sebastian replied, a hint of mirth in his tone. "Look what she's already done to Masterson."

"Good point," chortled another. "You can have her first. Wear her down."

"That's right." A third man laughed. "Better he get his eyes scratched out than the rest of us."

My stomach roiled. How many were there? So far, I'd counted four different voices, including Sebastian's. Spencer made five. It would take a miracle to get past all of them. The only course of action I had left was to appeal to Spencer's sense of self-preservation.

"Don't do it," I whispered. "He'll kill you."

"Get on with it already!" boomed a voice from behind me.

Spencer remained frozen as he stared down at me. I hoped he was seriously contemplating my words. "He'll find you and he'll kill you," I choked out. "You thought what happened to Elle was bad? Think of what he'll do to you when he finds out you and your friends raped and killed his wife."

"W-wife?" His eyes widened, and his mouth went slack. "You're married?"

I held up my hand, palm facing me, so he could see the ring on my finger. Even in the glow of the flames dancing in the fireplace, I could see the blood drain from his face. "Oh, God."

"Don't do this, Spencer. If you want to live, you need to let me go."

"Stop wasting time talking and fuck her already!" the man called again.

Spencer slowly turned to the men surrounding us, his face a sickly green. "But she's… She's Fox's wife."

Silence settled over the room for a moment, and I envisioned the men looking at each other, weighing their options. Was I really worth it? I held my breath as I waited for them to speak, praying the answer was no.

"We'll take care of it," said a new voice. "Go on. You wanted in; you know what you have to do."

My stomach roiled as I stared at my ex-brother-in-law. I didn't know what the man spoke of, but I could guess easily enough. He funneled information to them, arranged for innocent women and children to be bought and sold like cattle.

"Do it!" called the voice again.

"I… I'm sorry, Eva," he whispered as he took half a step forward toward me. I kicked upward, and my foot connected with his groin. He roared out a growl of agony, and I let out a scream of pure rage that was drowned out by a loud blast from outside.

Around us, chatter rose from the men as they scrambled from their seats, yelling for the guards.

"Go!" One yelled. "Get out there and see what's going on!"

Spencer was still slightly bent over covering himself, and I took advantage of the distraction. Rolling to my left, I maneuvered my knees under me and lunged toward the fireplace. A tool set sat at the corner of the stone hearth, and I reached frantically for the poker hanging from the rod. I let out a little shriek as a huge hand fisted into the fabric of my dress and yanked hard.

Using all of my weight as leverage, I threw myself forward, still reaching for the wrought iron rack. As Spencer pulled me backward, my fingers grasped the small shovel and it fell to the ground with a clatter.

I swept my arms clumsily toward the implement, and hope exploded in my heart as my fingers curled around the handle. Just as Spencer pulled me toward him, I rolled to my back and swung upward. The shovel made a wide arc through the air, and Spencer dodged out of the way just in time. It missed him by a narrow margin, and fury turned his face a dark, mottled red.

The momentum carried through, and I didn't have time to adjust myself for another swing. Spencer lunged forward, dropping to his hands and knees as he wrapped his hands around the handle. We grappled for control, and I dredged up every ounce of strength as I fought to hold on. With a growl, Spencer finally ripped it from my hands and threw it to the floor. The sound of metal striking wood rose from behind me just as a series of booms filled the air.

The sound of gunfire echoed through the cabin, and I instinctively covered my face as wood from somewhere overhead cracked and splintered, sending tiny shards spraying over the room. A mixture of hope and apprehension filled me. Was Fox here? Had he come to save me? I didn't have time to look as Spencer threw himself forward, and I screamed as his weight landed heavily on top of me.

One hand covered my mouth, and I could feel his pelvis pressing into mine as he covered me from head to toe. My heart kicked into overdrive, and I knew this would be my only chance. His head was only inches from mine, so I did the only thing I could think to do in that moment. I opened my mouth wide and sank my teeth into his throat.

Blood filled my mouth as Spencer let out a howl of pain, and I gagged at the irony taste. My stomach turned, and Spencer ripped himself away when I rolled to my side to throw up as all hell broke loose around us.

THIRTY-FIVE

FOX

The front door opened a crack, and a man appeared in the thin rectangle of light, pistol raised. Grabbing his forearm, I slammed it against the door jamb. He let out a sharp cry of pain as the fragile bones folded under the pressure and snapped in half.

The gun dropped to the ground as his muscles went lax, unable to get off a single shot. With my other hand, I brought the knife up in a wide arc and sank it into the side of his neck. The man dropped like a stone, and I dragged him out of the way.

Pistol raised, Xavier peered around the doorjamb, and the sound of a gunshot hit my ears a split second before the wood of the doorway splintered and flew into a dozen jagged pieces. I felt a shard hit my cheek, but the tiny bite of pain barely even registered under the need to find Eva and get her the hell out of here.

I couldn't risk returning fire without a clear line of sight, and I hunkered down as several more rounds pierced the door and surrounding wall. The window behind me shattered, and the tinkling of glass filled the air as it landed on the porch. I met Xavier's gaze and nodded once. I scuttled toward the now open window and nudged the curtains aside. I fired a single shot into the wall opposite, then ducked as the men inside returned fire at the window.

To my right, Xavier popped off a handful of rounds, and a distressed cry rose from inside the cabin as one of his bullets met its mark.

"Stand down!" He stepped over the threshold, pistol raised toward the men inside. I followed on his heels, sweeping the corners to make sure no one else inside was armed. Assured there was no one else, I took in the grizzly scene in front of me. Two men stood, hands raised in front of them, wide, fearful eyes locked on us.

Sebastian Moreau, along with a few other men I didn't recognize, still occupied the sofa and chairs arranged in a semi-circle around a huge stone fireplace in the large living room, apparently either too scared or too unconcerned to move. Only time would tell which.

What I saw next, though, made my blood run cold. Eva lay on her back in the middle of the rug, and a furious-looking Spencer knelt between her legs. Blood covered his neck and chest, and my heart seized in my chest.

There was a split second of calm, then all hell broke loose. The men began to move, pulling weapons and sending a barrage of bullets in our direction. I broke off to the right and threw myself behind a timber column as gunfire filled the air. I risked a peek, then fired twice in Moreau's direction. Wood exploded near my face, sending a trickle of blood seeping into my eye. I blinked it away, then popped off two more rounds and took out the man next to Moreau.

Everything slowed as we picked off the men, one by one. I didn't see Xavier, but I knew from the occasional flash of return gunfire that he was concealed behind the island in the kitchen. I stayed low as I moved from behind the column, intent on getting to Eva.

Xavier moved from his position in the kitchen and swept his pistol to the right, dropping an older gentleman concealed behind the chair closest to me. Spencer jerkily clambered to his knees just as I rounded the couch. I unloaded two rounds into his torso, watching with a sense of sick satisfaction as he tumbled backward, one hand wrapped around his waist as he toppled to the ground.

My attention was drawn back to Eva as she struggled to her feet, swaying under the effort. Blood caked her mouth and the brown liquid had saturated the top of her dress. Her hands were bound in front of her, and she had just taken a step toward me when a man darted out from behind an arm chair and yanked her in front of him, using her as a shield.

Around us, bodies littered the floor, but I didn't focus on a single one of them as I watched the man pull Eva deeper into the cabin. If he thought he was going to escape, he was dead wrong.

He met my gaze over her shoulder, the weapon in his hand shaking with fear. "Put your guns down."

I slowly did as he asked, and Xavier followed suit. I

watched impassively as the man took another step backward, then froze when he felt the barrel of Callum's gun press against the back of his head. "Let her go."

Cold calculation swiftly crossed the man's face, and I let out a low growl. "Think very carefully about your next move."

"I'm going to die anyway," he sneered.

"True," I replied. "But it's your choice how you die. If you hurt her, I'll draw out your death until it's so painful you'll wish you'd never met her."

The man glared at me but dropped his weapon to the floor and slowly released Eva. She darted forward, straight into my arms, and I caught her trembling body against me. I wanted to kill the man for ever laying a hand on her, for dragging her into this mess. But looking down at my wife, her hands curled into the fabric of my jacket, something occurred to me. I no longer cared about vengeance the way I once had. Eva was my life now, the only thing that mattered.

I lifted my eyes to Xavier and he nodded. Wrapping both arms around Eva, I covered her ears by pressing her face into my chest as Xavier put a bullet between the pleading man's eyes. Eva flinched as the gun went off but remained quiet, still shaking. The room fell silent except for the crackling of the fire and the labored breaths wheezing from Spencer's chest.

I met Callum's gaze. "We need to sweep the cabin."

With a quick nod of assent, he and Xander moved in tandem as they cleared the cabin. Once they were finished, Callum began the trek down the mountain to retrieve the car while Xavier headed outside to collect the bodies of the guards littering the lawn.

As soon as the men were gone, I tipped Eva's chin up to look at me, my gaze automatically moving to the blood ringing her mouth. I spotted several bruises and cuts, but none appeared to be too serious. But that was only the damage I could see on the surface.

"Come on," I said gruffly. "We need to get you cleaned up."

I sliced through the tape binding her wrists, and she grimaced a little as the tape pulled her skin. "I'm sorry, angel," I said softly as I guided her toward the kitchen. "Some water will help to loosen it."

"No, it's…" She made a face and ripped off the rest of the tape before looking up at me. "I couldn't stand to have that on anymore."

I nodded my understanding. I didn't blame her. Attention focused on the task at hand, I yanked open drawers until I found a towel. I ran it under the water faucet, then held it up to Eva's face. "We need to get this off."

I swallowed hard, trying not to focus on what had happened as I wiped the blood away. Once she was cleaned up, I tossed the rag in the sink and took her face in mine. Her upper lip was swollen, due no doubt to the gash cutting through the delicate flesh. Her hair was a mess, and her entire body was streaked with what appeared to be either dirt or ash from the fireplace.

The sight of Spencer kneeling over her flashed in my mind, and my body flared hot then cold with barely restrained fury. I battled it down and met Eva's gaze.

"Did they hurt you?" My voice broke on the words, and she shook her head as tears filled her eyes.

"No. You got here just in time."

Thank God. Her arms slid around my waist again as I pressed her cheek to my chest. I held her close as long as I dared, but I couldn't keep Eva in here any longer. She'd experienced too much death, too much pain, and I wanted to get her as far from this place as possible.

A scuffle rose from the front porch, and a few seconds later Xavier stepped inside. I kept Eva's face turned away as he dragged in the bodies of the guards and dropped them into a pile next to the couch.

Across the wide room, Xavier met my eyes. "Done."

"Thank you." I lifted my chin at him. "She'll be out in just a minute."

He left the cabin to give me another moment of privacy with my wife, and I disentangled myself from Eva's embrace. Taking her face in my hands, I made sure she was looking at me before I spoke. "I need you to go outside with Xavier."

She shook her head frantically, and her hands wrapped around my wrists. "No, I'm not leaving you. I—I can't."

Her entire body shook, and I wanted nothing more than to hold her close. But I had unfinished business that had to be taken care of. "Just for a minute, angel." I swept my thumbs over her cheeks. "I need to clean this up so no one will ask questions, and I need to know you're safe."

Her teeth cut into her bottom lip before she finally nodded. Shrugging out of my coat, I wrapped it around her shoulders then pressed a soft kiss to her forehead. I kept myself between her and the bodies as we moved toward the front door where I released her into Xavier's care. Once they were gone, I moved toward the fireplace and knelt by Spencer's side.

His neck was covered in blood, but I could see the tell-tale crescent indentations of teeth marks beneath the brownish stains. The sight of them filled me with a mixture of emotion as I began to understand what had happened. Pride for Eva suffused me. She was so strong, so damn brave, and it was for those reasons that I felt a tidal wave of remorse.

She never should have been in this situation in the first place. If only we'd gotten the information we needed a little sooner. Someone would have slipped up; we would have followed the trail, investigated more deeply and found that William wasn't truly responsible.

Of course, it had been incredibly well thought out. He'd been set up to take the fall, and their plan was executed perfectly. We'd assumed from the evidence that William was the elusive Araña we'd been searching for, and we could have easily taken him out and called it a day. Though I had my suspicions, I needed to know for myself. I turned my attention to the man sprawled before the fireplace, his skin a deathly hue.

Surprisingly, Spencer was still alive—though that wouldn't last long. He blinked up at me, eyes beginning to glaze over as the life slowly drained out of him. I turned his face toward mine and stared down at him. "You made a huge mistake taking my wife."

His mouth opened, and a tiny gurgle left his throat when he tried to speak. He swallowed and tried again. "Didn't... know."

"She was practically your sister. And you used her like she was nothing." I shook my head.

"Had... to," he gasped between breaths. "Orders. It was... her."

Piece of shit. "At least Elle can return to the States without having to worry about you."

His eyes widened for a second, and something flashed in the depths. "Glad she's... safe."

His eyelids fluttered closed, and I knew I wouldn't be getting any more answers from him—not that way, at least. I braced myself for the images as I wrapped one hand around his throat. I held on tight as the visions battered my brain.

My stomach clenched as I watched Spencer surrounded by the group of men in front of me. I watched the exchange of cash—and a new face, one we never would have expected. I watched as Spencer stood in a parking lot, a plane in the background. Beside him stood Eva's mother, Lillian.

"She knows too much." Something like regret was etched into her classic features, but she quickly blinked it away as she straightened and lifted her chin.

Spencer shook his head. "But—"

"Take care of it." She waved a hand toward the dark car. "You know how much I despise loose ends."

The image evaporated like smoke, but it told me enough. How a mother could be so cold and callous, I didn't know. But seeing the truth for myself solidified my plans—she couldn't be allowed to live.

I released Spencer, and my vision swam for a moment before I came back to myself. There had been no information about Rodrigo or the events leading up to Eva's abduction. That was disappointing for a multitude of reasons, not the least of which was that I would have to question her later. I wanted her to open up to me in confidence, not because I was interrogating her.

I rested my elbow on my knee and dropped my head into my hand. Fuck. I'd come so damn close to losing her tonight. Ever since I'd met her, Eva had given off this aura of being invincible. Deep down I knew she was just as human as the rest of us, but now, witnessing tonight's events, mortality pressed in on me, leaving me shaken to the core. She was a fighter, but she wasn't unbreakable.

I couldn't begin to understand her motive for going to her mother, but I knew there had been no malicious intent behind her actions. It was her mother, after all; no one had expected her to be the leader of a notorious international human trafficking ring.

I still wasn't certain of everything myself. As soon as we got home, I would have my men—a sharp pang shot through my chest at the reminder of Rodrigo's absence—research all of Lillian's recent activity. I hoped to hell that we would find Rodrigo, but I knew the chances of doing so would be slim.

With a heavy heart I pushed to my feet, then gathered the fallen men and arranged them once more in the chairs they'd vacated when we broke in. I spread the guards' bodies throughout the bottom floor to make it look as if they'd been moving around. I propped Spencer in the chair, his lifeless eyes wide and unblinking as they stared into the crackling fireplace. I followed his line of sight and smiled. "I like the way you think."

I cleared the house one last time, making sure that nothing of consequence remained. Confident that it was clean, I moved into the kitchen. Along the back wall near the oven I found the valve for the propane line, then turned it open wide. I was halfway to the door before the fumes even hit my nose, but I knew it wouldn't take long.

As soon as the gas reached the open flames in the fireplace, the entire place would go up like a Molotov cocktail.

I didn't bother to shut the door behind me as I left at a dead run—running toward Eva, toward my future and everything it held.

THIRTY-SIX

EVA

I paused in the driveway and threw a look over my shoulder at the cabin. A shiver snaked its way down my spine, and I pulled Fox's jacket more tightly around me.

"Come on," Xavier urged. "Callum should be here with the car soon."

I shook my head. "I'm not leaving him here."

"He'll be out in just a minute."

I met Xavier's gaze. "What's he doing?"

He stared at me for a second before responding. "Tying up loose ends."

My stomach twisted at the thought of the dead men littering the floor, but I couldn't dredge up any real remorse. Had Fox not shown up, they would have raped me or worse. It still didn't seem quite real. I'd never seen a dead body before, and it was strange to think that those men—even Spencer who I'd known for years—were never coming back. He'd fooled everyone, using his charming mask to hide the monster beneath.

Part of me was glad that Fox had killed him, killed all of them. But the deeper, more humane part of me wished that there had been another way to resolve it. In my heart, I knew it wasn't possible. Those men in there were responsible for the deaths of multiple women and children. I was only to be the next casualty in their long line of victims. They had the blood of thousands on their hands, and for that, I was glad they were gone.

Xavier's hand settled on my shoulder. "Please, Eva. I told Fox I would take care of you."

I threw another worried look at the cabin. It felt like forever had passed since I'd walked out the door. "How long has it been?"

Xavier sighed and glanced at his watch. "Eleven minutes."

Where was he? I opened my mouth, but my heart jumped into my throat as the front door flew open and a dark figure filled the space. As if my body instinctively knew his, I could tell it was Fox even from here. My body vibrated with the need to run to him, but I kept myself still by sheer force of will.

Fox's long stride ate up the driveway as he crossed over to us and gave an abbreviated jerk of his head. "We need to move."

Wrapping his arm tightly around my waist, he guided me across the driveway and down the slope at a fast clip. Suddenly, the splintering of wood and expanding gas filled the air as an explosion rocked the ground beneath our feet. I stumbled, and Fox dropped to one knee, pulling me into his chest for safety.

Reeling with confusion, I peeked over Fox's shoulder. The space where the cabin had once stood was now nothing but a raging orange inferno, dark smoke billowing into the air. My limbs shook, and my heart raced in my chest as realization settled over me.

One arm still wrapped around my waist, Fox swept a hand over my head. "Are you okay, angel?"

I drew back to look at him and nodded shakily. "I… I'm fine."

Headlights swept over the trees in front of us, and Fox helped me to my feet, then paused. "There's something I need to tell you."

His voice was serious—more so than normal—and I peered up at him warily. "W-what?"

His eyes darted toward the car before meeting mine again. "Your father is waiting in the car."

I couldn't keep myself from physically reeling backward at his news, and Fox grabbed my hips to steady me as I blinked up at him. "Why? Why is he here?"

I knew I sounded almost hysterical, but Fox shushed me with a soothing noise. "It's fine, angel. He didn't have anything to do with this. He helped us find the cabin."

I started to nod, then stopped abruptly. "But then that means…"

Fox's dark eyes held mine. "He was here, yes. But he was never involved in the illegal activity—at least, not the trafficking."

My teeth sank into my lower lip as I tried to reconcile my feelings. There were so many things I needed to tell him—about Rodrigo, about my mother. Fox squeezed my waist. "Trust me, angel. We'll talk about everything later."

He seemed absolutely positive that my father was

innocent in this regard, and, considering Fox's feelings toward my father in general, I felt I could trust his judgement. He would never put me in harm's way. I nodded and allowed him to lead me to the back of the SUV. Xavier opened the back door, and my heart clenched as I peered into the darkness. My father's face was illuminated by the lights coming from the dash, and the relief I spied in his eyes was instantaneous and real.

"Thank God you're okay!"

A tight smile lifted my mouth. "I'm fine."

At least, I would be when everything finally sank in.

"I was so worried about you," he continued as I slid into the middle seat. "When Fox called me earlier, I... God, I couldn't believe it."

For the first time, I noticed that his hands were zip tied together at his lower back. I threw a look over my shoulder at Fox who had climbed in behind me. His brows lifted a fraction as if to say, "what did you expect?"

I buckled myself in, then closed my eyes. A heavy arm draped over my shoulders, and I leaned into Fox as he pulled me close. All at once, I felt absolutely exhausted. I must have dozed, because I jerked awake when Fox's hands slid beneath my legs and he lifted me to his chest.

"I've got you, angel. Just relax," he whispered near my ear. He lifted me from the car then carried me toward the steps of the plane.

I stared up at them as we approached. Though I was loath for him to let me go, the steps were too narrow for him to carry me. I smothered a yawn, then patted his chest. "Put me down."

He lowered me to my feet, keeping one hand on me the

entire way up the steps and into the cabin. Fox directed me to the seats at the front of the plane, but instead of settling us on opposite sides of the aisle, he took a seat and pulled me over his lap.

I looked up at him. "I'm okay, you know. Really," I added when his piercing eyes met mine.

"I know. You're so strong, angel." His head dipped low next to mine, his warm breath caressing my ear. "But not this time. Not now. I can't let you go."

That was perfectly fine with me. I loved the feel of his arms around me, the strength and security he offered as I tucked my head into the crook of his neck. I closed my eyes and breathed him in, letting the soft beat of his heart lull me back to sleep.

The plane ride home was a blur, and the sun was up—looking much too bright and cheery—when we finally landed back in Chicago. We deplaned, then all five of us moved to another car in silence. As soon as we arrived home, Fox hustled me into the house.

"Antoine, please arrange a room for William," he tossed over his shoulder to the man next to the door

Fox kept one hand on my lower back as he guided me up the stairs and into the master bathroom. I stood there, feeling curiously blank, while he turned on the hot water in the shower then stripped my clothes off. He maneuvered me into the shower stall and pulled me against him. Fox murmured softly to me as he began to soap me off, his hands running up and down my back, over my hair. When he was done, he just held me close. For what felt like forever, we stood there entwined in each other's arms.

When the water turned cold, he silently toweled me off, then led me to the bed. Although I'd slept for a few hours in the car and on the plane, my mind and body were still exhausted. Guilt and grief weighed heavily on my heart, and I curled into Fox when he slid beneath the covers, pulling me with him.

"There's something…" My voice broke when I thought of Rodrigo, the way he'd shielded me with his body, protected me with his last breath.

"Not now, angel."

Fox's strong arms wrapped around me, and I pushed the thoughts away, focusing only on his touch as we fell asleep. Golden rays of afternoon sunlight poured in through the window when we next awoke, and I blinked up at the ceiling, still feeling numb and cold inside. The events of the past twenty-four hours still didn't feel quite real. It was almost as if I'd been watching it happen to someone else. But then Rodrigo's face came to mind again, and my stomach twisted, my heart clenching in agony.

He was gone. Because of me. I'd trusted the wrong person, and he'd paid the ultimate price. A deep ache settled into my bones, and I desperately tried to blink away the tears blurring my vision. What the hell were we going to do about my mother? She was still out there, and she needed to be stopped.

I felt a muscle in Fox's forearm twitch where it was wrapped around my waist, and I turned my head slightly so I could speak over my shoulder to him. "How did you know?"

He levered up on an elbow and peered down at me. "How did I know what?"

"About my mother."

He let out a soft exhalation. "Spencer."

My brows drew together. My brother-in-law had been shot almost immediately. He wouldn't have been able to—

My gaze jumped to Fox. "You read him. Your visions."

He nodded. "Yes. I saw everything."

I shivered, not entirely sure I wanted to know exactly what he'd seen. "I still can't believe it. Everything seemed so normal when I walked in there. Then…"

"I'm sorry, angel." He gave his head a little shake. His gaze drifted to the wall. "I had my suspicions when I couldn't get a hold of you. I called you and Rodrigo over and over but the signals on your phones disappeared."

His eyes held a trace of something I couldn't quite describe. Normally he looked so strong, so fierce. But now there was a vulnerability to him I'd never seen. My heart broke all over again for the loss I'd caused him. "I'm so sorry. I—"

My voice cracked, and Fox pulled me into his chest. "Shhh."

I clenched my eyes closed, but that didn't stop the tears slipping from the corners. I had no idea how long he held me like that before I finally calmed enough to speak. "What do we do now?"

"I'll take care of it."

I tipped my head up to him. "She needs to pay for the things she's done. She—"

"Eva." Fox's eyes were dark and serious, filled with something akin to guilt. "I need to do this my way."

I was no stranger to the failings of the legal system. My mother had far too many contacts; she would never spend a day in jail. I opened my mouth to ask what he planned, then immediately snapped it closed. I didn't want to know. But, despite everything she'd done, she was still my mother. I only had one request. "Just… Make it quick, please."

Fox dipped his chin. "Of course."

THIRTY-SEVEN

I studied William where he sat across from me. "Are you involved with the Helping Hand foundation?"

William shot me a questioning glance. "That's Lillian's pet project."

The foundation was created post-war in an effort to offer assistance to the women and children whose families had been torn apart. Lillian's maternal grandmother had started the foundation, and from what I could tell, it appeared as though the illegal transactions had begun when Lillian's father, Robert, got involved.

Robert Rhodes lacked anything resembling scruples judging from his dodgy business dealings. He had died from cancer several years back, and his wife, Beatrice, followed little more than two years later. Though they were unfortunately not around for me to question, I could pretty much guess what had happened.

Lillian's father, Conrad, had met and married Beatrice

Farnsworth in 1956. The foundation at that time was barely a decade old but had a sterling reputation. Lillian's maternal grandparents passed away in a plane crash several years later, leaving the foundation in the hands of Lillian's parents. From the manual entries of the accounting books, that appeared to be when the transactions first started.

The foundation grew by leaps and bounds, becoming more profitable each year. Unfortunately, no one questioned the significant donations from the questionable benefactors. Robert and Beatrice weren't fortunate enough to have a second child, and I could only speculate that Robert had groomed Lillian to take over his position.

Three years ago, the foundation had been flagged and an agent was brought in to investigate. Less than a week later he died in his home from an apparent heart attack. No charges were ever filed against the foundation, and any evidence they may have had on Helping Hand vanished into thin air. There was no way I would let Lillian get away this time.

I leveled a hard look at William. "Until this is over, you will remain here in my home."

His face flushed red with anger. "I had nothing to do with this!"

"That remains to be seen," I replied coolly. "Until my men assure me that you're not involved, I can't risk allowing you to interfere and potentially warn Lillian."

William shook his head. "If what you say is true—"

"It is," I cut him off. "Spencer told me everything."

As far as William was concerned, that was true. Spencer had confessed that Lillian was responsible—in a manner of speaking. The more my men investigated the funds moving through the foundation, the more we found an indisputable link to Lillian.

It appeared that she had set William up to take the fall. In fact, it appeared so genuine that I'd been certain of his guilt initially. William seemed to have no idea that there were millions of dollars sitting in an offshore account under his name. I wasn't about to enlighten him.

"What will you do?" For the first time, William looked truly unsettled.

I lifted one shoulder. "What needs to be done."

He was quiet for nearly a minute. "I've known Lillian half my life. Never did I ever imagine…" He trailed off.

I couldn't muster any sympathy for him. While Lillian's transgressions were far worse, he had once sold his youngest daughter into my possession. While I was grateful for that particular lapse in judgment, he was still a heinous human being. "This is as much for your protection as Eva's. You may technically be my father-in-law, but I don't trust you."

He blanched as though he hadn't considered we were technically related, even through marriage. "As I said before," I continued, "until I can fully determine your innocence, you will remain here under my men's supervision twenty-four hours a day. As far as everyone else is concerned, you're attending a conference on the west coast. The people there will vouch for you."

Though I knew he wanted to argue, William wisely kept silent.

"If there is any other information you would like to offer up, now is the time to do so."

He shook his head. "No."

I wasn't sure I believed him, but only time would tell.

"If you'll excuse me," I said, pushing from my chair, "I have a few things that need my attention."

"Of course." William left the office, and I blew out a breath. There was still so much to be done. Though Spencer and Sebastian were gone and the issue of Lillian was already underway, I hadn't determined how to deal with the rest of them. News of the fire had begun to spread but as of right now none of the men inside had been identified.

I was certain that, as soon as the media caught wind of who'd perished in the fire that night, Lillian would increase security. We needed to strike sooner rather than later without it appearing premeditated. It was a delicate balance.

I came to bed late that night, tiptoeing past the bed and into the bathroom so I wouldn't wake Eva. For a long while I stood under the spray of the shower, thinking about everything that had happened over the past week. It felt as if the weight of the world rested on my shoulders, more so than before.

In a short span of time, my wife had lost everyone close to her—if not physically, at least emotionally. Her mother and father had both betrayed her, and she still couldn't safely contact her sister any time she wished.

I flipped off the water, then toweled dry and made my way to bed. When I lifted the covers to slide underneath, my heart constricted when I saw Eva curled into a tiny ball on her side. Where she'd always gravitated to me before, now she'd pulled into herself. I wanted so badly to reach for her, but she'd completely withdrawn. I didn't know how to reach her.

Each time I saw her, I pictured that scene at the cabin. I

saw her covered in blood, cuts and abrasions marring her pretty face. She'd been through so damn much, and she needed to recover before I pawed at her like a dog. She deserved better than that.

Resigning myself to another lonely, sleepless night I turned onto my side and closed my eyes, fighting away the nightmare of the past few days.

THIRTY-EIGHT

EVA

I could sense Fox's disappointment with me. Though we'd shared a bed for the past four nights, he hadn't so much as tried to kiss me. The inches between us felt like miles. I wanted to curl into him the way I had before, wanted to revel in the refuge of his touch, but I stopped myself each time.

I wanted—needed—the physical reassurance of his touch. I wanted him to hold me the way he had when he'd rescued me from the cabin. Instead, he rose earlier every morning, long before I awoke. He came to bed later and slept on his side of the bed, turned away from me. It was like a wedge had been driven between us, and I was the one responsible.

And it wasn't just him. A somber pall hung over the household, and the guards seemed more serious than usual. Most of them ignored me completely, but I could feel some of them staring at me when they thought I wasn't paying attention, blaming me for Rodrigo's death. And they were right. It was my fault. I couldn't stand their sideways looks, the heavy sense of judgment hanging in the air, knowing that he would still be here if it wasn't for me.

I felt like everything was spiraling out of control. I still hadn't come to terms with everything. I couldn't believe my mother was responsible for something so horrible. It left me reeling, feeling more guilty than ever. I felt like I should have known—I should have seen the signs, or at least expected it. But there had been nothing.

My mother had used her position in a charity and taken advantage of the very people it was designed to help. I hated her for that, but I still worried about what would happen to her. She was my mother, after all, and I hated to lose her. It felt like I was being pulled in two very different directions—I loved her, but I wanted justice for the people she'd hurt.

Since the morning we'd returned home, I hadn't broached the subject and Fox hadn't offered any information. It stung that he wouldn't even tell me what he had planned, like he didn't trust me. I knew I only had myself to blame, but it didn't take the hurt away.

I felt like I was in limbo, just waiting to see what would happen with my mother, wondering if things would ever go back to the way they'd been between Fox and me. Things were strained between us, more so now than even when he'd held me captive.

I couldn't sleep, and I had no desire to eat. I felt sick with guilt, and grief hung over me like a huge black cloud. I was incredibly lucky that Fox had shown up when he had, and I couldn't remember if I'd thanked him for saving my life or not. He'd spent every waking hour sequestered in his office, and I didn't dare intrude. Once more, I felt like an outsider, and that hurt more than anything. The progress that Fox and I had made just a few weeks ago had slipped away in the blink of an eye.

My heart felt brittle and frail, like it was ready to crack wide open at the slightest touch. Part of me wanted to go to Fox, but I was terrified of the possible rejection. I wasn't sure we could ever go back to the way we were before, and that knowledge dug the knife of pain and regret even deeper.

Glancing down the hall, I kept an eye out for Fox's guards as I made my way into the kitchen for a drink. I stopped short when I saw my father sitting at the breakfast table tucked into the corner. He was looking out over the garden but turned at the sound of my footsteps. My father flashed me a small smile as I entered the kitchen, but almost as quickly it disappeared when he saw my hesitation.

I'd been avoiding him as much as possible, too, still unsure of my feelings toward him. He'd led Fox to the cabin to save me, but I couldn't forget that he'd practically sold me to Fox several months ago. I didn't know how to act around him anymore. I was emotionally exhausted from everything that had happened recently, and all I knew was that I was tired of being alone.

Swallowing hard, I forced my feet closer and gingerly slid into a chair across from him. "Dad."

He set his fork on the edge of his plate and studied me for a minute. "How are you?"

I offered him a tight smile. "Fine. You?"

"Doing well."

The conversation felt stiff and awkward, like two enemies being forced to share a space. I stared at him, and the words fell out before I could stop them. "Did you know?"

His face crumpled. "I know you probably won't believe me, but no. I had no idea. Until Fox told me what happened… I still can't believe it myself."

His expression bespoke of honesty and a slight bewilderment, like the news had blindsided him as well. I nodded a little. "I know, I can't wrap my mind around it either."

His gaze drifted outside, and I could practically see the regret etched into the lines around his eyes. For what he'd done, or for not realizing sooner what my mother was up to? I couldn't be sure. He seemed to have aged overnight. He looked older, more ragged and run down. He looked exhausted both mentally and physically—he looked exactly the way I felt inside. I watched him for nearly a minute before speaking again. "What are you going to do?"

My father took a deep breath. "Fox has requested that I stay here until things are… settled." He stumbled a little over the last word, no doubt thinking of how Fox might exact justice. "I told your mother I was on a business trip. Not that she'd notice or care," he murmured.

I knew my parents' relationship was primarily for show, and I almost pitied my father. "You're welcome here any time."

I hadn't meant to offer it but as soon I said it, I realized how much I meant it. He was still family, still my father. Though he'd made mistakes, I wanted to give him the benefit of the doubt.

His gaze jumped to mine. "Thank you. That means a lot."

Silence fell again for several moments, and I studied the wood grain of the tabletop before my father's voice drew my attention. "You look beautiful."

I smiled a little. "Thanks."

"Do you love him?"

"I do." Just saying the words made me want to cry. It reminded me of the day we'd said our vows, the laughter and teasing that had filled our trip to the island. My gaze dropped to my fingers and another memory filled my mind—the way he'd crossed my middle finger over the index, knowing that I wouldn't obey him.

A combination of guilt and shame clogged my throat, and I choked back a sob. Fox had come to mean everything to me, but I no longer felt as close to him as I once had. He was such a complex man. Hard to know, hard to love. But it made him all the more special. I would never love anyone else the way I loved him.

His gaze dropped to the ring on my left hand. "I never would have believed him capable, but… he cares for you."

My throat tightened, burning with unshed tears. I wished I was as certain of that as my father seemed to be. A week ago I would have agreed, but I'd ruined everything. I forced a smile to my face. "I know."

An awkward silence fell, and I finally pushed from the table. "I'll let you finish your dinner."

With that, I escaped from the room. The house was a blur through my tear-filled eyes as I moved quickly through the hallways and up the stairs. A soft sob escaped my throat as I reached the door to Fox's room. I couldn't bear to go in there right now, to be surrounded by his things, his familiar scent, knowing that he was so close yet so far away.

Slapping a hand over my mouth to stifle my anguished cry, I fled down the hall and threw myself into my room, then locked the door behind me. I moved to the window and blinked back the tears as memories assaulted me. I thought back to my first couple of weeks here, the way I'd escaped out the window. I'd wanted so badly to get away from him then. Now I would give anything to have him back.

I stood, unseeing, out at the garden for what seemed like forever before a soft touch to my shoulder startled me out of my melancholy reverie. Glancing over my shoulder, I met Fox's dark gaze. He looked tired and so very serious that I had to turn away. Tears blurred my reflection in the window, dark now that night had fallen.

"Have you eaten?"

I shook my head, unable to speak.

"Eva..."

There was a tinge of censure in his voice, along with an exasperation that tore at me. The tears I'd been trying so hard to hold back slipped free, and one rolled down my cheek. I fought to keep my breathing still so Fox wouldn't notice.

"You need to eat."

It was so reminiscent of the things he'd said to me months ago when I'd first arrived that it made the tears fall even harder and faster. My lungs constricted, and I wrapped my arms more tightly around my waist, trying to hold myself together.

"Angel." I dipped my head as he took one shoulder in

his hand and tried to steer me toward him. "What's wrong?"

I kept my gaze glued to the floor, unable to look at him. "It's my fault," I spoke haltingly, fighting like hell to keep the sobs from escaping. "He's gone... because of me."

"That's not true," Fox said softly. "You're not responsible for his death—your mother is."

Hearing that made it even worse, and I clenched my eyes against the burning tears. How could he ever begin to forgive me? "I don't blame you," I said slowly, my heart breaking a little more with every word I spoke between tears, "if you... if you don't want me anymore."

"Angel."

One huge hand slipped beneath my chin and lifted my face to his. Reluctantly, I cracked my watery eyes open to meet Fox's gaze. Dark eyes probed into mine. "I will *always* want you."

THIRTY-NINE

She threw herself into my arms at the same time I tugged her to me, holding her tight, her face pressed to my chest. Maybe it was just my imagination, but she felt smaller, frailer and more fragile than before. I knew this had been hard on her; it'd been hard on all of us.

Part of me still wanted to spank her ass raw for lying to me and going against my orders. But everything she'd endured was punishment enough. Unfortunately, Eva had learned her lesson the hardest way possible. It was obvious that she deeply regretted what had happened, and I wouldn't hold her actions against her. It didn't take away the sharp pang of loss, but I was grateful I hadn't lost her, too.

"I'm sorry we lost Rodrigo, but I count myself incredibly fortunate that you're still here."

Her body trembled, but she refused to lift her head from where it was burrowed in my chest. I could tell from the jerky motion that she was trying unsuccessfully to stifle her tears, and I moved my hand over her back in a soothing, circular motion.

I still hadn't heard from Rodrigo, and I feared we never would. It wouldn't be the first man I'd ever lost, but Rodrigo was closest to me. He was one of the first I'd saved, and he'd dedicated himself to the cause wholeheartedly. There was no doubt in my mind that Lillian would've had him dispatched. He'd seen and knew too much, and it was too much of a risk to let him live.

I didn't want to blame Eva for his death, but part of me resented that he was dead because of a poor decision. She'd gone to her mother out of some twisted sense of misplaced obligation, never once imagining the betrayal that lay in store. Eva was still so naïve and innocent sometimes, always looking for the best in people.

What I couldn't figure out was why Rodrigo had gone along with it. Maybe he'd been trying to appease Eva out of some misplaced sense of guilt. It was no secret that they'd never really gotten along. Maybe it was my edict that he start treating her the way my wife and partner deserved that prompted him to give in to her request.

Eva had taken full responsibility, saying that it was all her fault. But the fact of the matter was that Rodrigo should have known better. Considering at the time we assumed only William was involved, it was entirely possible that Lillian at least knew about his dealings to the foundation. Either way, there was no changing the past.

But what Lillian had done was unforgivable, and she needed to be dealt with. I currently had a man working on it, but I didn't plan to tell Eva. She didn't need that knowledge weighing on her conscience now, too. What she needed now was to forget. I wanted to baby her, comfort and love her. I hadn't touched her for the past four days, and each hour that passed without her in my arms was pure hell.

The night in the cabin had reminded me of just how vulnerable she truly was, and I hadn't wanted to push her. She'd been through a terrible ordeal, and I knew she had a lot of healing to do, both emotionally and physically. But what I hadn't seen was how much she'd needed me—and how much I needed her.

Keeping my touch firm, I swept my hand upward and cupped the nape of her neck. Her shiny green eyes blinked up at me, and I covered her mouth with mine. She responded eagerly, clutching at my back, pulling at the fabric of my shirt.

Bending my knees, I wound my free arm beneath her bottom and lifted her to my chest. Her legs automatically wrapped around my hips, her ankles locking at the base of my spine. Her arms looped around my neck, holding me close as I plundered her mouth, our tongues rolling over one another in an erotic dance. Holding her tightly, I crossed the room, bypassing the bed in favor of the floor-length mirror in the corner.

My dick swelled at the feel of her, and I slowly lowered her to her feet. Once she was steady, I began to strip her between kisses. Our hands roved frantically until we were both bare, and I turned her to face the mirror. I met her reflection there, her lids heavy as she peered back at me.

"Look at us." I settled my hands on her hips, then coasted them upward to cup her breasts. "Look how fucking perfect you are, how perfectly we fit together. How perfect we are for each other."

She melted into me, and I pulled her to the floor, pressing her to her hands and knees. "You belong with me, Eva." I kept my gaze locked on hers as I dipped my fingers inside her pussy, testing her, preparing her. "You're my wife. My everything."

One hand on her hip, I guided my cock to her with the other and pressed an inch inside, reveling in the way she stretched to accommodate me, welcoming me in. In the reflection, I watched her teeth sink into her lower lip, her expression one of anticipation and desire. I curled my fingers into the flesh curve of her hip then thrust hard.

She let out a little gasp as the motion rocked her forward, but I pulled her back to me and did it again, fucking her hard and deep as I took control of her body. Here with me, she didn't need to dwell on the past; she only needed to feel, to focus on us and the way we moved together.

Wrapping one arm around her waist, I lifted her so her back was pressed to my chest.

"I will always want you," I repeated to her once more as I cupped her chin in my hand and turned her head. Still buried deep inside her, I paused my movements and made sure she was looking at me—made sure she was hearing every word. "I only want you. I love you, angel."

Her mouth opened, but no sound came out, and a misty sheen covered her eyes. "I love you," I repeated fiercely. "You're mine, angel. Forever."

I kissed her hard, pouring every ounce of emotion I felt into the gesture. Her mouth moved under mine, frantic and hungry as her hand came up and her fingers curled into my head. "I love you," she panted when she broke away. "So much."

I kissed her, then started moving my hips again, pumping back into her. The intensity swelled and she pushed back against me, demanding more. I curled my fingers into her hips and fucked her mercilessly—commanding her, showing her she was mine. Only mine.

Watching her in the mirror was erotic as fuck, and I felt myself harden further at the sight of us moving together in perfect tandem. I slid one hand downward and stroked the tight, hard bud of her clit. Eva arched into my touch then shattered with a soft cry. She pitched forward, catching herself at the last moment to brace against my hard thrusts. Her head jerked up, those misty green eyes meeting mine in the reflection and spurring me on.

I pumped harder, faster, until heat swept over my body and I could no longer hold back. I kept my gaze locked on Eva's as I came deep inside her, and I felt the tremble of exhaustion in her muscles as I came down. I slowly withdrew from her, then scooped her into my arms and carried her to the bed. I settled her in the middle and drew the sheet up with one hand, never wanting to let go of her.

Eva curled into me, closer than skin, and I kissed her forehead. Her fingers danced lightly over my back, tracing my scars, and for once, I felt nothing. No pain. No shame. My love for Eva had changed all of that. She accepted all of me just as I was—she loved me. Hearing those words come from her lips—I couldn't begin to describe the feeling that swept through me. I clutched her tighter and drifted off to sleep with my wife tucked safely in my arms, right where she belonged.

A couple hours later, I awoke feeling sated, more invigorated and refreshed than I had in a long time. It felt as if a weight had been lifted from my shoulders now that

Eva was back in my arms. Her head rested on my shoulder while she dozed, and I sifted my fingers through her pale locks.

She came awake at the gentle caress, inhaling deeply before cracking those gorgeous green eyes I loved so much. Her hand rested on my chest, and her fingers curled slightly into my skin like she was trying to hold onto me.

I kissed the top of her head. "I'm sorry I pushed you away," I murmured into her hair. "I was so focused on everything…"

"I know. It's okay." Her voice was sad, and it sent a jagged shard of pain through my heart.

"It's not okay, angel." I propped myself up on an elbow and stared at her. "You're so damned strong, so good at putting on a brave face and pushing through. I think you're stronger than I am, sometimes."

I let out a little laugh, realizing for the first time how true that was. After everything she'd been through, she'd never complained—not once. Not when I'd held her captive, not even when she'd been kidnapped by the person she'd trusted to keep her safe. My wife was a fighter, and sometimes I forgot how sensitive she was deep inside. She had the most beautiful heart guided by the toughest, strongest mind I'd ever met.

I thought back to the way she'd cared for me after I'd been shot. Eva had set aside all of her insecurities and fears in order to care for me. Because that's the type of person she was. She flourished under pressure—but deep beneath the surface she was too compassionate, felt too much.

She'd protected me in my time of need, but I'd failed to do the same for her. It was my job as her husband, as the man who loved her, to care for her and make sure she was healthy both mentally and physically. I'd let her down, and the knowledge cut into me like a knife.

"I don't ever want you to be afraid to open up to me. You're absolutely incredible, and I wouldn't change you for the world. There's not another woman in this world who could handle the things you have. I should have seen how badly you were hurting, but I didn't. I wasn't there for you when you needed me, and I can't tell you how sorry I am for that."

She nodded a little, and I framed her face with one hand. "You understand that, right? You are everything to me—the only thing that matters."

A tear slipped down her cheek and across my palm where I cupped her face. I brushed it away, then kissed her. "I meant what I said, angel. I'm sorry I fucked up, but I will spend the rest of my life making it up to you, loving you."

She looped her arms around my neck and held me tight. She spoke into the crook of my neck as I held her tightly with one arm, using the other to stroke lightly up and down her back. "I love you, too."

I didn't know how badly I needed to hear those words, to hear that she felt as deeply for me as I did for her. Empty promises in the throes of passion were one thing; but I'd opened my heart to her fully and completely, and I was eternally grateful that she'd returned the sentiment.

More than that, I was thankful that she seemed to forgive my ignorance. I still felt like absolute shit for being so focused on revenge that I'd set my wife aside. It was the one thing I'd sworn I would never do, yet I'd reverted right back to my old ways.

I kissed the shell of her ear. "I'll try harder to be the man you need, angel."

Eva pulled back, hands clasping the back of my head as she stared deep into my eyes. "You're exactly the man I need, and the only man I want."

The call came the following morning. William and I sat in my office, discussing a way to turn his business around when my phone rang, diverting my attention. A host of emotions mingled in my chest at the sight of the unknown number lighting up the screen. This phone call could very well determine our future.

I swiped the screen to answer and lifted the phone to my ear, my eyes locking on William's. There was a brief moment of silence, then the caller spoke. "It's done."

Without another word, I ended the call and slipped the phone into my jacket pocket, all the while watching William. His quizzical expression gradually morphed into something deeper, and in that moment, I knew that he'd read the significance behind the phone call.

"Was that…?"

I nodded. "It was."

He ran a shaky hand through his hair. "I…" He dropped his hand and gazed across the desk at me. "What do we do now?"

"You need to go home. I'm sure the police will be there soon."

"Right." He looked a little lost, and I felt a brief pang of sympathy for the man. I was sure he'd cared for her in his own way.

He pushed up from his chair and was halfway to the door before he turned on a heel like something had just occurred to him. "Eva—what are we going to tell her?"

"I'll take care of it," I said as I rose. "You deal with the authorities and keep us posted."

With a tight nod, William left and I went in search of Eva. Predictably, I found her in the den near my office. I hesitated in the doorway, just watching her. She sat propped against the arm of the couch, her feet stretched out in front of her, the new laptop she'd purchased propped on her lap.

Her gaze lifted and met mine over the edge of the silver screen. "Hey."

I smiled and stepped into the room, then closed the door behind me. "I think we should make this your office."

She smiled and set the computer aside as I moved toward her. "Only if I actually find some work to do."

"You will." I knelt on the floor next to her and took her hand in mine. "I need to talk to you."

She must have read the truth in my eyes, because her mouth parted a little in a mixture of surprise and shock, her own pretty green eyes widening slightly. "Is she…?"

We both knew this had to happen, but I hated that it would hurt her. "Yes, angel."

She swallowed hard, still looking a little bewildered. "Does my father know?"

I nodded. "I sent him home. To deal with the police," I clarified at her puzzled expression.

She nodded a little. "H-how?"

"That I don't know, only that she's… gone." I squeezed her hand. "I'm sorry. I know this is a lot to take in."

Her face fell, and her bottom lip trembled, but she remained strong. I'd never admired her strength and independence more than I did in that moment. I eased her into my arms, pulling her head against my chest and pressing a kiss to the top of her head. I didn't know what to say to her.

This was a strange position for me to be in. I wanted to offer my condolences, but I wasn't sad that Lillian was gone. Never before had I ever apologized for the things I'd done, yet with Eva I felt the need to take her pain away.

Finally, Eva pulled back. "When do you think we'll find out? About… you know."

She was curious to see the proof, something I understood perfectly. I wanted to see it for myself as well. "Your father said he would call once the authorities left. Maybe it will be on the news. Would you like to check?"

Her lashes fluttered as she blinked rapidly, then nodded. "I need to know."

"Okay." Taking her hand, I pulled her to her feet and we made our way to the media room at the opposite end of the house. I flipped on the local station, and the headline proclaiming a fatal car accident immediately caught my eye.

"Police have shut down the bridge as they investigate the cause of a tragic accident that has claimed the lives of four Chicago residents," the pretty blonde reporter stated. Beside me, Eva sucked in a breath, her eyes glued to the screen.

The next shot panned to sky cams over the bridge and a mile-long line of traffic. "At this time, the victims have not been identified. We will continue to update you as we get more information, but now we'll take you to—"

I looped an arm around her and pulled her close, holding her tight as we watched for the next ten minutes or so until the reporters began to recap information for the new viewers tuning in. Emotions raged inside me as I lifted the remote and clicked off the TV.

"Come on, angel." I kissed her temple. "It's finally over."

FORTY

EVA

My father had returned home per Fox's edict as soon as he got the phone call yesterday afternoon to await the arrival of the authorities. It didn't take long. Only a few hours after the accident, the police had arrived on my father's doorstep. By the time the police pulled out of my father's driveway, news stations everywhere had been splashing her name all over the headlines.

There were no questions, no interrogations. As of right now, it just looked like a horrible accident. But the three of us knew better. Fox wouldn't tell me exactly what had happened, and I wasn't entirely certain he knew for sure, either. Part of me wanted to know the details, but I knew it was for the best that I didn't. This way, if the police began to suspect any sort of foul play, I could honestly tell them that I knew nothing.

I was relieved that she was gone. Sad. Angry. Part of me still didn't even believe it was real. Fox and my father agreed not to speak for the time being unless absolutely necessary. I wasn't certain what kind of act my father had put on for the police, but there was little doubt in my mind that his horror and grief at the news would be genuine. He'd worn the same slightly baffled, despondent expression ever since he learned of her treachery.

My phone rang, and I held back a cringe when I saw my father's name. "They pulled the car from the river, and they took her…" His voice broke. "Her body is at the morgue. They'll need me to identify her."

"I want to come, too," I said immediately.

"Eva, no, I can't let you—"

I shook my head. "I have to."

It wasn't that I had any real desire to see her, but I still didn't fully trust my father. After everything we'd been through, I needed the closure. I needed to know for certain that this was over. "What time?"

On the other end of the line, my father sighed. "I have an appointment with the medical examiner at eleven."

"I'll be there." I ended the call and turned to meet Fox's quizzical gaze. "I need to be at the morgue by eleven."

His dark eyes filled with a mixture of concern and anger. "Your father should be the one doing this."

I wrapped my arms around my waist. "He is. But I need to see for myself."

Fox shook his head. "That's not a good idea."

I narrowed my eyes at him. "She had me kidnapped. Drugged. Almost—" My voice cracked on the word raped.

A thousand emotions raged in his eyes. I knew he wanted to protect me from everything, but before we could move on we needed to put the past behind us. He nodded slowly. "Okay, angel. If that's what you need."

I took my time getting ready, and we pulled into the parking lot of the medical examiner's office at 10:58. Callum slid into a spot next to my father's white Mercedes, and my heart clenched as I saw him sitting in the driver seat, looking forlorn. As if feeling my gaze on him, his head turned and he flashed a wan smile as his eyes met mine.

We climbed out of the cars in tandem, then made our way inside. An assistant greeted us in the lobby before showing us to a private room. The doctor came in and introduced herself, then explained how everything would go.

"Most exams are recorded now to make the identification process easier on the family," she said, her kind brown eyes locking on mine. I nodded but didn't say a word. "If you'd prefer to see her in person, that can be arranged as well."

"The video will be fine," my father said, a slight tremor in his voice.

The doctor nodded her assent, then clicked a few buttons on her computer. An exam room came into view on the screen, and I immediately tensed. Fox, who had seated himself next to me, reached over and took my hand. I squeezed his fingers like a lifeline as the camera on screen panned over the body on the table. I viewed it almost impassively at first.

She looked unnaturally pale, and a handful of cuts marred her forehead and cheeks. Even with her eyes closed in repose, there was no mistaking her features. In my peripheral vision, I watched my father nod.

"That's her."

I heard them talking about releasing my mother's

personal effects and arranging a service, but I couldn't tear my eyes from the screen. I felt trapped in the past. Was it really just last week that I'd seen her in the living room of our family home, looking poised and unflappable? God, that felt so long ago. Now she was gone.

I stood abruptly, the legs of the chair screeching across the linoleum floor as I pushed it back. "Excuse me."

Without another word I left the room, walking past Fox and out to the car. I slid into the backseat and he cautiously followed. I could feel his gaze on me, but he quietly commanded Callum to take us home then fell silent. I stared out the window the whole way, lost in thought.

I had no idea how we got home; suddenly, I blinked and we were sitting in the driveway. Fox opened the door for me and I made my way into the house, then down the hall to the den, still not really seeing anything. I moved to the couch in the middle of the room and rested my hands along the back, staring sightlessly into the fireplace. The sound of the door closing, followed by the gentle clink of glass, met my ears, and a minute later Fox pressed a tumbler into my hand.

"I think we need this after today."

I dropped my gaze and looked at the amber liquid before lifting my eyes to the fireplace once more. I felt the smooth glass beneath my fingers, and all at once the emotions I'd been repressing for the past few days came rushing to the surface. A scream split the air, and it took a full second to realize that it was coming from me.

A howl welled up and out of my throat, all of the anger and pain I'd been harboring for the past few days bubbling to the surface. I flung the glass against the fireplace with a howl of pure rage.

"Why?" I shrieked. "Why did she do this? I hate her! I hate her!"

Fox stood by, watching impassively, and I rounded on him. "Why aren't you upset? You should be furious!" I screamed, my body vibrating with anger. "Look what she did! To you, to your friends, to—"

I broke off, unable to give voice to the horrible atrocities my mother had committed. Instead, I focused on the anger coursing through every cell of my body. I launched myself at Fox, battering his chest with my fists. "You should hate her!"

"I did, angel." He grabbed my biceps, stilling my movements. "I allowed it to drive me for years. But I don't need to be mad anymore."

I melted against him as he spoke. Gradually, the anger drained from me, replaced by a sharp sadness and the sting of loss. "I thought I needed revenge—I was wrong. I have you. I love you, and that's enough for me."

I burst into tears, and Fox clutched me close, gently rocking me side to side and murmuring softly. "Let it out, angel. Let it go."

Emotion poured from me as I cried into Fox's chest, wrapped in his strong arms. I couldn't explain the rapid swing from angry to sad as I wound my arms around his neck and held on for dear life. Fox kissed my hair, then my temple. I grabbed at him, pulling him down to my mouth, overwhelmed with the need to feel anything other than sadness and anger and loss.

The kiss was hard and brutal, and it helped to ground me in a way I didn't realize I needed. I ripped the shirt from his waistband, then yanked the edges apart, the sound of a button pinging softly off the coffee table registering dimly in the back of my mind.

Fox pulled my shirt over my head, then shucked his pants as I wiggled out of mine. He'd managed to get his buckle undone and had just pushed them down his thighs when I flung myself at him again. He caught and spun me, then lowered us to the couch. I attacked his mouth, all the while running my hands through his hair, over his shoulders, needing to touch every inch of him. With one hand, he palmed his erection and lined it up with my channel, then thrust hard.

The swift stroke took my breath away with its perfection, and a sense of rightness burst within me. He took me hard and fast, countering the pain I felt inside and driving it out of me with every thrust. He came at the same time I did, and I collapsed backward, out of breath and completely drained. Fox lowered his weight over me, pressing me into the couch, and I wrapped one arm around his neck. "Thank you."

It was everything I'd needed, and I loved that he knew me that well. He lifted up to kiss me once on the mouth, tender and sweet. "I love you, angel."

The investigation and autopsy took longer than anticipated, and the funeral wasn't held until almost two weeks later. Dozens of people stood around the gravesite, all dressed in dark colors, united by the somber looks on their faces as they mourned the woman they thought they knew.

My gaze flitted from face to face. How many of them truly knew her? Were any of them involved?

Tears slid down my face, and Fox squeezed my hand. "I'm sorry, angel. I know she was your mother."

"I'm not crying for her," I said as I swept away a tear with the pad of my thumb. I was crying for everyone her actions had hurt. Fox. Rodrigo. My father. Hundreds of women and children.

I watched as they lowered the polished wood casket into the ground but deep inside, I felt nothing. I had nothing left for her.

Fox released my hand, then slipped his palm to my lower back. "Are you ready, angel?"

I looked at the gravesite one last time, then nodded slowly. I was ready—to let it go, to put it all behind me so we could move finally forward in peace. I turned to my husband. "Let's go home."

EPILOGUE

FOX

FIVE YEARS LATER

The plane landed half an hour earlier than expected, but the early arrival didn't soothe my impatience. I was eager to get home and see Eva as quickly as possible. Not wanting to bother Hossam, I hired a local driver to take me to the beach house.

Almost as soon as I slid into the backseat, I remembered why I typically had Hossam drive. Though I was used to the winding, hilly roads, the native driver took them in record speed, coming close to causing an accident twice. By the time I reached the house, I felt like I'd lost ten years off my life and would take a week to recover from motion sickness.

The man grinned at me as I passed a tip through the window then sped out of the driveway, headed back to the airport no doubt to pick up his next victim. Though we'd been here for almost five years, I wasn't certain I would ever get used to the way they drove.

With a little shake of my head, I mounted the stairs, already scanning the foyer and hallway for my wife. The living room and kitchen were empty, and I spotted her through the window standing on the terrace. I couldn't help the smile that spread over my face, and my chest tightened the way it did every time I saw her, even after all these years.

I slid through the sunroom, closing the door quietly behind me as I stepped outside. She stood with her back to me, hands braced on the railing as she looked out over the beach. I kept my tread soft as I moved up behind her then slid my arms around her waist.

Eva jumped and let out a little squeak of surprise. "Jesus, Fox! You scared the life out of me." She turned in my arms, and her swollen stomach brushed mine as she looped her arms around my neck. "I wasn't expecting you for another two days."

I dipped my head and kissed her. "Johnson has everything under control back home." I slid one hand around to her belly. "Besides, I didn't want to leave you too long with you being so close."

Eva dropped her hand and covered mine. "I still have a couple of weeks left."

I shot her a wry look. "That's what you said with Liam."

She smiled and glanced over her shoulder to where our son frolicked on the beach below. "I'm sure it'll be fine," she replied.

I followed her gaze and lifted a hand in greeting to

William, who knelt next to my son. Elle and Hossam were seated in the sand a few feet away, watching their own son, Michael, as he and Liam studiously built a sandcastle.

Things had gotten increasingly better between William and the girls, and we'd invited him to come down and visit a couple years back, right after Liam was born. Now he spent about half the year here playing with the boys. I wasn't certain I'd ever forgive him for what he'd done to them, but he truly loved his grandsons and enjoyed being with them. I couldn't deny him time spent with them.

The boys laughed as they stacked up the sand, then demolished it, and I couldn't help but grin.

They'd been born only two months apart, and the women had been absolutely ecstatic when they found out they were pregnant at the same time. It seemed like kismet of some sort, and things had worked out almost perfectly. Now we eagerly awaited the birth of our daughter. The doctor had said it would be another few weeks, but I wasn't so sure.

"How are you feeling?"

Eva turned back to me. "My back hurts and my feet are swollen, especially in this heat. I'm ready to get her out already."

"My poor angel. Want a back rub?"

My wife's laughter filled the air. "I know how your back rubs end."

I leaned in and nipped her ear, then tugged her toward the house. "You shouldn't complain. Besides, I hear it helps the baby come quicker."

I wasn't wrong. By ten o'clock the next morning, I was holding our tiny daughter, Amelie, in my hands. Her face was still pinched and pink from her delivery, but she was the most beautiful thing I'd ever seen. Her tired little eyes blinked open, and I swore she stole my heart the moment she looked up at me. A few feet away, Eva watched on with an exhausted but ecstatic smile. I was still staring at Amelie in amazement when William strode through the door of the hospital room, Liam clinging to his hand.

I passed the baby to William then picked up my son whose bright green eyes, so much like Eva's, zeroed in on the baby. "So small, isn't she?" He nodded. "It's up to us to protect her. Will you watch over her when I'm gone, teach her to be strong and independent just like you?"

Expression serious, he nodded and I rubbed his back. "Good man."

His small face turned up to mine. "Can I hold her?"

"Of course." I settled him on the bed next to Eva then accepted Amelie from William. I laid her over Liam's lap and guided his arm under her head for support. I watched as he bent and kissed her forehead, already as fiercely protective of her as I was.

Eva looped an arm around them, holding them both, and kissed the top of Liam's head. "You're going to be a wonderful big brother."

A few minutes later, the baby began to whimper. Eva shifted the baby to her chest, and I scooped up Liam. "I think it's time for a nap anyway. Grandpa will take you home, but I'll be home in a bit, okay?"

I ruffled my son's hair, then set him on his feet. He and William left, and I closed the door to give my wife some privacy as she settled Amelie at her breast. The baby began to suckle and I took a seat on the edge of the bed, just watching them. I ran my fingers gently over the baby's downy curls, then dropped a kiss on her head.

Eva smiled, her eyes tired but filled with joy. "She looks like you."

She did, but I could see traces of Eva in her, too. "She's absolutely perfect."

Lifting my hand, I framed Eva's face and kissed her deeply. "I love you, angel. You've made me the happiest man in the world."

My wife. My family. It was nothing I'd ever expected my life to be, but everything I needed.

Thank you so much for reading the Retribution Series! If you loved these stories, don't miss the first book in the all new Rescue & Redemption series!

When Claire is drawn into a deadly ploy for revenge, police chief Grayson Thorne will do everything in his power to protect the woman he loves.

Turn the page for a sneak peek at Friendly Fire!

Thank you so much for reading the Sinful Duet! Want more of Fox and Eva? Sign up for my spam-free newsletter and get an exclusive bonus scene FREE!

FRIENDLY FIRE

CHAPTER ONE

CLAIRE

My fingers skimmed over the windowsill, resting in the empty space that had once housed one of my favorite pictures. It wasn't the first time something had been moved recently, but now it was just... gone.

The cleaning crew came through a few nights a week, and occasionally they'd moved things slightly as they'd dusted and performed routine maintenance. But the picture of my sister and me after graduation was nowhere to be found.

I'd even checked to make sure it hadn't fallen in the trash. That'd be a stretch, considering the bin was several feet away from the window and tucked beneath my desk. Perhaps one of the crew had broken it while cleaning and they'd been so embarrassed or worried that instead of coming forward, they'd gotten rid of it.

That, I could understand. I wasn't angry—I just wanted the picture back. I'd have to address the issue with Principal Sutton to see if he'd heard anything.

"Looking for something?"

I whirled toward the deep voice floating through my doorway and dropped my fingers from the sill. My gaze swept over the young man standing just outside my office, and I forced a professional smile to my face. Trent Jones was no stranger to my office, but was his expression just a little more smug than usual? I couldn't tell.

"Not at all." I gestured to the chair in front of my desk. "Have a seat."

His expression didn't change as he sauntered through the doorway and practically threw himself into the chair. His backpack hit the floor with a loud thud, and I pressed my lips into a firm line as he slouched insouciantly, one eyebrow cocked toward his hairline as he studied me, a challenging glint in his eyes.

His behavior had gotten worse recently, and he'd been caught fighting yesterday afternoon after school—hence his visit to my office first thing this morning. As guidance counselor for Cedar Springs High School, it was my job to help students. And Trent was screaming for help more than anyone.

Donning my emotional coat of armor I glided back to my desk and took a seat. "How is everything?"

He shrugged. "Same shit, different day."

"Language," I admonished, but there was no heat behind my words. Trent didn't have it easy. He was incredibly smart—probably one of the smartest kids I'd ever met—but he had a horrible home life and a giant chip on his shoulder. His parents were in the middle of a very brutal and messy divorce, each flaunting their new affair in front of the other.

For the past two years they'd dragged Trent through the proceedings, using him as a pawn. It was divorce ping pong at its best, played with children and emotions instead of sports equipment. I wished I could smack both of them.

"Heard there was an incident after school yesterday," I said as I settled back in my chair and crossed one leg over the other.

Trent clenched his jaw, then wiped his expression clean. "It was nothing major."

"I think giving Matt Cruz a black eye is pretty major," I said softly.

"He's a dick."

I pressed my lips into a flat line and studied him for a second. Having met Mr. Cruz, I couldn't exactly disagree. He was obnoxious and rude, and notorious for provoking other students. Unfortunately, he never got caught in the act, so he was rarely disciplined for his actions. I personally thought he needed to be knocked down a couple pegs. It would be incredibly unprofessional of me to admit that out loud, though, so I kept my opinion to myself.

"Tell me what happened."

It was as much an order as an invitation, and Trent rolled his eyes. "He was running his mouth about my mom again."

My stomach twisted with dread. "What did he say?"

Anger flared in his eyes. "Basically that she was fucking every guy in town except my dad."

I didn't bother to correct his foul language this time.

Cruz's words were a low blow, considering everyone knew his mother had slept with Trent's football coach last year just to spite her soon-to-be-ex-husband.

"We both know fighting's not the way to solve anything." *Even if the kid deserved it.* "Just do your best to ignore him," I said. "You'll be out of here soon enough and won't ever have to see him again."

Trent's gaze skittered away. "I'm still stuck in this hell hole for the next eight months."

He absolutely hated school, primarily because of the students like Matt Cruz. "Why don't you look into testing out? You could get your GED or join a work program. That would get you out of here, and you could get your foot in the door somewhere."

"And give them the satisfaction of running away with my tail between my legs?" His lip curled. "No thanks."

He could be so stubborn sometimes, but I had to admire his grit. "Don't let them determine your future. This is just the beginning for you. Prove them all wrong and make something of yourself."

He snorted. "Who the hell would hire me anyway?"

"If you're a hard worker, I'm sure there would be a ton of places willing to give you a shot."

"Right. Then they'll fire me as soon as the year's over. Assholes only care about themselves."

Trent had no reason to trust adults; he'd grown up with the two of the worst examples known to mankind. I decided to level with him. "You know what? You're right. People suck and they can be assholes sometimes."

His eyes widened fractionally with surprise, then immediately narrowed suspiciously. "What the hell would you know about it?"

"My parents did the same thing when I was twelve. Their divorce was long and messy, and all they cared about was hurting the other person. My sister and I never even registered on their radar. We bounced from house to house, counting down the days until we could leave." I leaned forward. "Kids always have it the hardest, especially during divorce."

"You don't know what the hell you're talking about." His mouth set into a hard line.

"Your parents have a responsibility to make sure you're getting what you need," I continued, "and so do I."

Trent jumped up, his face red. "I don't need your help!"

His anger didn't surprise me, but his huge form hulking over my desk sent my pulse skittering wildly. I slowly rose, clamping down on my control. "Trent..."

"Shut the hell up!"

He snatched up his backpack and stormed from the office, leaving me standing there, knees shaking. As my heart rate returned to normal, a sharp twinge moved through the muscle. Trent wasn't a bad kid. He was lonely, misunderstood. And mostly, I just felt bad for him.

I shrugged off my unease and fought to control my pulse. I couldn't wait until he finally graduated. I hoped he did just as I suggested and took off as soon as he could. The best thing he could do was get away from his parents' toxic environments. I'd met them on a handful of occasions, and I could honestly say I didn't like either one of them.

Despite Trent's misgivings, I knew he had the potential to do anything he wanted to do. He was a talented football player, though he'd quit as soon as he found out about his mother's affair and refused to join the team his senior year.

I wished for his sake that so many things were different. I'd give him the weekend to cool down, and I would use that time to check out a few local work programs. I was certain that someone would be more than happy to have him.

By the end of the day I had several prospects lined up. My personal favorite was a local construction company who was willing to take him on part-time. I'd spoken with the owner for nearly an hour this afternoon, and I thought it would be perfect for Trent. He could work with the crew in the morning, then use the afternoon to finish his coursework online.

I sat back in my chair, pleased that we were able to find some options. Getting Trent to agree to it would be a different story, but I'd cross that bridge when I came to it. He was like a wild stallion sometimes; you had to make him think the idea was his before he'd agree to anything.

My phone chimed from inside my desk, and I opened the middle drawer to retrieve it. A message from Gray lit the screen, and I couldn't help but smile. Gray had been my best friend for the past two years, ever since I'd moved here to take the position as guidance counselor at Cedar Springs.

One of the teachers had convinced me to attend a barbecue with her, and she'd introduced me to her family and friends. It was there that I'd met Grayson Thorne. Newly appointed to Chief of Police, Gray was smart and handsome, and he knew it. He'd immediately hit on me, and I shot him down. He'd laughed it off, thrown an arm around my shoulders, and we'd been inseparable ever since.

I scanned Gray's message. **Steak tonight?**

I loved that he just assumed I was free on a Friday night. A normal person would be out on a date or doing something fun. But not me. I was the predictable homebody, and he knew it.

I quickly tapped back a response. **I'll make a salad.**

The bell rang, sending teachers and students alike flooding from the building. I gathered my things then locked up my office. I wasn't taking chances this time. I waved to a few remaining teachers before climbing in my car and heading home. The football team had an away game tonight, otherwise I was sure Gray and I would have ended up there instead of hanging out at my place.

I left the front door unlocked knowing that Gray would be there soon anyway, then made my way up to my room. I stripped out of the jeans I'd worn today and tugged on the comfiest sweats I owned. After all, I wasn't trying to impress anyone.

I cringed as I skimmed my hand along my calf. How many days had it been since I'd shaved? Too many, undoubtedly. Not like I had a man who even cared about whether my legs were hairy or not. It had been years since I had dated anyone, let alone had sex.

The memory of my college boyfriend pinched my heart. Even though years had passed, in so many ways it still felt like yesterday. Once upon a time I thought he'd be my forever. But fate had other plans, and he'd been taken from the world all too soon.

For so long I'd held myself away from people, afraid that the same thing would happen to them. But all that had done was get me to twenty-seven, alone without even a pet to keep me company. I'd never had a dog or cat growing up. My mother didn't like animals and my father had traveled too much, even before they split up.

I should probably start entertaining the idea of letting my sister set me up with one of her husband's friends from work. Jane had suggested it more than a few times, but I'd always resisted. Wasn't Tinder the new place to meet people? As much as I hated the idea of online dating, setting up a profile and at least trying it might not be the worst thing in the world.

The front door opened, and Gray's voice reverberated through the house. "I'm here!"

A tiny smile curled the corners of my lips. Punctual as usual. That was exactly the type of man I needed. Someone driven who would give 100% in a relationship. Gray was such an amazing person on so many levels, and he'd shown me over the last couple of years what a man could be. He'd set the bar high, and every man I'd even contemplated going out with had fallen short. I wanted someone loyal and trustworthy, someone I could always count on to be there when I needed him.

I sighed. Finding a decent single man was like looking for a needle in a haystack. Forget Tinder, I should probably start with the Humane Society.

Keep reading Friendly Fire!

ALSO BY MORGAN JAMES

Romantic Suspense

QUENTIN SECURITY SERIES

Twisted Devil – Jason and Chloe

The Devil You Know – Blake and Victoria

Devil in the Details – Xander and Lydia

Devil in Disguise – Gavin and Kate

Heart of a Devil – Vince and Jana

Tempting the Devil – Clay and Abby

Devilish Intent – Con and Grace

Quentin Security Box Set One (Books 1-3)

Quentin Security Box Set Two (Books 4-6)

*Each book is a standalone within the series

RESCUE & REDEMPTION SERIES

Friendly Fire – Grayson and Claire

Cruel Vendetta – Drew and Emery

Silent Treatment – Finn and Harper

Reckless Pursuit – Aiden and Izzy

Dangerous Desires – Vaughn and Sienna

Cold Justice – Nick and Eden

Rescue & Redemption Box Set One (books 1-3)

RETRIBUTION SERIES

UNREQUITED LOVE – JACK AND MIA, BOOK ONE

UNBREAKABLE LOVE – JACK AND MIA, BOOK TWO

PRETTY LITTLE LIES – ERIC AND JULES, BOOK ONE

BEAUTIFUL DECEPTION – ERIC AND JULES, BOOK TWO

HIDDEN TRUTH – JOHN AND JOSI

SINFUL ILLUSIONS – FOX AND EVA, BOOK ONE

SINFUL SACRAMENT – FOX AND EVA, BOOK TWO

RETRIBUTION SERIES BOX SET 1

RETRIBUTION SERIES BOX SET 2

RETRIBUTION SERIES BOX SET 3

THE COMPLETE RETRIBUTION SERIES

THRILLERS AND MYSTERIES

SECRETS OF BROOKHAVEN

OUT OF SIGHT

OUT OF BREATH

OUT OF TIME

STANDALONES

DEAD OF WINTER

ABOUT THE AUTHOR

Morgan James is a USA Today bestselling author of contemporary and romantic suspense novels. She spent most of her childhood with her nose buried in a book, and she loves all things romantic, dark, and dirty. She currently resides in Ohio and is living happily ever after with her own alpha hero and their two kids.

Keep up with Morgan at AuthorMorganJames.com